Matty Groves

Also by Deborah Grabien

The Famous Flower of Serving Men
The Weaver and the Factory Maid
Plainsong
Eyes in the Fire

Matty Groves

Deborah Grabien

THOMAS DUNNE BOOKS / ST. MARTIN'S MINOTAUR ≋ NEW YORK

THOMAS DUNNE BOOKS.
An imprint of St. Martin's Press.

www.minotaurbooks.com

Library of Congress Cataloging-in-Publication Data

Grabien, Deborah.
    Matty Groves / Deborah Grabien.
       p. cm.
    ISBN 0-312-33389-7
    EAN 978-0-312-33389-8
    1. Haunted houses—Fiction. 2. Country homes—Fiction. 3. Art
festivals—Fiction. 4. Musicians—Fiction. 5. Hampshire (England)—Fiction.
I. Title.

PS3557.R1145 M38 2005
813'.54—dc22

                        2005046091

First Edition: October 2005

10 9 8 7 6 5 4 3 2 1

For Marlene Shannon-Stringer
and to the memory of Sandy Denny, gone too soon,
who sang the best version of the title song ever

To many of those I've thanked for the previous books in this series, the thanks still hold: all my anarachs (especially Betsy Hanes Perry, Beverly Leoczko, and Juliana Egley), Deena Fisher, Susan Stone Wilbanks, Rebekah Martin, and the incomparable Nilly Madar for additional input; Ken McClure, for falconry information, the members of my writers' support cadre (Rosemary Passantino, Melissa Dodd, Bea Taumann, Ken Howard Wilan, Reen Bodo, and Stephanie Trelogan); cool and groovy agent Jennifer Jackson (and everyone at Donald Maass Literary Agency); Dan Kotler; Marina Drukman for her perfect covers, and Ann Adelman, who copyedits so very well; and, of course, Ruth Cavin, who is, no doubt about it, the best editor ever.

Thanks are due, too, to the members of Fairport Convention, not only for allowing me to link their Web site, but for letting Ringan throw their name casually about.

And I certainly mustn't forget Nic, long-suffering, endlessly patient, and computer-brilliant husband of two decades, who shows me how to manipulate, for my own personal benefit, the fiendish yet wondrous invention known as Software.

Matty Groves

One

A holiday, a holiday
And the first one of the year
Lord Arnold's wife came into the church
The gospel for to hear

On a warm wet day in April, Ringan Laine came home to Somerset from a long, grueling few weeks in London to a piece of spectacular news.

The day certainly hadn't begun with any shining omens of good fortune. First, the cheque he'd collected that morning, for two weeks of session work with a well-known Canadian band, had been short of the amount agreed upon by signed contract, by rather a lot. After a noisy, unpleasant argument had got that mess sorted out, he'd headed back to his girlfriend Penny's flat to collect Lord Randall, his Martin guitar, only to discover a few spots of mould on the plush yellow lining of the expensive hardshell case.

Cursing, he'd headed for Glastonbury. The traffic between London and Somerset had been nightmarish, thanks to an overturned lorry spilling its cargo of eggs all over the motorway. By this time, Ringan's edginess of the morning had evolved into a bona fide roaring attack of bad temper. As if all this hadn't been enough to sour his mood, he'd noticed, too late to remedy the situation, that the Alfa Romeo was low on petrol. He'd spent fifteen minutes running on fumes, clutching the wheel and praying he wouldn't run out entirely, until he limped into an overpriced roadside service station, filled the tank, and allowed himself to breathe again.

It was still raining as Ringan drove down the country backroads between Glastonbury and Street, sporadic blinding downpours punctuated by anticipatory drizzles and small rainbows on the horizon. As he sprinted for Lumbe's, his renovated eighteenth-century labourer's cottage, the pelting water from above abruptly stopped entirely. After the day he'd had, this seemed like nothing more than one small alleviation to a day full of wide-ranging annoyances.

Ringan let himself into the cottage, kicking off his damp shoes and hurriedly opening Lord Randall's case to avoid any further accumulation of moisture that might warp the instrument. A rumble from somewhere deep in his interior reminded him that he hadn't eaten any lunch. That thought was immediately followed by the realisation that he hadn't picked up his post, or any milk or other groceries. That, he thought, just put the tin cupola on it; no dinner in the house except for things in jars, and what was worse, no tea, unless he wanted it black. And no beer, either.

Ringan swore aloud.

"Sounds like you've had a long day. Cheer up, mate, it's spring-time in Somerset. Welcome home. Penny not with you?"

The cheerful voice, sounding directly behind him on the front step, made Ringan jump. He'd neglected to shut the door as he came inside, preferring to let the fresh rain-washed breeze dissipate the mustiness of a cottage closed up for too long.

Albert Wychsale, Baron Boult and Ringan's nominal landlord, stood on the top step. He looked every inch the country squire out for a spring walk, in wellies and a mac that appeared to have been made for a much larger man. Drops of rain slid off the spacious coat and puddled on the ground beside him. He was carrying plastic grocery bags.

"Albert! Christ, you made me jump. Come in, I've only just got back. No, Penny's not here; you of all people ought to know that, you being her business partner and all. *Much Ado About Nothing* at the Bellefield, remember? The run wraps up Sunday after the matinée, and she's coming down Monday. What brings you to the poor working man's humble abode?"

Wychsale carefully peeled off his wellies and dropped them on the enormous seagrass mat just inside Lumbe's front door. Ringan noticed that one of the plastic grocery bags seemed to be heavily weighted; it was straining at its handles.

"I just thought I'd pop by with a few things." Wychsale had a look of too-casual innocence to him, so unconvincing that Ringan's curiosity was immediately piqued. "I remembered you saying you were due back today, and I thought you might not want to stop off for bits—so, I've brought some provisions with me, and your post as well. You asked me to hold it for you until you got back, remember? I, um, well, I thought you might fancy having it. Your post, that is. Here, let's put this stuff in the kitchen, shall we?"

"Yes, all right, let's. How remarkably civilised of you, Albert. I was just bemoaning not having stopped for groceries—that's what I was swearing about when you showed up." Ringan, suspicious and on high alert, followed Albert into the kitchen.

"You might want to put those groceries away. Were you planning on a cup of tea? Because I wouldn't say no, if you were offering. I've had a nice long tramp in the mud, and that calls for tea. Ah—here's Butterball, right on cue." Wychsale opened the bottom door long enough to admit the Wychsale estate's magnificent Persian cat. "Lord Puffbottom, I presume. I swear, he likes you and Penny better than he likes me. I can go days without sight of so much as his shadow. All he has to do is see the top of that Dutch door open, and he's in your lap."

"It's because he knows there's a free meal in it for him." Ringan filled the electric kettle and plugged it in, wondering, while Butterball wove a figure-eight between his ankles, leaving a scattering of golden fur along his trouser legs. Why on earth was the Right Honourable—the Right Hon, as Penny called him—being so excruciatingly coy? As he wondered, Ringan pulled items from the plastic carrier: milk, bread, cheese, butter, two small chops in butcher's paper, and, unbelievably, a split of 1990 *grand cru* French champagne.

Ringan blinked at the bottle in his hand. It was cold, expensive, and completely unexpected. It also had a tacky purple holiday ribbon wrapped around its neck. He looked up at Wychsale.

"Albert? What on earth is this in aid of?"

Wychsale, who had been stooping to stroke the purring cat, straightened up. He was smiling now, the mischievous-child look gone completely. "Found the champagne, did you? Yes, there's a reason and no, I haven't gone out of my mind—the explanation for the pricey bubbly's in your post." He jumped as Butterball turned his attention Wychsale's way. "Ouch! Wretched cat, remove your claws from my ankle, please. Here, Ringan, why don't you sort through that and I'll put this in the fridge?"

Ringan promptly turned the bagful of post upside down and dumped the contents unceremoniously across the table's well-polished surface. He sorted the pile with practised speed: takeout menus from various local eateries, mostly duplicates of menus he already had. A few music industry and National Trust periodicals—those could wait. Bill, bill, letter from sister Roberta, reminder of a friend's new CD release, postcard from Majorca from a modern music composer whose country pub he'd helped renovate. Finally, an envelope, on thick vellum paper, with a crest in sealing wax across the back.

Ringan looked at the crest. He looked at the engraved return address on the envelope. He looked up at Wychsale, his jaw slackening, his mouth opening and closing. He looked back at the envelope. No mistake; it was certainly addressed to him. His hands began to tremble.

"Yes," Wychsale said, "it's from Miles Leight-Arnold; Lord Callowen, that is. Did I happen to mention I'm heading up this year's Callowen Festival Selection Committee?"

"Oh my God oh my God you aren't serious you can't possibly be serious are you serious this isn't actually serious oh my God you actually are serious!" Ringan heard the words emerge as a sort of explosive run-together noise, and fought for breath. "Albert, are you telling me . . ."

"Why not read the letter? That'll confirm it. It'll also give you the dates and details." Wychsale was grinning like a mad thing. He poured milk into two cups and added a teaball full of leaves to each one. As fragrant steam eddied upward into Lumbe's rafters, Ringan, his hands shaking, carefully slit the envelope and unfolded the letter.

The body of the text was typewritten, with a handwritten postscript at the bottom of the page. "Dear Mr. Laine," the letter began.

> I am most pleased to extend an invitation to perform at the Callowen Arts Festival, to be held this year from 2 July through 13 July at Callowen House, Purbury, County Hampshire, to yourself and to the other members of the musical ensemble Broomfield Hill. . . .

Ringan read the rest of the letter in a state of disbelief bordering on ecstasy. His band, Broomfield Hill, would be the only musical act of this year's festival; the list of invitees included a world-famous American dance troupe; an actor who would have to take a week off from a sold-out show in the West End to do Callowen and certainly would do so without a moment's hesitation; and a Pulitzer-winning dramatist. Broomfield Hill would be expected to perform a total of five concerts during the two-week event, the choice of music to be left solely to the band's discretion, to an invitation-only audience of approximately forty people. The fee, half of which was payable upon Ringan's signed acceptance, was enough to draw yet another strangled noise from Ringan. Each member of the band would of course be housed at Callowen, along with a guest of his or her choice. The writer remained, most sincerely, et cetera, Miles Leight-Arnold, Lord Callowen.

Ringan looked at the handwriting, a confident, arrogant scrawl along the letter's bottom edge. Lord Callowen understood from his old friend Albert that Ringan's longtime companion was none other than Penelope Wintercraft-Hawkes. He hoped very much that Ringan would be able to convince her to come along for the festival, as he was a great admirer of her work. He looked forward to meeting them both. Following that, the signature, a single word: *Callowen.*

"You did this?" Ringan folded the letter and carefully put it away. "Albert, is there anything I can get you, as payback? Season tickets to the Isle of Wight, naked dancing girls, your very own pirate ship, complete with personal bath slaves and a crew of oarsmen? Anything? Name it. Just name it, that's all. Pardon my nattering, I'm a wee bit in shock."

"A pirate ship? Tempting, but no, I believe I'll pass, at least for now. Kind of you to offer, though." He passed Ringan a cup of tea. "You know, Ringan, I did nominate Broomfield Hill. But I wouldn't have if I hadn't thought you were one of the best in the business. This wasn't a question of nepotism. And I'd like to hear you people play live under better circumstances than the first time I heard you."

They were both quiet for a minute, remembering. The event to which Wychsale was referring had happened in the tithe barn, and it had been less of a performance than a full-scale exorcism of Lumbe's two resident spectres, Elizabeth Roper and William Corby. As renditions of Broomfield Hill standard covers went, that particular performance of the song "The Weaver and the Factory Maid" had been sketchy, to say the least. The performance had, of course, been complicated by the presence of three spirits, one of them a murderer . . .

"Well." Ringan shook off the sudden chill that the memory of Lumbe's haunting had raised in him. They were nearly a year old, the events of that day, and Ringan had been through a far more terrifying ghostly encounter since then. "We'll do you proud, Albert, trust me for that. I wonder about that note, though. If he wanted Penny so badly, why not simply invite the Tamburlaine Players? I mean, if we're talking about A-list performers . . ." The sudden realisation of the reason hit Ringan. "Damn. Sorry. Bloody stupid question. Forget I asked."

"I suggested the Tamburlaines, of course I did. I suggested them right off, first thing." Albert's face had a look of regret. "Miles mentioned this to me, but only in passing. Penny told us, remember? She gave me the whole story of what had happened to Donal McCreary's wife at Callowen, before McCreary joined Penny's troupe. Tragic, that; I gather McCreary has never really got over it. I think you'll agree that inviting the Tamburlaines under those circumstances would have been beyond tactless. Miles is a very old friend of mine, you know? And I'll say this for him: yes, he's a pampered aristo and yes, he may spend too much time and money indulging his eccentricities and obsessions, but he isn't a monster and even mentioning Callowen to Donal McCreary after what happened would be—what is it? What's wrong?"

"That's right, isn't it? I'm an idiot. I've only just remembered." Ringan spoke slowly, the memory of two supernatural encounters too fresh in his mind for comfort. "Callowen House is haunted. It's rather famously haunted, by a saucy little bit of highborn mystery who got caught with her footman lover, or whatever he was. There's a nice famous tune about it, one of the great ones, in fact. Haunted. Yes, indeed. And my almost-host wants me to bring Penny along with me. Oh, lovely. Splendid."

Wychsale's eyes had gone wide. Like Ringan, he had just made the connection between an invitation to spend two weeks at one of England's most notoriously haunted manor houses and the extreme, sometimes sanity-threatening sensitivity to the spirit world that Penny had already, and too often, displayed.

Ringan looked at Albert, saw his own dismay echoed in Wychsale's face, and spoke with true feeling. "Damn! Damn, damn, double-breasted pin-striped damn! Is there no getting away from all these ghosts!"

The following Monday afternoon, Penny Wintercraft-Hawkes treated the Tamburlaine Players, the theatre support staff, and three of the troupe's pet critics to an uproarious wrap-party lunch in the private room of the Beldame in Ashes pub. She then kissed everyone concerned, locked up the Bellefield Theatre at Number 1,

Hawthorne Walk, and headed down to Somerset as fast as her vintage Jaguar would legally carry her.

She was in need of a rest. The three-week run of *Much Ado,* one performance per day for twenty-one straight days with additional matinées at the weekend, might not have seemed stressful to an untutored eye. After all, the play was a staple in the Tamburlaine repertoire, and the details of earlier productions were there for Penny's use.

But the circumstances were all new. For one thing, this was the very first summer season at the Tamburlaine's newly renovated home base. For another, they were returning from America, having done nearly a month of Elizabethan tragedy at a prestigious festival on the West Coast. The jump from tragedy to comedy with less than two weeks to prepare had been tricky, since the responsibility for everything from scheduling rehearsals to checking the existing costumes for damage sat squarely in Penny's lap. There was also stubbornly lingering jet lag, the result of an eleven-hour flight from Seattle to London with a heavy cold. Penny had worked through the pre-production and the run itself, but there had been moments where she'd found herself praying to stay on her feet for just one more performance. It was time to relax.

She drove well instinctively, mentally commanding herself to stay within the posted limits. The last thing she wanted was a summons for speeding, and besides, the knowledge that she'd be sleeping in the big feather-bed at Lumbe's that night was pleasant and luxurious. The truth was, Penny was tired of London at the moment, a rare state of mind for her. She loved the city, but the weather had been stereotypically bad and she had yet to shed her cold. The countryside definitely beckoned.

As traffic thinned out towards Somerset, Penny let her mind relax and wander a bit. The run of *Much Ado* had been profitable enough, not spectacularly so, but after all, it had only been for three weeks, a sort of mini summer season. This was the sort of production that, in a rented theatre, would be lucky to break even and cover the costs. Instead, it had actually made a bit of money, enough so that Albert Wychsale was going to see a small return on his investment in the Bellefield. Two short dramatic runs since laying the ghost of Agnès de Belleville Maldown to her rest, and both had shown profits. Albert, Penny ruminated, should be pleased. She herself certainly was.

The reviews had been kind, as well, but she had expected nothing less; the Tamburlaines could do Shakespearean comedy in their sleep, and do it well. If the notices on *Much Ado* lacked the rapturous near reverence of the ones invoked by the February opening production of *Iphigenia,* well, *Much Ado* was a comedy and didn't really lend itself to reverence. *Iphigenia* was an entirely different thing. And there had been circumstances to lend that production an additional edge . . .

Penny felt her memory shy away from the events that had triggered her desire to produce the Euripides tragedy. The memory of the woman who had haunted not only the Bellefield but in fact the entirety of Hawthorne Walk was taking far too long to fade to manageable proportions.

She turned onto the A39, deciding to make a quick stop in Glastonbury proper to pick up some wine and some decent coffee. She hadn't spoken to Ringan for nearly a week; somehow, their schedules had simply refused to mesh. They'd left messages on each other's machines, and Penny wondered if she was imagining that Ringan's latest message had a sort of undertone to it. Actually, he'd sounded mysterious ever since he'd got back to Lumbe's. The more she considered it, the less she believed it was all in her mind. It was very unlike him. There was certainly something going on.

Penny stopped near Glastonbury Abbey, taking a few minutes to stretch her legs. The weather was glorious, the soft green day easing gently into a cool April evening. The air smelled like a Monet painting, freshly scented with the best of early spring. Flowers rioted colourfully in window-boxes, and clouds moved, stately and non-threatening, towards England's coast. She got back into the Jaguar and drove sedately the few miles south-east towards the town of Street. She pulled onto Lumbe's drive, saw Ringan's Alfa, and headed for the cottage.

As Penny let herself in, the aroma of cooking met her head-on. She stopped in her tracks, sniffing. The cottage smelled wonderful, a smell far beyond anything in Ringan's repertoire of burgers, sausages, eggs, and soup.

"Hello? Ringan?"

He poked his head out of the kitchen door. "Hullo, lamb. Are you hungry? I've got dinner waiting."

"So I gathered." Penny sniffed, sniffed again, and felt her taste buds stand to attention. "This place smells like Cordon Bleu heaven."

Penny dropped her overnight case on the seagrass mat and followed Ringan. She pulled up behind him, staring at a beautifully set kitchen table, complete with an ice bucket; protruding from the bucket was the neck of a bottle of what, even at this distance, Penny recognised as champagne of a vintage not to be taken lightly. In a corner by the door, the cat Butterball looked away from his milk to regard her briefly.

Penny turned to Ringan. He was grinning like a loon.

"All right," she remarked. "What's going on? Have you won the pools? Signed a new record deal? Got yourself pregnant?"

"None of the above. And better than all of them. Lord, where are my manners? I haven't even said hello. Hello, love." He slipped an arm around her waist, pulled her close, and kissed her, long and deep. Penny, her spine going limp as she relaxed against him, thought the kiss had a definite taste of masculine triumph to it.

"Well," she said, when he finally released her, "nice to see you, too, dear. And how very nice to be back in Somerset. That was definitely the smooch of a satisfied man. Seriously, what's happened? And who did you hire to cook whatever smells so good?"

"I borrowed the Right Hon's cook. Don't know what he did, but it required lamb and root vegetables and rather a lot of something I think he called *demi-glace,* which I gather is some sort of super-gravy. Also, he asked if he could raid our kitchen garden for herbs. I told him to use whatever he wanted. Smells superb, doesn't it? I say we eat it."

"Yes, let's." Ringan held her chair out, and she settled in. "A 1990 *grand cru* champagne? Rob a bank, did we?"

"Actually, it was a gift from your business partner. I thought we'd pop it after dinner. To celebrate, you know?"

"Right, that's it. I refuse to be tormented any longer." Penny leaned across the table. "Rupert Darnley Laine, if you don't tell me what's going on, and tell me right now . . ."

He told her. Penny let out a whoop that could have been heard in the tithe barn, had anyone been there to hear it.

"Callowen! We're going to Callowen! Oh my God, this is so amazing . . . and Miles Leight-Arnold is a fan of mine? He wrote that down, really? I want to see that letter, damn it."

"After dinner, with champagne. Let's eat first. I've been fighting off temptation for about two hours, and I'm starved. It took superhuman control not to help myself to a bit, but this is a celebration and I was a good lad and haven't even tasted a bite, because it was for both of us."

The lamb stew, redolent of spices and mysterious herbs, tasted like heaven. Ringan offered dessert, French pastries from a local bakery, and uncorked the champagne. As they touched glasses in a silent toast, Penny saw that Ringan's brows had drawn a bit. She lifted her own at him.

"Penny for them?"

"My thoughts—well." Ringan took a mouthful of bubbly, looked momentarily appreciative, and set his glass down. "You know, lamb, there's more than one side to this invite. Not all the sides are appealing."

"You're thinking about what happened to Donal's wife, aren't you?" Penny forked buttery pastry into her mouth, chewed, and swallowed. "About the fact that there might be a ghost there?"

"There's no 'might' about it, Penny—Callowen's haunted, all right; it's been documented for about three hundred years now, with probably dozens of witnesses. Hell, it's in all the books. We're talking about one of England's most famous hauntings." He was quiet for a moment. "But there's something that worries me more than just the plain fact of the haunting. You see, it isn't just a house with a ghost. It's a house with a ghost and a traditional song about the ghost."

"Damn!" Penny set her champagne flute down. "Not good. We've had two of those already, and neither time was any fun at all. Am I likely to know the song? Does Broomfield Hill cover it?"

"Oh yes. We cover it—Jane does an incredibly poignant vocal. Best version ever, in my opinion, was done by Fairport Convention, and sung by Sandy Denny. It's on their *Liege & Lief* album. Joan Baez covered it too, years ago, so it's even known in America. The song is 'Matty Groves.'"

"Really?" Penny blinked. "The Callowen ghost is out of that song? Are you joking? That's incredible. Does Matty Groves stagger through the halls bleeding all over unsuspecting guests, or something?"

"No joke. The family is called Leight-Arnold, and they go back damned near to the Conqueror. The ghost is the wife in the song, Lady Arnold. You know, the one who snuggled up to the young stud Matty, and got ratted out by her much older husband's servant. The husband came roaring back, found them in bed together, and used his pricey sword to whack both Matty and wife, after offering Matty first whack, mind you. The story's a classic bit of melodrama, which just happens to be true."

"'*I'd rather a kiss from dead Matty's lips Than you in your finery.*' Wow. I love that song, even if I can't so much as hum it properly. It's one of the famous Child ballads, isn't it?" Penny poured half the remaining champagne into her glass and knocked it back as if she needed it. "Ringan, you said documented. Dozens of witnesses. Could you be a bit more specific?"

"No, not really, although I do remember a pretty famous story I was told years so, when we first started covering the song, some high-powered politico—literally Winston Churchill or somebody—was staying at Callowen during the Second World War. He and a whole flock of people, all cabinet ministers and belted earls and whatnots, watched the lady step out of her own painting and float off down the stairs." Ringan grinned sardonically. "She's apparently not a shy ghost, not at all. I don't know if the story's true or if it's pure apocrypha, but they said it happened in broad daylight, and not just the once. Will that do for a start?"

"I think so, yes." Penny sounded dazed. "Ringan—is there anything about her being, well, evil? Malevolent? You know, in the Agnès de Belleville vein of big bad dark things that go bump in the night?"

"Not that I know of, but then I'm not really up on it. I don't hang with Lord Leight-Arnold, although the Right Hon apparently does. Let's ring him up. He might very well have some gen on the haunting."

"Yes, it actually was Winston Churchill. He was at Callowen several times during the war. I remember my father talking about it at the time, after he'd come back from Callowen himself. Just a day trip for my father, of course; he wasn't staying there."

Ringan and Penny were seated in sturdy chairs on one of the terraces overlooking the lawns at Wychsale House, watching the panoply of stars in the night sky overhead. Penny hadn't wanted to wait until morning; at her prompting, Ringan had called Albert, explained what they needed, and accepted the prompt invitation to come up and have a drink.

They'd driven the short distance in Ringan's car. A soft breeze riffled Ringan's beard and lifted Penny's dusky hair from her neck. Somewhere to the west, hidden under tree and cloud, an owl called imperatively.

"Was your father a friend of Lord Callowen?" Penny sipped her brandy; in the nacreous light, her skin was alabaster, or creamy marble. "The Lord Callowen of the day, I mean?"

"Friends? No, not really. I don't think so, anyway. I was a child, of course, but I don't remember that any of the Leight-Arnold family ever came up here for a weekend, or even for dinner. And even though I was at school with Miles, he didn't know where our house was, or who my family was, or anything. We got friendly over time." Wychsale regarded Penny curiously. "Do you know, I'm rather surprised you don't know the family yourself. Surely, they're rather in your milieu? Arts patronage, theatre, the festival. Didn't you go to Oxford? Because Miles has a daughter, Charlotte, who was at Oriel. I think she did Classics or something. She's close to your age, maybe a year or two older. She's a folklorist, if I recall. Big on Ye Olde Ways."

"Really?" Penny shrugged. "We've never crossed paths, for some reason. If you were at school with him, then Miles Leight-Arnold must be a contemporary of my parents, but I don't remember them ever mentioning his name. Well, I mean, you can't know everyone, can you?"

"True." Ringan was grinning at the unconscious snobbery of the remark. "I think I must meet the daughter of this particular house—Charlotte, is it? Folklorist, and money for miles? Obviously, we're a match made in Heaven."

"Slut," Penny said affectionately. "Albert, if your family and the Leight-Arnolds weren't close, why was your father at Callowen? War-related stuff?"

"Exactly. My father was stationed at home, and Callowen House was a major centre for high-powered gatherings. They had rather a lot of high-end communications and spying equipment being stashed there. Not surprising, when you consider Purbury's setting. You can get to the Army base on Salisbury Plain or to the Navy at Portsmouth with no trouble or time spent at all. That house was ideally situated for the south coast hush-hush."

"Location, location, location? Right. That would explain what the PM was doing there." Ringan was fascinated. "So your father actually worked with Winston Churchill? The Winston Churchill, cigar, vee-for-victory Winston Churchill? I can't tell you how completely that floors me, Albert. Did he ever actually see Lady Arnold's ghost? Your father, I mean."

"Not that I ever heard," Albert said regretfully. "Wouldn't that have been superb? I'd have loved to have had my father come home with a good ghost story. But he never said he'd seen her. If it's any good, I did gather he heard about the incident with Churchill direct from the horse's mouth."

"Now, this I want to hear." Penny reached for the brandy bottle. "Tell, Albert, please. I really want to know a bit more about this particular ghost."

"Well, Dad came home from Callowen and I remember he said the Prime Minister had been there. I don't really remember how old I was, but if Churchill was PM, it had to have been before 1945. So I'd have been about six. Amazing, really, that I remember the story so clearly."

"Maybe not," Ringan said gently. "After all, wasn't it right around that time you had your encounter with Elizabeth Roper's ghost, on the stairs at Lumbe's?"

"Oh God, yes. So I was primed to remember, I suppose; you're quite right, Ringan." Wychsale lifted a hand and gently brushed at a moth that was inspecting his glass. The moth, not seeming to notice, fluttered off into the dark. "That insect is going to make some bat very happy before the night's done," Wychsale remarked. "Anyway, Dad said he'd seen Churchill angry, that he'd seen him austere, dangerous, sarcastic, smug, chilly, and devilishly funny, but that he'd never seen him shaken off his balance before. And when my mother asked him what had happened, was it Hitler, had there been bad news, my father said no, Churchill and a few hats from MI5 had been halfway up the Great Staircase at Callowen, and the resident ghost, Lady Arnold, had popped out of her picture, materialised at the head of the stairs, floated down to the Great Hall, and faded out. Churchill told my father she'd gone right through an Under-Secretary of the Navy, and that the chap had disgraced himself by screaming and running off."

Ringan choked on his brandy, sputtered, and set his glass down hastily. "Sorry," he said, when his throat was clear and he could control his voice. "I'm just constantly amazed at the things that shock you sassenach aristos."

"You mean, that the ghost didn't worry anyone as much as the loss of self-control did?" Penny's smile faded. "Albert, as interesting as that story is, it isn't really telling me what I was hoping to find out. Have you heard anything, ever, from any source at all, that so much as hints at Lady Arnold's ghost being dangerous? Has she yelled boo at a downstairs maid and caused a heart attack? Has she ever appeared as a skeletal monster with a demonic face and woken someone from a sound sleep? Sent anyone screaming madly into the night from anything other than being thoroughly startled? Have you ever heard that she's caused a living breathing human being harm in any way whatsoever? Or does she just manifest on odd Public Days, and float in and out of Callowen House, looking decorative?"

Wychsale and Ringan were both watching her, trying to see her better. It was too dark to read her face properly, and both men were puzzled by the intensity in her voice.

"I've never heard that she was dangerous, no." Wychsale was thinking back, trying to remember. "Even the naval bloke suffered nothing worse than a bad fright and the indignity of non-stop teasing from all the other witnesses, and she went right through him. No lasting side effects from the encounter, if I recall correctly. From what I gather, she's got a history as a rather sad, very pretty creature, more pathetic than terrifying."

"That's just the impression I got, as well." Penny looked from Ringan to Albert. "Now think about that for a moment. Pathetic, pretty, sad, no lasting side effects. Do those descriptions of Lady Arnold's ghost match the description of whatever killed Sinead McCreary?"

There was a long silence, broken by Ringan. "Crikey," he said, and sounded grim. "No, love, they don't. Not in the least. I remember what Donal said about that, only too well. He said whatever it was that passed through his wife was grotesque, misshapen, wrong. And besides, she died of it, or at least Donal thinks so. You know, I was reasonably good at maths, and this does rather seem like simple addition, doesn't it?"

"Oh, my." Wychsale sounded dazed. "Oh dear, dear, dear. Yes indeed. I can add that up, as well. We have a problem."

"We?" Penny lifted an eyebrow.

"Yes, we." Wychsale puffed his cheeks and blew out air. "I'm head of the selection committee this year, so I'm there for the entire festival. Damn. More than one ghost at Callowen, and we're going there for two weeks. The only answer is that there is more than one ghost, and unlike Lady Arnold, it's a dangerous one that the Leight-Arnold family either doesn't know about or doesn't want to talk about. Dear, dear, dear. Would anyone like more brandy? Because I need some."

Two

And when the meeting it was done
She cast her eyes about
And there she saw little Matty Groves
Walking in the crowd

A few miles short of Purbury, Hampshire, and the hundreds of acres of extensive grounds surrounding Callowen House, Jane Castle pulled her elderly Vauxhall off the road and succumbed to a quiet little nervous breakdown.

It was the afternoon of June 1. Jane, following Lord Callowen's directions and presumably along with the other three members of Broomfield Hill, was making her way towards England's most prestigious private arts festival. She'd been in a state of barely controlled euphoria since Ringan's initial phone call; in fact, she hadn't really believed him until the invitation itself arrived. She was still considering framing it, or having it gilded in twenty-four-carat leaf, or something equally suitable for the most mind-boggling bit of post ever to pop through the slot in her front door.

Euphoria, yes. Yet here she was, sitting in her car with her flute on the seat beside her and her suitcase in the boot, literally trembling on the edge of panic. She took a tenuous hold of herself, applied a few of the breathing techniques she used for her singing exercises, in hopes of getting the situation under some sort of control. *In, hold, count to five, exhale slowly, two-beat, repeat . . .* Now that she thought about it, she'd put a ridiculous amount of work into making sure that suitcase had been packed with just the right clothing. *In, hold, count to five, exhale slowly* . . . My goodness, she thought, am I really that big a brown-noser? Why should I give a single solitary damn what Miles Leight-Arnold or his handpicked crowd of critics and whatnots think of my grey cashmere sweater? And really, what was I thinking, bringing that sweater, when I know grey isn't my colour . . . *In, hold, count to five, exhale.* . . .

After a few minutes, the technique began to do its job, and Jane, her diaphragm expanded and her lungs full of clean fresh country air, began to calm down. A bit of soul-searching brought the cause of her panic to light. It wasn't the Leight-Arnold family prestige that awed her, it was the prestige of the festival itself. That feeling was putting her at a disadvantage before she ever got there. And that simply would not do.

A few cars passed the idling Vauxhall, their drivers casting curious glances at Jane as she sat, doing battle with herself. She turned the engine off, and explored her nerves. So, she thought, I'm intimidated by the festival? That's absurd. I'm an invited guest. Broomfield Hill is an invited act. I should be prepared to enjoy the next two weeks, and just look at me, cowering like a puppy, afraid to drive through the front gates.

She shook her head sharply, admonishing herself aloud in the otherwise empty car. "You're being ridiculous. Stop it at once. You are one of the best flautists in England and you're certainly one of the best vocalists and you were invited because you're good, and just because people like Jean-Pierre Rampal have played here, and Miles Davis, and Andrés Segovia, and what in hell am I doing here? in, hold, count to five, exhale slowly, oh God I think I'm going to be sick. . . ."

She made it from the front seat of the Vauxhall to the nearest hedge just in time to avert disaster, leaving the bulk of her breakfast in the grass. Shaken and furious with herself, Jane wiped her colourless lips, summoned the rags of her personal pride, and got back into the Vauxhall. Right, she thought, that is absolutely it. Enough of this nonsense. She drove down the road, and came to a full stop in front of an enormous pair of wrought-iron gates with a crest above them in lattice-work.

The gates were closed. They also seemed to be chained.

Jane, feeling yet another surge of paranoia, pushed it forcibly away. She sat and waited, and considered what to do next. As she was wondering, a gnomelike little man in tweeds materialised, opened the gates, and waved her through. She hurried the Vauxhall onto a wide curving road of crushed white stone, and glanced in the mirror. The caretaker or kobold or whatever his job title might be was chaining the gates open.

A sudden horrid fear seized Jane that she was the first person to arrive. Oh no, she thought, that I simply refuse to deal with. If I'm the only car that's got here, I'll just pull off to one side and wait for someone else to show up. I flatly refuse to be first. . . .

The road curved between high hedges and yew trees. Jane found herself insensibly soothed; there was something about the road, the calm, the soft green stateliness of the trees with their poisonous berries, that reminded her of a blissful week spent driving around the French countryside. The road curled and dipped, allowing for tantalising glimpses of rolling lawns and brilliant colour.

Jane drove slowly, pausing to roll down her windows. The Hampshire air was soft and uncontentious; she thought she tasted the barest tang of salt, wondered, and then remembered that Callowen House was not far from Portsmouth and the coast. She touched her tongue to her lips. Just as she did so, the curving white road opened out into a huge circular drive. Jane found herself staring at Callowen House.

Callowen, home of the Leight-Arnold family since its grant by charter from Edward III in 1372 to the first Lord Callowen, was exquisite. If anything remained of the original manor, it wasn't immediately visible; the house looked primarily late Tudor, Elizabethan, or perhaps Jacobean. It had straight columns in white stone, soaring heavenwards in a kind of semicircle, framing the main entry; it had long, elegant wings in a creamy-reddish stone on either side. Three floors of leaded windows looked down at the circular drive where Jane sat, gawking; atop a long, elegantly peaked roof, chimneypots jostled for position. Off into the summery distance, a gentle roll of hills supported grazing sheep and bits of vibrant colour that spoke of extensive gardens. The entire scene was reflected and repeated in a lovely broad ripple of water that looked like a man-made lake.

Jane blinked at the vistas, at the house, at a sky that seemed softer and of a sweeter, deeper blue than any sky had ever been. So enchanted was she that the sharp, imperative rap on her window made her jump and stifle a shriek. She rolled down the window, and found herself confronting the most extraordinary-looking human being she had ever seen.

A woman stood beside the Vauxhall. To Jane, tiny and fine-boned, she looked like an Amazon, or perhaps a Valkyrie; the woman had to be at least six feet tall barefoot, and she was not, at this moment, barefoot. She had round eyes, set wide apart under red-gold brows and lashes, but the eyes themselves were two disturbingly different colours: one was a vivid, copper-flecked green, the other a dark brown. Her hair, pulled off her neck and piled into a recalcitrant bun, was of so improbably beautiful a shade of red-gold that Jane knew it must be natural. She had cheekbones a supermodel would have envied. She also had long dimples. Her mouth seemed to be under imperfect control, wanting to move about in all directions, even in repose. As a sort of finishing touch to this peculiar package, the woman appeared to be wrapped in several layers of mismatched burlap.

"Hello." The voice was unexpectedly beautiful, a crisp, educated overlay atop soft Hampshire, deep and lilting. "Welcome to Callowen. You look awfully familiar. Are you one of those boring theatre people Da insists on every year, or have I just dropped a brick? Not that I mind."

"Um—no, I'm Jane Castle. I play flute with a band called Broomfield Hill. I'm a guest—I mean, I have an invitation." The woman gazed at her intently, apparently in astonishment or disbelief. Mad, thought Jane, this is unbelievable, I've fallen into the hands of a complete nutter. Oh joy, oh rapture, oh lucky me. A note of desperation wavered in her voice. "We're playing the festival. Honestly. I can show you my invitation—you did say this was Callowen House?"

"Oh my God, of course. Jane Castle, Broomfield Hill. You play that amazing music with Ringan Laine, you indecently lucky person, you!" Before Jane could frame a response, or even properly consider one, the woman yanked the car door open and dragged her free. Jane managed to grab hold of her flute case and pull it out of the car behind her; some vague notion of bopping the nutter with it, in order to give herself time to leap into the Vauxhall and escape, flashed through her brain. "I'm so chuffed to have you here, you can't imagine," the woman told her. "Jane Castle! Stupendous! I'm a huge fan of yours, simply worshipful, honestly. Although, you aren't actually stupendous, now that I look at you. Quite teeny, really. Far smaller than I'd have thought. But music, and with Ringan Laine! How yummy!"

"Um—right." The madwoman had got hold of Jane's free hand; she was clutching it in a painful grip and pumping it wildly, while beaming down from her Olympian height. "I'm sorry," Jane said, rather feebly, "but my hand—I'll need it to play my flute, you know, and really, you're awfully strong. I'm losing sensation. Could I—would you mind . . . ?"

"Oh, lord, sorry sorry sorry." Jane's hand was released, but the madwoman continued her high-voltage beam. "And of course, since I got all excited and forgot to introduce myself, you probably think I've escaped from the local corn bin. No need to phone the butterfly collectors, really. I'm Charlotte Leight-Arnold, daughter of the house."

"This," Penny said exuberantly, "is going to be fun."

Ringan muttered something. His comment was mostly lost, carried away by the wind rushing through the car. The lost response had sounded remarkably like "not on my planet," or words to that effect. Penny, her hair streaming out behind her, grinned to herself. She'd insisted, not only on Ringan driving, but on his putting the cloth top of the Alfa down. She was on her way to Callowen, she had no responsibilities for two weeks except to enjoy herself and dodge whatever ghosts might wander her way. All was right with the world.

Still, if she'd heard him properly, Ringan wasn't agreeing, which was rather odd. She cast a considering glance at his profile, saw the set of his jaw and the taut angle of his black beard, and realised something. He was nervous. Which, of course, was absurd. Ringan, nervous? Ringan was never nervous about anything, ever.

"Ringan," she said, her voice pitched to counterpoint the vibration of the engine, "stop looking so scared, for heaven's sake. Miles Leight-Arnold isn't going to eat you. He'll likely fawn all over your shoes—well, maybe not fawn, I suspect he's not much for fawning. But honestly, don't be nervous."

"I'm not nervous!" he yelled. The tip of his beard was now quivering.

"You're nervous," she told him. "You get incredibly Scots when you're overtaken by any strong feeling. Did you know that? And you just told me you weren't 'nairvous.' So, you are, nervous, that is. But why? Five performances in fourteen days, all in one place, to an adoring audience—what's nerve-inducing about that? And stop yelling—that's absolutely the wrong technique. Just modulate your pitch. You're a singer, you ought to know that."

"Right." Ringan eased his foot off the accelerator. "Sorry. So I'm nervous. And I'm perfectly well aware that the blueblood in charge of all this won't eat me. But—it's Callowen, damn it! People in the arts wait their whole lives for an invite like this. Beyond prestigious. Did you look at the performance invite list? The Blue Gum Dance Troupe—they're right on the level with Alvin Ailey. Julian Cordellet—his show on Shaftesbury Avenue is up for all sorts of awards, and I hear he's taking it stateside to Broadway next season. And Allyson Greyer—my God, Penny, the woman has a Nobel Prize for literature."

"It's a Pulitzer for drama, actually." She was smiling affectionately at him. "A very prestigious list of invitees, darling, yes. But you left someone off."

"Oh God. Did I?"

"Yes. You forgot Broomfield Hill. And that won't do, because you know, there's no better traditional music ensemble on earth right now, and it wouldn't do to slight the band members by forgetting that."

Unexpectedly, Ringan pulled the car onto the shoulder of the road. The kiss left Penny breathless.

"I love you all the way to the moon and the stars, and back again," he muttered into her hair. "You know that, right?"

"Yes, I do, and aren't I lucky?" She touched his cheek. "I was serious, though. Don't devalue yourself. Don't devalue Jane or Matt or Liam, either. And for heaven's sake, don't devalue what you do, and what Broomfield Hill does. It's not just keeping the music alive in the modern world, there's a lot of people doing that. The point is, no one else does it half so well. Which is why you're going to Callowen, and they're not. Speaking of which . . ."

"We'd best get a move on? Right. We're nearly there, I believe. The exit for Purbury should be just ahead."

They came to the open gates, were waved through by the same gatekeeper Jane had encountered earlier, and followed her trail along the curving white road. Ringan, having got the nervous attack out of the way, was relaxed and even anticipatory. At length, they emerged on the huge circular drive in front of Callowen House, and pulled to a stop.

"Jane's here." Ringan had spotted the Vauxhall, third in a line of ten or so cars, apparently awaiting relocation to some unseen spot. "I hope she wasn't the first one here. She'd never forgive us."

"Oh, good, we're not the first, then. I loathe arriving before anyone else. Too shymaking." Penny climbed out of the Alfa. "I wonder if we're supposed to just go ring the—oh, never mind. Here's someone coming down the stairs. Ringan, who in the world is that enormous woman—do you recognise her? And why do you suppose she's wearing homespun pink and purple flour sacks? And isn't that Jane she's dragging along behind her?"

Before Ringan could answer, Charlotte Leight-Arnold, with Jane clutched firmly by the arm, had swept down the front steps of Callowen House and skidded to a stop.

"You're Ringan Laine. Truly. You *are*." She was three inches taller than either Ringan or Penny, and her odd-coloured eyes seemed to want to focus on different points of interest. "I'm utterly chuffed to meet you, no, honestly. I am, truly. I mean, goodness, I hoped Uncle Albert would put your name up for this year. I'm so tired of all those dreary little drama types, cluttering up the place and emoting left and right. I mean, I ask you, who in hell wants Shakespeare in the morning, before you can even brush your teeth? Declaiming all over the house? Music! That's what we want."

Ringan blinked. At his side, Penny's shoulders suddenly began to shake a bit. She put one hand up to cover her mouth.

"Ringan." Jane, who had managed to extricate herself from Charlotte's hold, spoke urgently. She had a very strange look on her face. "This is Charlotte Leight-Arnold. She lives here. She's—she's rather an admirer of yours."

"Understatement." Charlotte laid her hands, which were long-boned and beautiful, on Ringan's shoulders. She hadn't so much as glanced at Penny. "That's a complete and absolutely deliberate understatement. The truth is, I've wanted to shag you for years. No, really. I mean, since I saw Broomfield Hill at Cropredy, about ten years ago. I decided then, I simply had to drag you off into some poorly lit, uninhabited corner of the carpark and ravish you. And here you are! How lucky!"

She was beaming, the long dimples now deeply etched grooves down the length of her face. Jane edged away; this was the same loony, high-powered look that had nearly sent her off screaming, earlier in the day. Ringan, slack-jawed and speechless, stared at Charlotte. He opened his mouth, closed it again, and waited for Penny to demolish her.

A strangled noise came from just beside his right shoulder. Penny now had one hand entirely covering the lower half of her face. Her shoulders were taut with the effort of holding still. Right, Ringan thought bitterly, just like her, to choose this of all moments to find the situation funny. Seeing that no immediate help could be expected of his lady-love, he made a huge effort and pulled himself together.

"That's—very flattering." Inspiration seized him. "You're Charlotte? Did you mention an Uncle Albert, and can I assume that's Albert Wychsale?"

"Of course. None other. Did he tell you I was madly in love with you, and wanted to do you? Honestly, I didn't think he knew." There was not a speck of self-consciousness in Charlotte's speech, no indication that she was aware of having said anything unusual. It came to Ringan, unnervingly, that Charlotte Leight-Arnold, rare among humans, had absolutely no inhibitions. Jane, nearly lost behind the welter of flapping multicoloured burlap, caught Ringan's look and jerked her head towards the front door. She made no attempt to meet Penny's eye, whether from terror of triggering an explosion or unwillingness to provoke howls of laughter was unclear.

"Um, no. No, I don't believe he mentioned anything like that." Ringan turned around and got Penny by the arm. She took a step forward. There was a singular smile on her face. "If you're Charlotte, then I must introduce you to Penny. You would have missed each other at Oxford by just a bit—Albert told us you'd been at Oriel, and so was Penny, doing Classics. This is Penelope Wintercraft-Hawkes."

"Oh." Charlotte put out a hand. "Hello. You were at Oriel? You're younger than I am."

"Yes, a bit. Not by much, though. I'm thirty-seven." Penny took Charlotte's hand, and spoke cheerfully. "A pleasure to meet you, and to be here. Lovely to see Callowen at last. One of the members of my acting troupe, Donal McCreary, had a bad experience here, so we can't come back unless we come without him, and I wouldn't. But you wouldn't mind that, would you? Shakespeare in the loo before teeth and all that, rather our speciality."

"Oh. No, true. I wouldn't mind less theatre. It's not my thing, at all, in fact it makes my back teeth lock up. Blah blah forsooth avaunt ye, and all that. Ugh. And of course, all those wretched little tunes Shakespeare wrote. He was tone-deaf, you know, and should never have gone near music." Charlotte was studying her frankly. "So, you're not here to perform?"

"No, no." Penny locked eyes with her hostess, and smiled suddenly. It was a genuine smile, not threatening, but Jane took an involuntary step backwards, and Ringan stiffened. He knew that smile. "I'm here because I'm shagging Ringan. Have done, for a good, what, eleven years now. I'm afraid, by the time you first saw him at the Cropredy Festival all those years ago, you'd have already been too late. So, here we are. Very much a couple, shagging and all. So I'm afraid you'll just have to do without. Can you cope?"

There was a long silence. Jane had her teeth clamped on her quivering lower lip, and Ringan was aiming indeterminate silent prayers to whatever might be listening. Penny, her head tilted, watched Charlotte's face. It was obvious to the others that Charlotte herself was seriously considering the question.

"Yes, I suppose so," she said finally. There was no rancour in her voice at all. "It's a pity, because honestly, there's very few blokes out there I ever want to even share air with, much less have wild sex with, and he happens to be one. But if it's no go, well, *c'est la vie*."

She suddenly turned the beam on Penny, full strength. Jane watched Penny's dimples curve up, and let her breath out.

"Welcome to Callowen. We're having some of the staff move the cars around the back, to the garage. Let me get someone out here, and they'll bring your bags and whatnot upstairs. Did I say, welcome to Callowen? Because, well, welcome. Both of you."

". . . a poorly lit, uninhabited corner of the carpark. Oh my dear God!"

Penny, lying on the bed in a comfortable guest room, was trying to catch her breath. She'd been wailing with pent-up laughter for a good ten minutes, unable either to stop or to get any control of it whatsoever. Ringan, becoming progressively more the dour Scot the longer the laughter went on, stood at the side of the bed, looking warlike but not really angry. He was well aware of the fact that, once the surprise and the sense of unreality at even being here in the first place wore off, he was going to see just how funny that exchange downstairs had been.

"Understatement! Deliberate understatement! Wanting to shag you for years. No, truly. Damn, now I've made myself sick with laughing. At least she's got taste." Penny struggled upright, and wiped her streaming eyes. She had scraped her tangled hair off her face and pulled it back in an elastic band, and the resulting ponytail bobbed as she moved. "What a way to begin the festival. And don't you sit there glaring at me, Mister Quickie in the Dimly Lit Carpark. If you had any proper gratitude, you'd be thrilled I'm finding this all so funny. I could just as easily be going after the lady with some bit of medieval ordnance they've undoubtedly got ordinance stashed in a glass case somewhere." She began to giggle again. "'Did he tell you I was madly in love with you and wanted to do you?' Damn, now I've started up again, just imagining Albert's face as she was telling him that. Oh, lord, lord, I think I've pulled a muscle. Right, I must stop howling. It hurts. Music! That's what we want!"

She went off into another paroxysm of laughter. Ringan stared at her balefully.

"I'm never going to hear the end of this, am I?" Ringan asked conversationally. "Do you know what I'd really like to do? At this exact moment, that is? Put you across my knee and take a slipper to you, that's what. You're an evil, evil wench."

"Oooooh, spanking. You sexy man, you." She leered at him theatrically. "Well, if you're mad enough to try it, let's have Charlotte in first. I'm sure she'd love to watch."

Ringan's sputtered reply was cut off by a knock at the door. It opened to reveal the three other members of Broomfield Hill.

Liam McCall erupted into the room first. His long black hair was pulled back into a braid, he'd forsaken his usual torn jeans and crammed his six-foot five-inch height into good ones, and his general air of manic exuberance seemed dampened. On the other hand, Matthew Curran, the band's placid accordion and concertina player, was looking energised. Jane bought up the rear.

Penny sat up on the bed, tucked her legs under her, and waved. She was grinning evilly. "Hello, Broomfields. Welcome to Callowen. Aren't you glad you aren't any of those dreary little drama types? Who in hell wants Shakespeare before breakfast? Musicians! That's what we like! Would any of you fancy shagging Ringan, in a carpark?"

"Ta, Penny, but I'd rather not. Generous of you to offer to share, though." Matthew was grinning as Ringan, framing a threat of dire consequences, took a purposeful step towards Penny. "Yes, we've met Lady Charlotte. I'm a bit shorter in the flesh than I am onstage, apparently, but that's all right, I'm still very nice, but of course I'm not Ringan, and welcome to Callowen. Molly gaped at her like a water-starved trout. My wife takes a while to get up to speed, coping with the unusual. And Charlotte Leight-Arnold? Unusual. Yes indeed."

"The woman's a nutter, a raving head case," Liam said explosively. "Mad as a sack of frogs. Mental, spoiled, and rude with it. Only an Englishman would let her run loose. Why she's not bricked up in a secret room somewhere in this mausoleum, I don't know. If her Da was an Irishman, now . . ."

"What did she say to you, then?" Ringan asked, with the vague hope that she might have outdone herself.

"She tugged Liam's beard." Jane was looking out the window. "Just reached right out and gave it a tweak. She asked him how he didn't get it caught in his fiddle every time he played. Told him he ought to cut it off. Left him speechless, something I honestly didn't think physically possible. God knows, I've been trying to do that for donkey's years. She's mad, of course. Do you believe this view? You can see nearly to the coast."

30

"I don't think she's mad, Jane. Not at all." Penny had sprawled across the bed on her stomach, her long legs bent up behind her. She looked about fifteen. "I just think that whether from genetics, or eccentricity, or social standing, or maybe just enough personality not to give a damn, she honestly sees no reason not to say whatever comes into her head at any time, about anything at all. It's scary as hell, isn't it? But I like her. I like her enormously. I don't think this little quirk of hers allows her to have a single manipulative or ugly bone in her body. And that's an awfully rare attribute. She brings out this strange protective streak in me. I didn't even know I had one. Not the protective type, at all."

They all stared at her. She raised both eyebrows. "What? That's my take on her. I think I could get quite fond of her, quite quickly, too." She considered for a moment. "Unless, of course, she actually does drag Ringan off into the carpark and ravish him," she amended. "Then, she dies."

"I'm curious about something." Matthew had taken a small guidebook from his pocket, and was leafing through it. "Ah, here we go. Molly picked this up from the National Trust, when she found out we'd be coming to stay at Callowen. It says here that the place is a famous haunted house."

"It is haunted, yes. Winston Churchill said so." Ringan heard his own words, realised how peculiar they sounded, and hastened to explain. "Albert Wychsale told us—his father was here at Callowen in the forties, and Winston Churchill and a handful of government dignitaries actually had an encounter with the resident ghost."

"Oh. Well, it says here that her name was Susanna, the Lady Susanna Leight-Arnold, and that she's the Lady Arnold in 'Matty Groves,' the song, that is. And I wondered. Because, well, if she's an ancestress and she haunts the place, are we planning to do it? The song, I mean? While we're here? Or would that just be beyond tactless?"

"That's a good question." Penny swung her feet to the floor. "Damn, my other shoe's gone under the bed. Are you, Ringan?"

"Don't know yet," he said briefly. "I was going to ask Lord Callowen if he wanted it. I mean, we don't actually need to do it. It's not as if we haven't got a set list, without summoning her out of her picture. Totally our host's call."

"Ringan, my love, you've just reminded me, there's something we haven't done." Penny, both shoes located, headed for the door. "We came up a side stair with Charlotte, so we haven't seen that portrait yet, the one Lady Susanna traditionally pops out of."

"No more have I seen it. Let's all go." Jane moved towards the door, where Penny waited. "You know, I really am curious about her. Maybe she'll materialise for us, just to oblige. Apparently, she's not timid about it, not if she wafted past Winston Churchill in broad daylight."

They made their way down panelled hallways, past priceless bits of antique *chinoiserie* in regularly spaced alcoves. Penny seemed to know instinctively where she was going, and Ringan reflected that she must have spent school holidays at houses which, if not this grand in scope, would certainly have been of a similar period and layout. Below them, in the Great Hall, they heard the distant sounds of people arriving. As they followed Penny, the muted clamour became less distant.

"Here," Penny said gaily, over her shoulder. "It should be right down this next—ah. Here we are, then. Hello, Charlotte. You're looking all puzzled and bemused. What's up?"

There was no reply. Penny stopped, the others slowing down at her heels. Charlotte Leight-Arnold, with two dazed-looking academic types behind her, stood motionless at the head of the Great Staircase.

While everything at Callowen seemed to bear the label of "Great," the staircase, at least, wore the appellation with pride. Running straight from the hall to the first-floor gallery which led to the guest and family wings, it was exquisitely carved From the area's local oak. Standing at the top looking down, or standing in the Great Hall looking up, produced a very *trompe l'oeil* effect: From a vertical perspective, it seemed as if the staircase had been built as a modified hourglass, narrowing noticeably at the halfway point. In actuality, the entire structure was the same width, a gracious three or so yards, for its full length. The hourglass look was produced by the addition, at either end, of standing fluted pilasters of age-mellowed wood. The effect was oddly welcoming, almost as if the house was opening gracious arms.

"Charlotte?"

Charlotte's head turned, slowly. Her glorious pile of red-gold hair, shakily controlled to begin with, was perilously close to escaping confinement altogether. Penny saw her vivid face, now curiously blank.

"Charlotte! What is it? What's wrong?"

"I said you looked familiar." Penny opened her mouth, bewildered, and then saw that Charlotte's odd-coloured eyes were directed past her, towards Jane. "Didn't I? Awfully familiar? I was right. Look. It's you. Well, almost you."

She pointed a finger. Everyone, including the two as-yet-unidentified guests on the stairs, clustered around to look.

The portrait of Lady Susanna Leight-Arnold, as painted by the Dutchman Daniel Mytens, had been executed on a canvas approximately seven feet by four, and made even larger by a wildly elaborate gilt frame of bas-relief curlicues. It hung in solitary splendour at the head of the stairs. This was a perfect setting: the lady stood, bathed in light from all directions.

She'd been young when Mytens painted her, no more than twenty or so. She'd dressed up for the sittings, in a gown of celestial blue velvet, split down the middle to reveal a white brocaded silk underdress beneath, and full slashed sleeves to match. She wore a collar, the fabric standing remarkably to attention, in what must have been uncomfortably stiff lace. Even the bunchy, high-waisted dress of the early seventeenth century couldn't disguise her ethereal slenderness; it was there in the roguish arch of her neck, the lines of her face, the sculpted wrists.

Nor had Mytens made any attempt to render her features in the smug, satisfied style so prevalent among the court paintings of his era. There was none of Van Dyck's flatness or stillness. The eyes, a dark heady blue, looked out on the world and seemed to be on the edge of winking enticingly. The Lady Susanna, in fact, as captured nearly four centuries earlier by the distinguished Dutchman, was enchanting.

"You," Charlotte repeated. "How odd. Are we related?"

Jane stared at the Lady Susanna. Dark blue stares met, one painted, one incredulous and a bit uneasy. There was certainly a pronounced resemblance. It was there in echoes of colouring, in the cast and smallness of bone, in the shape of face and mouth, the way the Lady Susanna stood.

"No, I don't think we are." Jane swallowed. There was something disturbing, not about the painting, but about knowing she'd had someone this close to a double, so long dead. "That's not me, I mean, we aren't really alike. The hair, for instance. She's got your glorious gold, not my dishwater blonde."

Charlotte had, in fact, exaggerated. There were certainly differences, as many differences as similarities. But the similarities were striking, and impossible to miss.

"Showing our guests our naughty ancestress, Char?"

The deep voice from behind them brought everyone's head around. A man stood there, late middle-aged, extremely tall, and completely bald. He had a high forehead and a bony, warlike nose, contrasting oddly with a mobile, generous mouth that immediately proclaimed his genetic ties to Charlotte. He was dressed conventionally, in country tweeds and sturdy walking shoes; he needed only a spaniel at his heels to complete the picture.

There was no spaniel, however. Instead, jessed to one heavily gauntleted forearm and held carefully away from striking distance to his face, was a full-grown peregrine falcon. The bird was unhooded. It was also uneasy.

One of the academic types gasped, and moved hastily backwards. The bird, startled by the suddenness of the movement, lifted its wings. There was a flurry of feathers and colour and noise, as the hawk bated, fluttering angrily from its perch. Silver varvels bearing the Leight-Arnold crest, dangling from the ends of the leather jesses, jangled like harsh bells with the animal's motion.

The man spoke sharply, and the bird answered, a high harsh scream that echoed through the house. Then the wings folded down, the powerful shoulders twitched uneasily, and the terrifying talons closed once again on the leather of the man's gauntlet as the bird settled.

"Silly young fool," the man admonished his deadly pet. "Don't you act up, now, that's no way to behave. You mustn't scare the guests. Charlotte, you need to introduce me, unless I can guess." He looked up at the clutch of people at the top of the stairs, all of whom seemed to be holding their breath. His gaze travelled from one to the other, and stopped at Penny.

"I know who you are," he said, and came up the stairs. The members of Broomfield Hill parted like grain in a summer wind. Penny, with one wary eye devoted to watching the bird, stood her ground. "Penelope Wintercraft-Hawkes, isn't it? It's an honour. I saw your production of *Iphigenia* a few months back, opening night, in fact. Albert Wychsale took me along. Marvellous stuff. I'm Callowen, by the way. Welcome to you all. Will you introduce me to everyone? Or perhaps my daughter will?"

Penny made the round of introductions, stopping at the academics. Charlotte stepped in and took over; one was a professor of European folklore from a German university, the other the author of several scholarly and obscure books about the origins of jazz in North America. A servant, happening around the corner of the gallery, was pounced on by Charlotte and sent off with the two grateful academics to their respective rooms.

"That—what a very imposing bird you've got." Jane was staring at the creature in fascination. "That's a peregrine, isn't it? Or a goshawk? Does one usually have them indoors?"

"Peregrine. Goshawks are shortwings, with darker plumage and copper eyes; they're easy to tell apart, really, the breeds. This is Gaheris. Two-year-old tiercel. Gorgeous, isn't he? And no, most falconers, not—indoors, that is. Gaheris is fine indoors. He's beautifully trained and bonded with me, and he's wearing short jesses. Used to people. Besides, my house, my hawk." Lord Callowen, stroking the speckled breast feathers, glanced up at Jane, and did a classic double take. His eyes narrowed. "Hello! Are you family?"

"That's what I asked." Charlotte broke in eagerly, before Jane could reply. "Doesn't she look just like the Lady Susanna?"

"That she does. A bit unnerving really. You're—Jane, was it? Of course, Jane Castle, Broomfield's flautist. Any chance you've got some of the old Leight-Arnold DNA about you anywhere?"

"No. I mean, we, my family, we go back a good long way, and we're about two steps above the yeomanry, with a lot of healers and musicians." Jane realised she was babbling, and bit her lip. "Anyway, there isn't any nobility in there anywhere. No."

"Huh. Coincidence? Hard to believe. Devil of a lookalike." Callowen and the falcon Gaheris both pinned her with their stares: the two pairs of eyes were oddly similar, since both were yellowish amber. Indeed, with Miles Leight-Arnold's bony ridge of a nose and powerful shoulders, the resemblance between man and bird went well beyond the eyes. It came to Ringan, watching in silence, that Callowen had chosen his dangerous pet precisely because they were physically so well matched. "Wrong side of the blanket, maybe? Possible, d'ye think?"

"I—no, I don't." Jane shook her head firmly. "My mother does genealogy as a hobby. She's got the complete lists. Kind of you to think we might be related, very flattering really, but we really can't be."

"Ah well. I wondered, you know, because it isn't just your looks. Women in my family have been musical going back to when they first left Normandy in 1066—Char's just the latest in a very long line. And one of the Leight-Arnold women got called up for witchcraft, under Cromwell. The Lord Protector didn't like girls knowing all about healing herbs. You said musicians and healers. So I wondered."

There seemed to be nothing to say to this. Liam spoke up suddenly, for the first time.

"The Lady here, in the painting. Susanna, is it? Or rather, was it? She's the one who walks?"

"Not walking." Charlotte had moved to her father's side, and was murmuring to the falcon Gaheris, lightly and rhythmically stroking the bird's cere, the waxy skin above its nostrils. Gaheris was calm, almost placid, under her touch. Ringan, who had never before seen a hawk in the flesh and was finding it difficult not to stare at it, thought that, had the bird been a cat, the damned thing would have purred and kneaded. "More like floating. Or drifting."

"Or zooming," Callowen added. "It's strange. She comes out of the picture, looks over her left shoulder, jerks her head around, comes down the stair fast and gets faster as she goes, and then veers into a sharp left turn about halfway down. The muniments say the original staircase was a well construction, with a series of bends, rather than a straight one, so perhaps there was an incident on the stairs, but who knows? She does the same thing every time. No one's ever seen her anywhere else in the house." Callowen put his right hand out and grasped Liam's. "You're Liam McCall, yes? Flute, fiddle, and concertina. Char should be delighted. She's a huge fan."

Penny's lips twitched. Ringan, watching her with foreboding, was relieved when Liam went on.

"Has the Lady Susanna been seen in recent times?"

"Not for a couple of years." There were more people in the Great Hall now, the sound of car doors slamming, the swell of conversation. Callowen lifted his voice. "Must go down and greet the incomings. I wouldn't worry about Lady Susanna. She doesn't seem to like the festival much, since she's never once been seen while it was on. Maybe it's too noisy for her. In any case, we've got a welcome dinner tonight at seven. There should be a note about it in each of your rooms. We do dress, but if you didn't bring anything really suitable, just do what you can. We'll see you tonight." He turned to go, and both the man and the bird swivelled their heads. "I'm glad you're all here," he told them, and went.

Three

"Come home with me, little Matty Groves
Come home with me tonight
Come home with me, little Matty Groves
And sleep with me 'til light"

"So," Ringan asked, "what do you think of the setup?"

It was past midnight of their first night at Callowen, and Penny and Ringan were curled up in the comfortable oversized bed. Their suitcases were unpacked and everything was put away for the duration, their teeth were brushed, the bedroom door was locked. Even their shoes, as was the custom, had been left outside their door for cleaning and polishing. They had learned the hard way to lock both doors of the bathroom before use, since the bathroom in question connected their room to Jane's. She'd been rather vocal about being disturbed. Ringan, who'd accidentally done the disturbing, had backed out hastily with promises to be careful. He'd kept the grin off his face until the door was closed.

Now, stuffed to capacity with a five-course meal crowned by the traditional roast beef of Old England, Penny and Ringan lay side by side, and chatted in low tones with the ease of long custom. Despite their joint elation at being where they were, neither had the faintest urge towards lovemaking. As Ringan put it, the act of digesting all that food was going to require that he give it all he had. It was more than either of them would normally eat, short of Christmas dinner.

"The setup, as in the festival arrangements? Or as in the family itself? Because I'd have to say this entire place and everyone in it qualifies as interesting." Penny shifted from her back to her side, facing Ringan, and propped herself on one elbow. The half-opened curtains let a soft summery glow of moon into the room; as the evening breeze lifted them slightly, the room danced with shadows. "You've heard my views on Charlotte. As to her father, well, I find Miles impressive."

"He's all of that," Ringan agreed. "And it isn't just that bloody eagle he carries around with him, either. That's a man with enough self-confidence to float an armada. Is that money, or social standing, or both? The poor wee Scots boy wants to know."

"Come off it," she said, and grinned. "That confidence of his? Both, but also genetics. I expect the first Leight-Arnold to ever slide down the chute came out lifting his brows at the midwife, and looking vulpine. And the one who helped the Conqueror at Hastings probably looked down his nose and complained about the weather and the smell of the serfs. Family arrogance, meet Ringan Laine." She saw his teeth, a brief flash of white as he grinned. "Charlotte has it, too," she continued. "In carloads, I'd say. It really makes you wonder about Charlotte's mum, doesn't it? I gather she died of cancer when Char was at school. But as to the setup, if you meant in terms of how to deal with it, you're asking the wrong person. It's nothing to do with me, is it? Not really. I'm an accessory. I'm just here to be an ornament, talk theatre when appropriate, and eat my head off. Oh, and to shag you just enough to keep Charlotte at the edge of frenzy, or at least let her think that's what I'm doing. This is your moment of glory, darling, not mine."

"True. Speaking of talking theatre, wasn't that Julian Cordellet you were partnered with at dinner?"

His voice was a bit too careful, and Penny bit back a grin of her own. While it was nice to know he could still get jealous after so many years together, it was also disconcerting. And since pretending to be casual was something foreign to his nature, he was very unconvincing.

"It was indeed Julian Cordellet, but you got the verb wrong. He was talking theatre, not me. I was listening," she said cheerfully. "I was the talkee, as in being talked at and talked at and oh, yes, talked at. You were right about the one-man show at the Haymarket. He's taking it to Broadway next year. I now know more about it than anyone, including the devastatingly handsome and self-absorbed Julian himself, or even his proctologist." Ringan snorted rudely, and Penny relaxed. "Seriously, Julian's a sweet, charming man, but he could talk the teats off a cow. I grunted elegantly and interpolated the occasional glottal. Who was the lady with the pearls you were partnered with? While I was managing to get a word in edgewise about every four minutes?"

"No idea, except that she seemed to be Canadian and involved with dance. I know she has something to do with a revival of Morris dancing in a suburb of—Toronto, I think she said. And her first name was something I couldn't pronounce. She said it was her mother's maiden name, which sounded very weird. I gather she's invited as part of the selected audience."

"That's right, isn't it?" Penny pulled the duvet up around her shoulders, against the chill of the Hampshire dawn that would slip into the room as the night eased along. "If you've got performers, you need an audience. I wasn't even thinking about who the rest of the guests were. I never thought to take a count. Did you?"

"No, but it wasn't necessary; I asked. There's an audience guest list of forty-nine people. Forty-six showed up, three couldn't make it."

"Only three no-shows? Wow. Apparently people don't say no when Miles puts out the welcome mat. By the way, are you going to do a version of the Callowen family anthem? Or the Leight-Arnold Fight Song, or whatever they consider it?"

"What, 'Matty Groves'? Yes, but only at the last performance. I had a word with our host and he said he liked the idea of doing it only once, and closing this year's festival with it seemed the best. We're doing both, opening and closing. It's tradition, apparently; the first and last performances at the festival are always music, and since we're the only musical act this year . . ." His voice trailed away into a half-swallowed yawn.

Penny eased herself back down, and stared at the room's high ceiling. Blackness, patches in the shape of leaves on Callowen's prized yew trees, fluttered across the wainscoting and blended with the night as the breeze stilled and started up again.

"Ringan?" She reached a hand out under the light summer duvet and touched his hip. "What Miles said, when Liam asked about the Lady Susanna. He said she'd never been known to manifest during a festival, and that she always showed in the same spot, and did the same thing. He sounded as though he believed it. Do you suppose he doesn't know?"

"Oh, lord." Ringan understood at once. "About whatever it was that came through Sinead McCreary? There's a nice comfortable thought to have just before I drift off for the night. I don't know, lamb, honestly. But I expect we'll find out, or with any luck at all, we won't find out, since whatever it is will stay elsewhere for the next fourteen days. And I agree with you. He really sounded as though he mightn't know, or at least might not believe it." He yawned cavernously. "Me for some kip. That last glass of wine did me in, and we need to set up for a sound check in the morning. Good night, Pen. If anything at all wakes you up, wake me up. I'm serious. Don't try and deal on your own."

The breeze lifted the curtains, and settled them again. Over the next few hours, the patterns on the ceiling changed in subtle ways as the moon moved in its courses, first waxing, then waning. Penny and Ringan, both deeply and dreamlessly sleeping, saw none of it.

Two rooms away, on the other side of the big comfortable bathroom, Jane Castle lay asleep. Unlike the others, she was dreaming.

It was a dream that began with herself some twenty years ago. She was a student again in London, although no younger than she was now. And here was a face she never dreamed about: Colin, her study partner and, coincidentally, the first man she'd ever slept with.

Where were they? She couldn't tell, but it seemed to be rural, even rustic. Here were tall hedges, a stone bench, a riot of roses, all with names she knew from her mother's garden as a child, but only a few of which she could remember: "Lady Fortevoit," for instance, she knew that one. And what was the yellow rose called, that sweet-smelling climber that she avoided because everyone knew yellow roses attracted bees and wasps? She couldn't remember. The name of the yellow rose, the name of everything, edged her mind and slid just beyond her grasp as she reached for it. It was very frustrating.

Come here, little pretty one. Hush. Come here to me. Such a pretty thing, such a pretty little bird. You will be kind, won't you? You'll not tell on me? You'll not make me punish you?

Was Colin trying to tell her something? Yes, he was, his lips were moving, but they weren't Colin's lips and he didn't look like Colin any more. In the manner of those who inhabit dreams, the young lover had metamorphosed into someone else. The young dreaming Jane, who wasn't entirely herself, tried to place his features. It was no good. Not only could she not name him, she had never seen him before.

Or had she? He was familiar, after all. She knew him from somewhere, yes, but the connection was tantalising, impossible to pin down. A thin bony face, pale eyes a bit too close together and with something not right about them, a stark nose like a raptor's beak, thin brownish hair cropped close to the skull. Who . . . ? The face teased away from her, becoming indistinct. Then it came back, zooming in like a new camera being manipulated by an amateur, hard and fast and disorienting.

He leaned closer to her, too close. She was on her back now, looking up at a wheeling sky. His lips brushed her face; teeth, small sharp teeth, scraped along her upper lip and grabbed it. The teeth fastened and bit lightly, not enough to draw blood, but enough to leave an echo of hurt behind them. The biting stopped; the lips moved away, parted to whisper, to brush against her ear. He whispered her name, lovingly.

But it wasn't her name, and there was no love in it. And suddenly, as will happen in dreams, she was frightened.

The sleeper jerked a bit. Her head pressed back against the pillow, back and away, as if in protest. Had Jane not been sleeping alone, had someone been awake during the march of the hours, he or she might have noticed an anomaly: the leafy pattern on the ceiling was gone, replaced by a solid black bulk of something through which no light seemed to penetrate. And had the walls of Callowen House been less solidly built, or had the proprieties of modern life not mandated keeping both bathroom doors closed, Penny and Ringan might have woken from their postprandial stupor to hear Jane whimpering.

Next morning after breakfast, Penny enthusiastically took Charlotte up on her offer of the loan of a good horse, and Broomfield Hill got their first look at the Callowen House ballroom, which would host their five performances.

This took up one entire wing of the ground floor. It was an enormous room, designed to easily accommodate four hundred people, half of whom would have been twirling across the hardwood floors in full-skirted evening dresses. There were alcoves, hung with velvet curtains in a deep, lustrous blue; there was a full-sized stage at one end of the room. The entire space was flooded with light, pouring through the cut glass of two dozen French doors that ran the length of the ballroom's walls, from floor nearly to the ceiling. It was a lovely room, built to house the entertainments of a more gracious age.

For an acoustic musician, the place was a close to perfect venue. Miles Leight-Arnold employed an expert sound technician named Jack Halley, whose job it was to make the festival performers as happy as the surroundings would allow. Jack, a friendly man in his early sixties, had worked with everyone from the RSC to the Beatles to the BBC. He'd devoted his considerable ability to this one room for the past fifteen years, and there was virtually nothing he couldn't do to manipulate the acoustics. He was waiting for Broomfield Hill in the theatre with Miles Leight-Arnold when the band members found their individual ways there and met, shortly after breakfast.

Ringan arrived first. He'd eaten eggs and toast in company with Penny, two members of the Blue Gum Dance Troupe, and about fifteen people who had all stared admiringly while he self-consciously ate his toast and drank his tea. He'd waved at Charlotte as she hurried in, and watched in fascination as she wolfed down coddled eggs, sausage, several rashers of bacon, and toast. Apparently, a huge breakfast was par for the course on mornings when she planned to ride.

Ringan had kissed Penny, told her not to fall off any of the nasty horses, ducked a swipe at his head, and gone off to the theatre. Broomfield Hill's first performance of five was scheduled for that evening. The set list, ten songs of which four would be alternated for subsequent performances, was in place; all were Broomfield standards, and they'd rehearsed extensively in the days leading up to the festival. The only concern was the acoustic viability of the room.

"Good morning." Matthew Curran wandered in right behind Ringan, stopping just inside and staring around him, at the ornamented ceiling, the expanse of perfect parquet floor, the vast doors through which he had just come, folded back upon themselves. "Ringan, is that a riding outfit Penny's wearing? Molly's off to explore the flower gardens; my wife's a pistol for roses. Crikey! Gorgeous space, this is."

"Thanks. We like it. And Penny's riding with us. Char's offered her a horse." Callowen nodded over Matt's shoulder. "Here's Liam, just coming. Where's the lovely Jane? Can't check your sound without your high end, can you?"

"Isn't she here?" Ringan cast one practised look around the converted ballroom, and whistled. "Nice," he said appreciatively. "Yes, where is Jane? She was just sitting down to breakfast when I was finishing up, but I'd expect her to be here by now. Tell you what, why don't we set up for a sound check? If she's not here by then, I'll go fetch her. It's not like her to be late, not at all."

45

"True," Liam grunted. "Usually she's all over us, scolding like someone's nursemaid if we're not there early. She'd best not be sickening for something."

Leight-Arnold, having introduced them to Jack, took himself off and, as he put it, all the way out of their way. As Ringan set up his guitar stand and put Lord Randall, his instrument, out to allow the strings to settle, he was aware of a growing uneasiness in himself. Liam was right. Jane was the last member of Broomfield Hill to be late for a sound check, or for anything else. Where in hell was she?

She arrived just as he was getting ready to go hunt for her. As he opened his mouth to give her a bit of hell, the words withered in his throat.

"Jane! Are you all right? You look as if you haven't slept."

"What? Oh. I'm fine." She was holding her flute case limply in one hand. She looked terrible, almost fragile. There were pronounced blue-black shadows under her eyes, her mouth seemed slack, and there was something about her speech, a kind of vagueness, that was disquieting. "I don't think I did sleep very well. Nightmares, I suppose, but I don't remember them. Are we setting up? Sorry to be late, but I had to go back to my room. I forgot my flute."

"You forgot your flute? Are you sure you're Jane?" Liam was staring at her. "You look like death warmed up and served on toast. What in hell's wrong? Was there a mouse in your bed? A pea under the mattress?"

"No, I told you, I'm fine. Where do I—oh, right. Stage left, as always. Come on, woman, wake up now. Time to get yourself organised for a sound check." She seemed to be a bit more alert. "I didn't have my second cup of coffee yet. That's probably it. Oh! Look!"

She pointed out through one of the open French doors. On the wide lawn in the near distance, four horses and their riders cantered. Two of them, thoroughbred chestnuts, carried women. Even from here, Charlotte's flame of hair was visible, escaping from under her riding cap. The straight-backed silhouette, handling the rather frisky second chestnut with casual ease, was unmistakably Penny.

The other two horses were magnificent. One was black with a white blaze down its nose, carrying someone Ringan couldn't identify at this distance. The other was an enormous silver-coated gelding with Lord Callowen a dominant, black-habited figure on his back. That the rider was Callowen was made obvious by the presence of the falcon on his arm.

Ringan and his bandmates stared out. Charlotte called out something to her father. He nodded, and released Gaheris into the morning air. With a high-pitched cry, the falcon fluttered, then gained altitude as the powerful wings caught a thermal updraft. Higher he went, soaring heavenward, his eyes to the ground and his back straight as the horizon itself.

The rider on the black pointed. Everyone, the riders out of doors and the musicians inside, watched the falcon Gaheris.

The bird, impossibly, seemed to stop in mid-flight. Then, faster than the human eye could translate into sense, he was in freefall, his wings against his sides, plummeting towards earth. Ringan, horrified, thought he heard a distant scream, and then realised the bird, far from being in danger, was in a controlled dive. He was on the hunt.

Leight-Arnold clapped his booted heels to the silver gelding's sides. The horse leaped forward, marking the hawk. The other three followed, Charlotte at full gallop, the other two more sedately.

The unidentified male rider turned his head and spoke to Penny, cantering easily at his side. Whatever he said amused her; Ringan knew that motion of her head, the tilt of her chin, that meant enjoyment or appreciation. There was an odd intimacy about the unknown rider's movements, a sensuality and grace in the way he leaned towards her. The movements were familiar, as well, and suddenly Ringan was able to put a name to him.

"Julian Cordellet," Ringan said, under his breath, and felt something close hard around his heart for a moment.

Behind him, unnoticed by the others, Jane Castle was swaying on her feet. Something was fighting its way through her waking mind, something she had heard or seen in the dark, buried shadow patches of the night just past. A bird, a pretty bird, who had said that? Surely, someone had said something to her about a pretty bird? There had been something about the hawk's dive, about the concentrated power and intent. It was a killing dive, he would go straight down with the lethal steel talons and the long sharp beak; was that a beak? Were those nares? Or was that a bird's face at all? Of course it was, it must be, but what colour were the eyes of the falcon, what colour, there was something, but she couldn't remember, she didn't want to remember, it was coming straight at her, too close to her face, her body, hunting her, a controlled dive, there was something and it wouldn't come, she wouldn't let it come . . .

"*No*," she said, loudly and firmly. As her bandmates turned to stare at her, she lifted a wavering hand to her face.

"Get the hell away from me," she said, and fainted.

"Oh God," Penny said. "Oh no. Poor Jane. And you say she doesn't remember, not any of it?"

"Nothing." It was Liam who replied. Ringan, since shouting for help and following a shaken Jane to her room as she went slowly upstairs to lie down, had been strangely pinch-lipped, and completely silent. "Not a damned thing. She said something when she was just coming to—something about eyes, the wrong eyes, and also about a pretty bird, but she couldn't remember why that had come into her head. Creepy. Damned creepy. Reminds me of the bogles in the barn, last year at Ringan's."

Molly Curran came out of Jane's room, through the bathroom, and into Ringan and Penny's room, where everyone was waiting. She closed the bathroom door behind her; everyone heard the click as the lock slid home inside.

"How is she?" A confusion of voices pitched the question.

Molly saw the concern in their faces. "She's fine," she told them reassuringly. "Much better, in fact. She said she's going to have a cup of tea and a hot shower and she'll be ready for the sound check and fine for the show. Matt—what's going on here? What happened to her?"

"I don't know." There was trouble in Matt's face. "But something's wrong, that's all I know. Her face, her voice—I've never seen Jane look like that. It was—she looked as if she was staring through a window into Hell. Liam just said he was remembering last summer, in the tithe barn at Lumbe's, but she didn't look nearly so—lost—back then, surely."

"Does she have breakdowns? Seizures or epilepsy or anything like that?" Charlotte, her riding cap discarded, chewed on a strand of hair. The riders had been called back; Callowen had gone off to put his bird in the mews, and Julian Cordellet had not accompanied the two women upstairs. "I mean, you know, blackouts and that kind of thing," Charlotte went on. "Sort of mental bits that aren't quite right? That any of you know about, I mean, or maybe, I don't know, what is that thing called, oh, right, bipolar? Is she?"

"No." Ringan's voice was chilly and detached. "She doesn't have seizures and she isn't bipolar and just in case you were thinking of asking, no, she doesn't take drugs and she isn't much of a drinker, either. So don't ask it. The answer's no."

The last sentence had a bite of dislike to it that was completely unlike Ringan. Everyone turned to stare. He flushed, his skin mottling.

"Sorry," he muttered, "I'm not trying to be rude, but I won't have this glossed over. The plain truth is that there's nothing wrong with Jane. There never has been anything wrong with Jane, and I ought to know; we've been working together, playing together, travelling and rehearsing and whatnot, for fifteen years at least. I'd put her among the sanest people on earth, and also the most dependable. Besides, she was fine yesterday—you all saw her. Something happened, I don't know what, and apparently, Jane doesn't remember, not yet, anyway. But whatever it was, it happened between dinner last night and breakfast this morning."

"And just what do you think it was?"

The voice came from the doorway. Miles Leight-Arnold, with Albert Wychsale right behind him, was standing in the hall, just outside the room. He was still in his riding clothes, and his boots gleamed against the soft pale carpets.

"What's all this I hear about Jane being ill? Here, Miles, let me past, there's a good chap." Albert edged into the room, and went up to Ringan. "How is she? Can we do anything for her? Do we know what happened?"

"Molly says she's better. She's taking a shower at the moment." Ringan was meeting Callowen's gaze, two pairs of steely eyes in a deadlock, neither blinking or backing down. "I could take a damned good guess at what happened, and I expect Lord Callowen could as well. I'm not sure this is the moment to do it, though. Or the place to do it."

"Why would this be the wrong moment?" Matt, sensing the undercurrents, seeing the awareness and dismay on Wychsale's face, spoke in bewilderment. His usual placidity was transmuting into something close to anger. "Seems to me this is the only moment. We have a performance tonight, remember? If something is happening to one of our bandmates, what good is it going to do if you're all standing about, looking fierce and discussing timing? What's all this, then? Talk to us."

Penny was staring at Ringan. In the last hour, he seemed to have become someone completely separate from the man she'd kept company with for over a decade, someone dark and formidable. He was angry, she could see that, even though she had no idea why. But there was something else just below his visible anger, a dark edge honed and ready to slice, that had nothing to do with the man she knew and loved. He had not so much as glanced her way since she'd walked into the room. He had not met her look, spoken to her, acknowledged that he knew or cared that she was alive. She'd never seen him this way, and she couldn't take any more of it. Enough was enough. Besides, if he meant what she thought he meant, this was more her business than his.

"I believe he's talking about what happened to the wife of a member of my acting troupe."

The sound of her own voice—calm, cold, and very measured—astonished her. She certainly felt neither calm nor cold. Something was churning inside, hot and emotional and unpleasant. "What happened here, that is, at the festival. It would have been about a dozen years ago, shortly before he joined the Tamburlaine Players. Her name was Sinead McCreary."

Penny watched Miles Leight-Arnold, but on the periphery of her vision, she saw other faces change. Albert Wychsale had known what was coming, she could see that in his very expressive grimace. Ringan, for the first time, turned to watch her. And Charlotte was genuinely surprised.

"Sinead McCreary? The Irish actor woman? I remember her. She went riding with me, the first morning she was here. She adored horses. I liked her. Funny woman, I mean, she made me laugh. What do you mean, what happened to her? I never heard anything had—"

"Be quiet, Char." Callowen spoke authoritatively. He was looking very steadily at Penny. "I heard she had a stroke, not long after she was here. I don't know what you think that has to do with her presence at Callowen, but don't you think Ringan's right? I damned well do. This is hardly the place or the time."

His tone was precisely what he might have used to a stupid child, or a social inferior. It was the final straw. Penny, already shaken by Ringan's strangeness and what was happening to Jane, suddenly and gloriously forgot both her manners and the fact that she was a guest in the Leight-Arnold house, and proceeded to lose her temper.

"No. As it happens, I don't think Ringan's right," she told him. "Do you know, I don't know what I dislike more, your assumption that I'm mentally defective or your assumption that you can bully me into shutting up. How dare you address me in that pompous, arrogant way? Who in hell do you think you're talking to, a housemaid? I'd love to give you the benefit of the doubt, really I would.

I'd love to be able to assume you honestly don't know what happened the night one of your resident incorporeal Bad Boys went right through one of your invitees and left her permanently damaged for what remained of her life. I can't. You know all about it, don't you? The very fact that you're trying to shut me up proves it. So don't dare talk to me as if you thought I was one of your servants, or some stupid schoolgirl. It's not only bloody rude, it's inaccurate. I am not a fool. I am not your inferior. And I will not play *noblesse oblige* with you, not now, not ever. Is that quite clear?"

Someone gasped. Penny, in a complete rage, swept on.

"You're willing to talk about the pretty, pathetic little thing that floats out of the Mytens painting. Oh, yes, that's because she adds a cachet, and she's an ancestress, and anyway, she doesn't hurt anyone. But you're damned if you want to talk about this one, is that it? You don't even want to admit it might exist, because it's ugly and nasty and dangerous. No greater glory to the Leight-Arnolds off this one, is there? Well—fine. So long as it doesn't hurt anyone, fine. I don't give a damn. You can be in denial from here to Hell. But it did hurt someone, didn't it? Her husband was there and he saw, and twelve years later he's still grieving for her. And now I think it's hurting Jane, and I won't allow it. So don't you look down your nose at me and try and intimidate me into shutting up. That, Lord Callowen, is simply not going to happen."

She stopped, her breath rasping through her nostrils. Ringan walked over to her and dropped his arm around her waist. He stood beside her in a gesture of solidarity, his hip pressed against hers, facing Callowen, once again the Ringan she knew.

In the absolute silence, Miles Leight-Arnold grinned. It was an expression of genuine appreciation.

"Feisty, aren't you?" he said. "You're quite right, I knew there was some tale about McCreary's wife. Thing is, that was the only time in history we'd ever heard anything like that, so we didn't altogether believe it. McCreary believed it, though. That's why we never invited the Tamburlaines—tactless. Still think it's rubbish, though. If there was something dark here, something else here, why wait for Sinead McCreary? There have been no tragic deaths at Callowen for centuries, not since the Lady Susanna and her fancy man were killed by Lord Edward. Doesn't make sense. Why show up then, and just the once? But I didn't mean to make you angry, or insult you. Shouldn't have spoken that way, it was damned rude of me. No way to treat a guest, certainly not an honoured one. I apologise."

Penny opened her mouth to reply, but was forestalled. Behind them, the noisy old-fashioned latch gave its distinctive click. The bathroom door swung open, and Jane Castle, swathed in an over-sized bathrobe and with her hair wrapped in a towel, stepped into the room and stared at them.

"Hello," she said, in honest surprise. "Are we having a party? And shouldn't everyone be getting ready for tonight?"

Four

"Oh I can't come home, I won't come home
And sleep with you tonight
By the rings on your fingers I can tell
You are Lord Arnold's wife"

Everyone present would later agree that Broomfield Hill's opening night performance at the Callowen Festival was one of the best they'd ever done.

Sometime between breakfast and dinner, the ballroom had been expertly transformed into an intimate nightclub. Comfortable chairs alternated with small tables, the curved rows making optimum use of the room's acoustics. At the rear, inside the enormous fold-back doors, one of Callowen's staff served drinks to the guests. The atmosphere was a perfect blend of relaxation and anticipation.

Penny, ensconced in an end chair in the second row, had dressed for the occasion. Her clothes would have been suitable for someone else's opening night in the West End: designer silk, high heels, and full makeup. She'd spent some time on her hair, and touched up her nails. Diamonds, Ringan's first Christmas gift to her, dangled from her ears. This, after all, was Ringan's big night. If she was attending in the guise of Official Ornament, she was damned well going to be ornamental.

His coldness and strangeness of earlier in the day were not forgotten, but for the moment she had pushed them to the back of her mind. She was going to tackle him about it, there was no way she was letting it go, but it would have to wait. Right now, nothing was more important than Broomfield Hill's Callowen debut.

"God, I'm nervous." Molly Curran edged past, dressed for evening but still comfortable in a silk sweater and skirt. She was balancing an overfilled glass of cider in one hand. "Matt's not nervous, mind you, just me. Oh, you saved me a seat! Thanks, Penny."

"I'm nervous as well. How ridiculous are we? I mean, how many opening nights have I seen? And hell, for that matter, how many opening nights have I been personally responsible for? And how many shows has Broomfield done? A thousand, at least." Penny held the table steady as Molly set her cider down next to Penny's tonic and lime. "Cider? Brave. No booze for me tonight. I'm edgy. Molly, did you talk to Jane at all during dinner? I thought it was smart of them to set things up buffet-style, instead of that stuffy formal sit-down thing of last night, but I was so busy circulating and avoiding talking to—I mean, being chatted up by various strangers—that I never got next to her. Is she all right to play, do you think?"

"We had a few words at the dessert trolley. She seems fine—very much her usual self. No nerves about tonight at all, and no after-effects, or so she said. I don't know if she's remembered anything more about it—I didn't like to ask, not just before showtime." Molly leaned across the table and lowered her voice. "Penny, I don't want to pry, but can I ask you something?"

"Of course." Penny, who liked Molly very much, gave her an encouraging smile. "Ask away."

"Matt told me about what happened at Lumbe's last year. And I gather, from something Ringan said during rehearsals, that you'd had another experience with something I'd really rather not have to believe in, in your new theatre—did I congratulate you about that, by the way?"

"Yes, just now." Penny grinned at her. "Come on, Molly. Just ask me. What's up?"

"All right, then, I will. The thing is, I got the impression from all this that you're—I don't know the right word—a sensitive, or something? Anyway, susceptible to ghosts and things. Assuming there really are ghosts, I mean, which please don't think I'm assuming. And you told Lord Callowen this afternoon that there was a ghost here, maybe more than one, and that it was nasty. So what I want to know is, are you all right? I mean, are you feeling anything, well, *off* about this place?"

Penny opened her mouth to reply, but closed it again as the house lights blinked twice and then went down. The stage lights went up, and a wave of applause echoed through the ballroom. Broomfield Hill had taken the stage.

It had been a while since Penny had seen Broomfield perform live. Her schedule and Ringan's had taken them in different directions, and she had long ago lost her taste for rehearsals, with their stop-and-start, argue-and-tinker mode of work. She had almost forgotten the incredible tonality Lord Randall produced in a room this size, the effect of Jane's flute on the ganglia at the base of her spine, the consonance of musical language between Matt's concertina and Liam's fiddle. And when Ringan and Jane sang together, the power and beauty of those two voices blending were enough to make Penny want to cry.

For the first song, "False Knight on the Road," Penny simply sat and listened. The lyric, which told the story of a schoolboy outwitting the Devil, was accompanied by a steady build in tempo, in which the guitar acted as a percussion instrument while the other three stitched harmonies in rapidly escalating call-and-response movements. Penny, who loved music but was unable to sing so much as a note, fought back her usual desire to bellow atonally along, and applauded enthusiastically when the song was done.

As Broomfield moved through their ten-song set, however, her mind took hold of Molly's question, and looked at it from all angles. Did she, in fact, feel anything? Was she, the admitted, albeit unwilling, sensitive, at all affected? Did she feel one single hint of the supernatural?

The answer was surprising. No matter how many times Penny

turned the question over, the answer was the same: no, she didn't feel anything peculiar and she didn't seem affected. In fact, for all the sense of ghostly presence she was getting from Callowen House, she might as well have been shopping at Harvey Nichols or getting her nails done. Whatever she felt, it wasn't haunted.

She considered it, a bit wryly. Here she was, in a house with at least one historically documented ghost and almost certainly a second one with enough power to damage and destroy, and she felt, and sensed, absolutely nothing out of the ordinary. Good grief, she thought, am I actually piqued by it? Have I got so used to being the centre of all the ghostly attention? What a petty, pampered little twit I'm getting to be. . . .

Broomfield had settled into their routine, and were offering up one of the best shows Penny had ever heard them do. It was obvious she wasn't alone in thinking so. She saw her opinion echoed in the faces of the band; it was there beside her as well, in the usually placid Molly's enthusiasm. Five songs, six, seven; the crowd, that handpicked collection of academics, critics, musicians, and actors, was loving every note, singing along, clapping and stamping in rhythm. Eight songs, nine; they came to the closer, a vibrant, ringing version of "The Bonny Lass of Anglesey," ended with a flourish, bowed, and were promptly cheered back for a two-song encore.

Penny, amused by her sudden status as a representative of the patient womenfolk traditionally found attached to musicians, waited off to one side while a crowd of people gathered around the band. Over the next quarter-hour, business cards were proffered, questions asked and answered, opinions spouted and debated. The band members smiled, nodded, made intelligent conversation, and in Liam's case, flirted energetically.

Penny wandered back towards the bar, in search of another tonic and lime, and found that several of the Callowen staff were circulating among the guests with trays that held champagne flutes and fresh strawberries. She accepted both fruit and bubbly and stood, dipping and sipping, watching Ringan and waiting for him to finish. He looked to be enjoying himself immensely, and she was aware of a surge of pride in him. He'd certainly earned this triumph; keeping the folk tradition alive was a damned good reason for thanks, but the fact that Broomfield Hill had done it so consistently and so well over the past fifteen years was amazing and praiseworthy. Even when it hadn't paid the rent, Ringan had never walked away from it . . .

"Penny for your thoughts."

She jumped galvanically and nearly dropped the crystal champagne flute. Ringan's pet phrase had come from just behind her left shoulder, in Charlotte Leight-Arnold's voice.

"Goodness, you look quite startled." Charlotte, dressed in layers of what seemed to be tie-dyed crinkled silk, was poppy-cheeked and very obviously happy. "It's only me. Truly. Weren't they just splendid? Don't you adore Ringan?"

"Well, yes. I do, rather." Penny watched with a surge of affectionate amusement as Charlotte caught the attention of one of the servants and beckoned at him imperiously. The man was clearly familiar with the festival, or at least with the daughter of the house and her habits; he got just close enough to dextrously swap a full glass for her empty one, while avoiding the obvious danger posed to his full tray of expensive glass and equally pricey sparkling wine by Charlotte's thrashing silk sleeves.

"Splendid, splendid, just fantastic. They were. They really were." Charlotte was beaming at Penny with a kind of tipsy goodwill, but now she turned her head and stared at Ringan. "And you get to head off to bed with him as well. Utterly lucky."

Fortunately, since Penny honestly had no clue to how to respond to this comment without replying that yes, that was precisely what she had in mind because music, especially Ringan's music, always did have that effect on her, they were interrupted. Julian Cordellet, indecently handsome and self-assured in a dinner jacket that had obviously been cut by the hand of a master, strolled up.

"Penny, my dear, what a superb show Ringan gave us. Quite

stunning. Are they always this good? Good evening, Ms. Leight-Arnold—you look wonderful."

Charlotte, still beaming but with the glaze of mild boredom settling across her face, responded in a distracted fashion. Seeing an opportunity, she patted him on the arm and edged her way over towards Ringan. Cordellet, obviously highly amused, ignored this implicit dismissal and followed her. Penny bit back laughter; Julian, it would appear, was somewhat smitten.

"Ringan! What an incredible show!" Charlotte grasped his arm, the silks swinging wildly. "It was perfect, it really really was. Did you feel it was amazing, while you were playing?"

The odd eyes were aimed straight at him, and the vertical dimples were more like deep grooves. She had a very strong grip. Ringan, looking past her in search of inspiration or divine intervention, found himself staring into Julian Cordellet's chiselled face. The actor smiled at him, a warm friendly smile, and Ringan felt something surge up in him, dislike that was close to violence. What in all hell was this?

(It's privilege, that's what it is, why should he have so much, looks and money and prestige, he's never had to sweat for any of it, look at him swagger, a fine figure on horseback he made as well, with your lady at his side, whispering into her ear, I'd wager she strutted and rose to him, the common little jade, what right does he have, this is yours by right, yours . . .)

Nausea, a bitter dark taste at the back of his throat, surged up in Ringan. He was suddenly dizzy, the elegant room moving unpleasantly around him. He took a firm hold of himself, managed a smile in return, and saw by Cordellet's face that the actor had seen, and registered, Ringan's initial reaction.

Ringan, swaying a bit, looked rather frantically around, trying to steady himself. Damn, he thought, damn damn damn. This is a perfectly nice bloke. Why do I keep having to fight down the urge to hit him with a rock, or choke him to death? What in hell's got into me?

"Ringan, darling, are you all done with being triumphant?" Penny, as if in response to his silent plea for rescue, had materialised at his side. She looked sleek, elegant, and very high-powered, and was obviously enjoying herself. He had never been so thankful for her presence. His head was thumping.

"Yes, love, I suppose I am."

"Good, because these high heels are pinching me and I'm longing to kick them off and wriggle my toes a bit." Penny slipped her arm through his, and felt the slight pressure. It was an old signal between them: *let's go, come on, let's get out of here.* "Hello, Julian. Hello again, Charlotte. Sorry, I'm officially kidnapping Ringan. Wasn't it a sensational show?"

"It certainly was." There was a faint crease between Cordellet's black brows. He looked like the epitome of romantic screen lovers or heroes. "I just came over to congratulate your significant other on a brilliant set. And having done that, I'll let you go put on pink fuzzy slippers. Good night all. Lady Charlotte, can I get you some more champagne . . . ?"

Penny and Ringan, one giddy with champagne and the other oddly silent, headed upstairs. It was a perfect summer night in the English countryside, beautifully warm and scented with night-flowering blooms. The front doors had been propped open, along with those in the ballroom. Various guests had wandered out into the moonlight and were conversing on the broad terrace or the lawns. Somewhere in the woods, a nightjar called out, lacing the air with its voice.

They unlocked their bedroom door and squeezed through together, Penny giggling slightly as she moved firmly against a sensitive bit of Ringan's anatomy. As Ringan pushed the door closed behind them, his arm around Penny's waist suddenly tightened painfully.

"Oi! Loosen up, will you?" She turned to look at him, questioning, and saw something in the set of his face that she'd never seen there before. Taking in air in a fast, shallow breath, Penny felt her heart stutter.

Ringan's eyes, narrowed to slits, were points of dark light. They were concentrated on her; they were danger, they were fear. There was ruthlessness in that look, and a brutal carnality of a degree unknown to Penny. That look pinned and held her in the circle of his arm. His mouth was a thin line, the bones of his face jutted. He looked, in fact, terrifyingly masculine and completely alien.

"Ringan?" She heard her own voice, rather small and raspy. "Ringan, what is it? What's wrong?"

He tilted his head slowly, his eyes opening wide. Penny, in the grip of an unaccountable lassitude, felt a scream rise from somewhere far down. She clamped her lips shut against it; not to be denied, the scream mutated and became a strangled noise in her throat.

This wasn't Ringan. Whoever was looking at her, with loathing and desire and the visible intention of causing damage, wasn't the man she had walked through the door with only moments ago.

"What troubles you, pretty bird?" He jerked her close, and rubbed his beard against her ear. "Look at you—so very afraid. You'll not tell on me? Give me away?"

"Ringan," she whispered, "no, you aren't . . . how . . . who . . . ?"

"Shut your mouth."

"Let go of me—you—what—"

He bit her. His teeth, sharp and small, came together at the top of her ear. She felt the grind of the bite, a moment of white horror, a trickle of warm blood, sliding down the side of her neck, pooling for a moment, leaking towards her dress.

Penny screamed, a genuine scream this time, small but intense. It circled and died amid the room's sculpted ceiling, and was lost in the plush carpet.

Come on, she thought, *you're not weak, get out of this room, push him down, run, go;* but she had no energy, no strength, no will. She shoved at his jaw with a hand that might have been without nerves, so limp and weak was it, pushing as hard as she could at his face with the heel of her palm. He jerked away, just enough for her to manage a single step backwards.

"Trying to fly away, wee one? We'll pinion the wings, then, and see how far you fly then." The arms around her jerked into agonising strength, as unnatural as it was unbearable. Her arms felt weighted, leaden, nearly too heavy to lift. Her bones were suddenly too dense to manage.

"Stop that fool struggling," he told her harshly. The thin voice, contemptuous and without a trace of Ringan's Scots accent, was familiar. She knew it, she'd heard it, or had she? She couldn't remember, or pin anything down. The only certainty was the presence of danger, of immediate threat. It was palpable in the air. "Are you trying to raise my anger? You'll do what you're told, lady."

"No," she said. "No, I don't think so. I don't—I don't know who you are. This is all wrong. Let go of me. Let go!"

"I told you to stop struggling." He was very strong, much stronger than she'd realised. She wasn't going to be able to break the grip on her waist. Ringan wasn't anything like this strong. She pulled back and tried to muster what remained of her own unnaturally depleted energy, wrenching hard against the confining grip on her waist, hunting for any vestige of her own strength, wondering from a hundred years away what was happening, was this real, who was he, was this . . . ?

"I told you not to anger me. You won't learn. You won't do what you're told. I'll have you sent off, to beg in the street, where you came from. Cast off, as you should be. I'll have your boys taken from you."

She stared at him, speechless, trying as if from a great distance to make sense of words that held no meaning for her. The dark uncanny light was aimed at her now, a stare like a hiss of contempt. She had never seen anything so twisted as his smile. "You won't learn? I'll have to teach you, then, you nameless little scum."

He drew one hand up and slapped her. The blow rocked her head back, and left a small smear of blood where tooth met lip.

He was dragging her now, the bed merely paces away. Whimpering, she dug her feet in. One three-inch heel caught in the dense pile of the carpet; the other twisted and broke where it met the bottom of the flimsy shoe. She went down, off-balance, crying out.

He caught her as she stumbled, one hand twisting painfully in her hair, and pulled her the remaining few steps, tossing her face-down across the duvet. They were the same height, within a stone of each other in weight, but she might as well have been made of bird bones, so easily did he handle her. He held her there effortlessly, as a rider might hold an unbroken horse, clamped hard between powerful thighs. Something was wrong, all wrong; no heat came from those muscles, hard up against her. No heat came from his body at all. He was stone cold. And she had no strength, none.

He was hurting her, hurting her vilely. One hand tightened around her neck. It suddenly came to her that this creature, whatever it was, might actually be meaning to kill her.

His free hand groped for the delicate fabric of her dress. He found the hem, gripped, and pulled viciously. She heard it tear.

"No," she managed, not knowing who she was speaking to, who might be listening. "This isn't happening, it isn't it isn't no no no not happening let go get off let go no."

The fingers on her neck dug in hard, pushing her face into the duvet. It came to Penny, with a sense of complete unreality, that she was about to be raped and possibly murdered by someone or something using the body of the man she loved, the man she'd come upstairs to have sex with in the first place.

It was too much. Something broke. With her mouth muffled by the Leight-Arnold's excellent linens, she began to laugh.

It was wild, and hysterical, and her laughter spiralled and echoed around the high corners of the luxurious room. As if from a distance, knowing that if what seemed inevitable actually happened she would never be able to touch Ringan or look him in the eye again, she felt her own laughter shudder down the length of her pinioned body, and waited helplessly.

The fingers loosened their grip on her neck, then eased altogether. He rolled off her, and away.

"Oh God," he said quietly. "God, what just happened? What in hell did I just do? Penny, I'm sorry, I'm so sorry, I don't understand what—I didn't mean—oh, God, God, sweet Christ."

His voice was his own, Ringan's normal tones and his usual Scots accent thicker than usual. Penny's frenzied laughter transmuted into tears. She began to cry, slow, agonised sobs that wracked her body. Ringan, trembling uncontrollably himself, turned without thought to gather her in to the curve of his own body, then just as quickly let go of her, remembering. He couldn't touch her, not now. He'd given up all right to that.

"No," she managed, "don't let go. Hold onto me, Ringan. Don't you dare let go. I need—I need something, I don't know, reassurance, something." She stiffened then, and pushed him away; her own strength had returned to normal, but her voice was beyond her control. "You are Ringan, aren't you? You're you?"

"I seem to be, love, yes." Christ, he thought, Jesus Christ, what just happened? His stomach was moving unpleasantly, his flesh wanted to leap on his bones. He tasted the sweet coppery tang of blood on his tongue. "Yes. Me."

He held her, sheltering her while she cried herself out, his arms light and exerting no pressure. She pressed her body against him. After a while, the dry heaving sobs tapered off to normal breathing, punctuated by hiccups.

Laughter, light and distant, touched their ears, followed by the soft indistinct hum of conversation. Outside, going about their business in the warm summer night, people wandered on the lawn under their windows.

"Ringan?" Penny's face was a mess, her skin patchy and blotched with crying, her cheek smeared with drying blood. "What is going on here? What's happening? First that thing with Jane, whatever it was, and now—this? I don't understand. What's happening in this house?"

"I don't know, lamb." Ringan closed his eyes, forcing his memory to acknowledge what he had done, to confront what he had nearly done. He couldn't make sense of it—he couldn't believe it, by any way other than to see it as something he had watched on a distant screen somewhere. Teeth coming together—no, he'd imagined that. Had he done that? Surely, he hadn't—it wasn't possible, not even with that metallic aftertaste.

When he opened his eyes again and focussed, the first thing he saw was the cut on her lip, the ugly streak of blood brown and dry. The uproar in his stomach, already making itself felt, expanded with remembered horror and helpless outrage.

Oh Christ, he thought, I did do this. I hit her. I let something use me to hit her. He tasted bile at the back of his throat, reminding him of something, another odd moment, but he couldn't place it. He found himself swearing a silent oath: He was going to track down whatever it was that had used him to damage Penny. He was going to hunt it down, put a name to it, and then it was going to pay. He was going to savage it, hurt it, find some creative way to destroy it where it could watch itself die. Hatred moved along his nervous system like a dark tide. He'd never felt this way before.

"Could this be a ghost?" Her irises seemed clouded, and her voice was tremulous. "Because if it is, then why can't I feel it? It's always been me they react to. I'm feeling nothing unusual, except weak, as if I'd been made of water. Jane, you—I don't understand anything. What's going on here?"

"I can't even begin to guess what's going on here," he told her hair. "And I'm certainly not saying it's a ghost, because how in hell could it be? Never mind that you can't sense it—ghosts can't touch people, can they? They're all about fear, and special effects. Even Agnès de Belleville—Jesus, Pen, she killed a man and she had to do it with smoke and mirrors. They can't touch people. When have we ever seen a ghost physically damage anyone, even while passing through a living person? Betsy Roper walked straight through you on her way to her own exorcism, and all you felt was pity. Not even a headache, right?"

"That's right." There was a very faint smile glimmering around the corners of her wounded mouth. "I'll admit I was right royally gobsmacked by the experience, but no damage at all, and certainly nothing physical. So—not a conventional ghost?"

"How could it be? This—what I remember, it was all lust and frustration and self-hate." Ringan pressed his lips together for a moment; the memory of that need, surreal as it was, was horrifying. "It was all about something wanted and something denied, something he—it—wasn't entitled to. I could feel it. Whatever it was, it was a deep dark hole of bad feelings."

"It was also a rapist—I got that much from it. Whatever it was planning on doing, this was something I think it had done before. I felt it, familiarity, an old story, you know? Not something new. And I'm thinking it was possibly a killer as well." Her voice was very quiet. She lay still, curled up, seeming fragile in a way she had never been, in a way he didn't like at all. "Maybe this is a different sort of ghost, Ringan. Maybe this is whatever it was that destroyed Sinead McCreary. Maybe it just didn't bother going through Donal to get at her."

Ringan reached down to touch her hair, and his hand came away bloody. She flinched, sitting up.

"My ear," she said. "It hurts. Ringan, what? What did I say? Where are you going?"

He made it to the bathroom, but only just. Five minutes later, having rinsed his mouth out several times and got his knees to stop shaking to the point where he could walk almost steadily, he brought Penny a damp flannel and some ointment. He could still taste his own vomit.

"Ta," she said. She'd calmed down completely, and was holding a bit of fabric to her ear. Ringan wondered where she'd found a black silk handkerchief, realised it was the piece he'd ripped from her frock, and battled his unruly gorge back down.

"Here," he said. "Leight-Arnold's left us a well-stocked cupboard—makes you wonder, doesn't it? Do his visitors usually need a lot of first aid? Only the best for his honoured guests. I've brought a damp cloth—your mouth is cut, as well as your ear. Penny, my darling, my only one, is there anything I can do to show you how sorry I am? Anything?"

"Actually, there is." She handed him the ointment, and pulled him down beside her on the bed. "Two things. You can deal with the mess you made of my ear, because I can't see it or reach it properly. And then I think you should take those clothes off and come to bed, and let's have a good long cuddle."

He blinked at her. Her face, level with his own, was vital and alive, and somehow energised with something he couldn't quite define. Determination? Anger? Whatever was driving her, it was impossible to argue with. Yet he had to try; her safety, and his own sanity, demanded it.

She caught and interpreted his look, and ran a fingertip across his lips before he could speak. "Stop staring at me as if I was some sort of enabler, or circus freak, or something." She sounded very fierce. "I'm quite sane, and this isn't a case of loving my would-be rapist, or any of that rot. It wasn't you. You know? Get that through your head—*it wasn't you.*"

"It was my body," he said, flatly. "It was my teeth caused that wound that you're asking me to bandage up. I'm remembering now, lamb—bits, just fragments, but enough. It was the back of my left hand that cut, which by the way is going to be tricky as all hell to explain until it heals up. And had this—this thing—had its way, it would have been me, the rest of me, doing irreparable damage. That's the reality, Pen. It won't do to shy away from it. It got at you through me. I let it in."

"So? You didn't know it was coming. You didn't even know it existed. Now you do. Forewarned, forearmed, et cetera, and whatever aphorisms I may have missed." She examined his face, found it stony and unyielding, and sighed. "It's this way, Ringan: we came up here to make mad passionate whoopie to celebrate your triumph, and I'm damned if I'm going to be done out of it because some wretched evil creature of the night isn't getting any, and thinks he can horn in on mine. All right, maybe not mad passionate whoopie, I'm a bit shaky for that, but at least a nice long cuddly snog. You owe me, dammit. First, please, could you do my ear up?"

She lifted her hair away from the mangled ear. Ringan held the flannel and ointment in a slack hand.

"Suppose it comes back?" he asked quietly. "You'd be defence-less. Pen, love, the truth is, right now, I'm afraid to touch you. I'm afraid to come near you."

"If it comes back, I'll just clock you over the head with some-thing large and heavy, tie you up, and give you to Charlotte to play with." She saw how drawn he looked, and sighed. "It won't come back, Ringan, not tonight. Don't ask me how I know—I don't know how I know, but I do. But I felt the thing—a sort of hungry ravenous need, and then the exact moment when it rejected me completely. I did something: I scared it. I think perhaps when I laughed at it? Anyway, I know for a fact, this damned thing doesn't want me. So it won't come back for me, not tonight, anyway. Trust me. I know."

She spoke with absolute knowledge. Ringan looked at the blood on her mouth, thought about leaning forward and kissing her, and compromised.

"Sweetheart," he said, "are you sure?"

She managed to grin at him, an enchanting cheeky look that etched a lopsided dimple from nose to jaw. "Quite," she told him, "but actually, let's save it for a bit later on. Right now, I want to sneak down the backstairs to the ballroom and boost some of their ice. My lip hurts. And . . ." Her voice wavered. "I think I want to get out of this room for a while, after all."

Jane Castle, after an hour spent wandering in the Callowen or-angery with a music critic from a London daily, let herself be given a late supper, pleaded exhaustion, and headed off to bed.

She was in a peculiar frame of mind. Her occasional boyfriend, Peter, was elsewhere for this trip; she hadn't considered asking him along, and she doubted he'd have accepted, even to see a stately home. What was really bothering her, surrounded by couples and a guest list that had specified plus-ones, was that she wasn't missing Peter at all.

As she chewed roast partridge and nodded mechanically at the critic's memories of an earlier Callowen Festival, Jane's mind took hold of the issue and confronted it. She wasn't regretting Peter's absence. More than that, she was actively glad to be here on her own. And now she thought about it, the feeling was almost certainly mutual. He generally was elsewhere when anything resembling commitment was in the offing. Peter was willing to stay at Jane's flat, go to dinner, indulge her with the occasional day out in the country, but when it came to displaying that he considered himself one half of a couple, Peter was more like Houdini, wriggling loose from imaginary chains, doing a disappearing act. Apparently, this not only didn't worry her, she approved of it. What on earth were they doing together? Maybe it was time to end it. From the way she was feeling, it would almost certainly be painless. . . .

Jane bid the critic an absent-minded good night, and headed off to bed. Her mind was still active with the question of Peter. Why hadn't she asked him? Insisted he come along? Why didn't she want him here? The answers came quickly, and with no pain at all. She liked her own privacy, and as a general rule, she felt no need for a man on her arm. But for some reason, since getting to Callowen House, her thoughts had insisted on taking unexpected little meanders down some unexpectedly dark, uncomfortable alleys.

She unlocked her bedroom door. In the distance, echoing lightly over the manicured lawns and away towards the town of Purbury, church bells sweetly spoke the half hour. Half past midnight. She closed the door behind her, swallowing an enormous yawn. She was suddenly limp with exhaustion. Her mind wandering idly, Jane looked back at the evening. That had been a very good show tonight. There was something to be said for the intimacy of a folk club, where the audience was handpicked and knowledgeable and guaranteed to behave themselves. No drunks, no hecklers, no too-loud conversations disrupting the music.

She locked her bedroom door and let herself quietly into the bathroom. Odd; Ringan had left it in a mess, with a damp stained flannel in the basin, and some antibiotic ointment uncapped and left out on the edge of the sink. Jane, swallowing another monumental yawn, felt a sudden dizziness. The cloth was wet, and that stain—surely, that wasn't blood? No, it couldn't be, not possibly. They'd both been fine when she'd seen them last. And this was an awful lot of blood. She thought for a moment about knocking on the connecting door, checking on them, but all was silent in the next room. Besides, she was just too groggy to cope.

She brushed her teeth and washed her face. It was a painful effort; her desire for sleep seemed to increase exponentially with every passing moment. Her vision was blurry and her eyes felt gritty. Where had this tiredness come from? she wondered, but the thought died away as if snatched by a vagrant gust of wind. Her mental processes seemed as heavy as her own eyelids.

She put out the bathroom light and pushed the connecting door shut behind her. Her curtains were wide open, her window was slightly so. The air in the room should have been crisp, light, scented with summer. Instead, it was heavy and hard to breathe.

She lay down on the duvet, looking up at the ceiling, unable to summon enough energy to get into bed. She couldn't keep her eyes open at all. Something was wrong, about that stained cloth in the bathroom. And something was wrong with the ceiling. Where had it gone? What was the thick black shape, looking down at her with hunger and want?

This was wrong. This was all wrong. This mustn't happen. She mustn't allow it to happen . . .

Jane began to fight, pushing her unnaturally drowsy awareness to stay awake, to call out, to get out of the soft warm bed and safely out the room. It was no use. As sleep took her, she had a moment of sudden clarity, as cold as it was inarguable: she was being hunted. As the thought hit, she tightened her hold on herself, on her own awareness of herself, and went down into the world of dream.

Down she went, down into the dark. She knew a sense of cold, then warmth, as she spiraled like Alice through the rabbit hole into Wonderland. And then, dreaming, Jane found herself sitting in her garden.

As she had been the previous night, Jane was aware of the fact that she was dreaming. Tonight, however, she was prepared. Something of her waking self had come into this cool shadowy place of symbol and memory, where physical day-to-day reality was supposed to have no meaning. Jane herself had brought it, this nameless invisible thing, essential to what made Jane Castle a living entity, complete unto herself. Sitting in her garden, a garden she knew nothing of but which was hers nonetheless, she held her awareness of self like a talisman against whatever hunted her.

It took a few moments before her senses began to function. She heard birdsong, sweet avian chatter on the warm summer air. The air itself smelled delicious, roses and ripe fruit and the soft sharp tickle against the nostrils of newly cut grass. She held something— not her flute, but some sort of wooden frame. A picture, brightly threaded—she was doing embroidery, fancy-work of some kind, or at least the body in which she waited for whatever was coming was occupying itself with this frame and needle. She pushed the needle through the muslin, then pulled it back, looping a strand of dark blue. After a moment or two, she rested her wrists—were these her wrists? she wondered, they seemed thinner and more finely boned than they should be—against the peach-coloured stuff of her gown. Detached and fascinated, Jane lifted a small foot and regarded the dainty fabric shoe. Whose body was this? It certainly wasn't hers . . .

He came into the garden down a path to her left. She felt no sense of threat, only a certain nervousness. This was no hunter or, at the least, he meant her no harm. She knew the step, the cadence of the heels of those boots as they rang along the hard stone path. She turned her head, and smiled up at him.

"Putting the roses to shame? You're looking lovely, little wife." Solidly built, black-haired and dark-eyed, the man was much older than she. His voice held warmth, affection, a touch of almost paternal pride. "What have you there, Sue?"

She smiled, and showed him the frame with its fancy-work. He wrinkled his face. "My poor Susanna, you must be so bored. Too warm for a ride? You could take Andrew along. He'd go with you—shall I tell him?"

"No!" She felt her face stiffen, and then relax. *Andrew.* Something about that name, about the older man's suggestion, had frightened her. And there was something secret, something she had to keep to herself, or rather this person he'd called Sue had to keep to herself. She heard her own words—they came higher, clearer than Jane's own normal voice. "No, Ned, it's too warm to ride, and I'm not dressed for it. I don't want any company, except yours. I— I don't want Andrew."

"And there's naught I'd rather do than bear my lovely girl company. But I've got business in Purbury. I won't be long, and I'll see you at supper, I hope. I'm leaving Andrew behind; you call him if you need anything." He bent and snatched a kiss. Then she was alone in the garden once again. The embroidery frame lay in her lap, her fingers clenching and unclenching.

The interloper, the black shadow of the hunter, fell on Jane as she sat wondering, trying to make sense of random thoughts and feelings that weren't her own. Unlike the man she'd called Ned, this man came silently. She knew, as she smelled him, that silence and stealth and wanting to stay invisible until there was no way to move away safely were his natural modes of being.

The touch of his hand on her neck brought something near to panic. Breath followed the hand, then a hated, familiar whisper.

"Alone, are we, little one, my fair Susanna? Aye, I see y'are. Your lord's saddled up the grey and gone off to Purbury without you." His whisper, ardent and ugly, held a mocking tone. "He told me to look after you."

The hand on her neck slid inside the bodice of her gown. Possessive and chilly, it cupped around one breast. Frozen in Susanna's body, sick and dizzy, Jane understood what was going on. She opened Susanna's mouth, wondering what would come out.

"No," she told him, "leave me be, Andrew. I want nothing of you. Take your hands off me!"

"Not likely." The hand slid back out, tightened viciously on the base of her neck. He jerked her around to face him. The malice in his touch would have been disturbing in anyone, at any time. "Were you going to tell him, then? I'd like to hear you do that. My noble cousin Edward's little commoner wife, trying to turn her lord against his own kin. D'ye think he'd believe you, you little lowborn scut? You, with no standing, nothing but our name, the Leight-Arnold name, and Edward's goodwill to protect you? What happens if you lose that goodwill? He'd cast you off without a look back, he would. You'd not see your son again. No, I don't fancy you'll tell him."

He leaned over, and ran his tongue along her jaw. Hot breath moved along her skin. "You'll do what you're told, little bird."

Susanna cowered back. Jane, using her own vision, drank him in, coldly committing as much of him as she could to her memory, knowing it mattered. Here it was, then, the hunter exposed. This was the black shadow that had stalked her. It seemed he was family; he'd called Susanna's husband, Edward, his noble cousin—that was the man Susanna herself had called Ned.

He told me to look after you.

So, this must be the man called Andrew. He was skeletally thin and very tall. There was a definite resemblance to the man called Edward, in the strong bones and hawk's nose, but there was no warmth in Andrew's face. Instead, there were flecks of foam at the corners of his thin lips. And his eyes—no, this was wrong, it was indecent and jarring and wrong. Those were Charlotte's eyes, different colours, all strangeness and familiarity together, pinning Susanna as one hand caught in her yellow hair and pulled her behind the towering hedge of climbing roses, and down on her back. The wrong eyes, in that feral bony face, weakened her, sapping strength and will.

Right, Jane thought strongly, this is where I get off. Waking up now. I'm waking up, I'm waking, this isn't me, time to yell and shout and wake up wake up wake up . . .

She wasn't waking. She was trapped here in Susanna Leight-Arnold's brutalised body, unable to move him, unable to twist free, one hand was over her mouth and she could feel him, he was evil, an evil thing, hateful. She was losing herself, going down into Susanna, disappearing into the well of terror and the stench of madness that came from Andrew in waves, her energy, her sense of self being sucked dry. . . .

"Jane! *Jane!* Oh God, Ringan, she isn't waking."

The voice, a lifeline, came from a safe place, a sane place. It pulled Jane free of Susanna Leight-Arnold, the rose garden, the vicious cold power with its mismatched eyes, and back into herself. Up she came, through the rabbit hole, back to the world of light.

Jane opened her eyes.

"Christ." Ringan's voice, Jane thought dreamily. The room, it's my room at Callowen, Ringan or someone put the reading lamp on. No shadows. Good.

"I'll kill him," she said conversationally, and then blinked at herself. What was she talking about? And what was wrong with Penny's face? Her mouth . . . "Bloody evil rapist," she went on. It was her own voice, not Susanna Leight-Arnold's. But what in hell was she saying? Were these her words, or Susanna's, or both? "Oh, he's a dead man. I'll have his bollocks for earrings, I swear to Christ, I will. Bastard, bastard, evil filthy bastard! Maybe I'll wear them round my neck, on a nice bit of chain. I don't care if Edward divorces me. How could he leave me alone with Andrew? How could he? How can he not know what Andrew is?"

"Jane! Ringan, her eyes, look at her eyes, there's something wrong. She can't focus them. God, what happened in here!" Penny, six inches taller than Jane, sat and gathered her in. Her voice sounded peculiar, as if she was having trouble forming certain words. "Jane, wake up now, please. Come all the way back. It's gone. Don't cry, Jane love, it's gone for now. You're safe."

"He's not gone. He's never gone. And I'm not crying." She was, though. Her body shook with something wanting to get out, and her face contorted. "Right, sorry—no, it's me, I'm all right. How—why are you both in here?"

"We heard you call out. You were shouting—saying something,

but we couldn't make it out. You left your side of the bathroom unlocked. And after what we went through an hour or two ago, we'd have kicked the door down if you hadn't."

Ringan's face and voice were equally grim. Jane lay passively against Penny's supporting arm. She could barely move; each individual muscle of her body felt as though she'd had the strength surgically extracted from it.

"Jane," Penny said. "Jane, listen. Can you tell us what happened? We need to know. It's important."

"Of course I can," Jane snapped. Did they think she'd forgotten already? That she was ever likely to forget? "There was something: I was dreaming. There was a man, a horrible man, horrible. He called me little bird. He hated me. He was hating me, despising me, wanting me—oh God, I feel so *sick*."

It came back to her for a moment, all of Susanna's horror, her fear, the odd-eyed evil pressing down against her into the grass, Susanna's isolation and helplessness. "God," Jane whispered. "God, God, tell me I was dreaming that. Please?"

"I can't." Ringan sat down beside Penny. He was shaking. "Whatever it was, you very likely weren't dreaming it. There's something here, something in the house. I almost raped and killed Penny a couple of hours ago. Or something did. Someone. I think whatever, whoever it is, or was? He's feeding off you, somehow. I think he, it, got at you last night, as well. And Penny thinks he—it, whatever this thing is—was responsible for killing Sinead McCreary."

"Anything, Jane." Penny touched her own sore mouth gingerly with a fingertip. "Anything at all you can remember. I know it's tricky, I know it's horrid and an awful lot to expect, but here's the thing, he's a killer. He's a killer and a rapist and he's manifesting all over the shop and I don't think he's likely to stop on his own. So we have to do it; stop him. He got to you last night, didn't he? I'd lay odds on it. We need to go to Miles Leight-Arnold with this, all of us. Anything? You said a relative? If we knew who he was—"

"Andrew," Jane said clearly and coldly. "His name was Andrew."

Five

*"Tis true I am Lord Arnold's wife,
But he is not at home
He is out to the far corn fields,
Bringing the yearlings home"*

The following morning, after breakfast, Miles Leight-Arnold found himself the target of a most unwelcome ambush.

The atmosphere in the library at Callowen House was tense and expectant. Miles, on his way to the mews for his hawk and the stables for his horse, found himself taken by both arms, figuratively speaking, and frogmarched off for an urgent tête-à-tête. Penny, Ringan, and Jane had formed a raiding party, telling him there was a need for immediate, and private, conversation. Since they'd had the sense to approach Charlotte first, and had told her the entire story of the previous night, she was firmly with them. Rounding out the group was Callowen's old friend Albert Wychsale.

As a result, Miles was feeling overmatched and betrayed. Once the library door was closed, he made an immediate tactical error, and tried to take command of the situation.

"I can't stay long," he said tersely. "Very busy this morning, and there's a show tonight. Is there a problem?"

Penny was equally terse. "Don't be a fool," she snapped. "Look at my mouth, and my ear. Of course there's a problem."

"What is it, then?" He wasn't backing down an inch. "Don't want to be rude, but really, I've got a schedule—"

"Oh, Da, please do stop going on about nothing, and listen for a second." Charlotte stepped forward. "Listen. We've got a—a sex-ghost in the house."

That brought his head around, to glare at his daughter. "What in hell is that supposed to mean?" he demanded. "What kind of language is that?" He was purple with outrage.

"A ghost, the kind of ghost that goes round trying to roger living people." The odd eyes were focussed on her father's face. "I don't know what they're called. But we've got one. We do, truly. He got at Penny last night—look at her mouth, and her ear. And he got at Jane, twice. And we have to do something."

"Rubbish." Miles, while he still sounded stubborn, was clearly shaken. "A—a ghost that wants to—to interfere with the living? Ridiculous prurient nonsense. I've never heard of such a thing."

"I have." Albert spoke up, mildly but firmly. "I think what we're talking about is something called an incubus, at least if it's male. Apparently, this one is."

"Not apparently, Albert. Definitely." Jane spoke up. She looked fragile, and tired. Her resemblance to the Mytens painting was very strong this morning. "I know who he was, too. Or at least, I know his Christian name. But first—tell me something. Susanna's husband, that Lord Callowen—was he called Edward?"

"Yes, he was. And if you're trying to get me to believe the man raped his own wife, or anyone else, I'll tell you straight out, you're wasting your breath." Miles licked his lips, and suddenly a memory of her dream, foamy spittle at the corners of the rapist's pitiless mouth, came back to Jane. She stared at Miles and began to sway.

"Jane!" Ringan jumped forward and got one arm around her. She raised a hand to her eyes, breathing raggedly for a moment, and then shook her head.

"I'm all right." Her voice was paper-thin. "It's only—he did that, licking his lips, sort of half-smiling. He kept doing that, licking the foam on his mouth. Just before he went for her—the Lady Susanna. Andrew—he had cold hands, and Charlotte's eyes. Ned—Edward—he left Andrew there to keep her company. 'Little lowborn scut,' he called her. He was daring her to tell Lord Edward. He said Lord Edward would cast her off, she'd be sent away, not see her sons any more. I didn't know she had a son. But he said that, and he licked the spit off his disgusting mouth, just before he . . . before . . ."

She sagged against Ringan. Ringan, every inch the militant Scot, glared at Miles.

"You're not going to wriggle out on this one by saying it's rubbish. Get that through your head. And you aren't going to come the lord over me or anyone else, either. I don't give a copper-plated damn if this is your patch, the festival, the house, whatever. We nearly lost both Penny and Jane last night. Look at Jane—she's a wreck. So we could walk out right now, hand you back your precious fee and just pack it in and go, but there's the question of ethics, isn't there? Something's bringing this bloke out of the woodwork. Suppose he doesn't go back in again, just because we pick up and leave? Suppose Charlotte's next up on his rounds? Could you live with that, the rape of your own daughter? Because we can't. We won't. We've got to send him back, send him away. We've got to find out about him."

Black beard jutting and rigid, Ringan readied himself for a fight. But Miles Leight-Arnold wasn't arguing. Instead, he was staring at Jane.

"Have I got this right?" he asked slowly. "A man called Andrew. You saw him, spoke to him, in what, a dream? And he had eyes like Char's? And you saw Lord Edward, Susanna's husband?"

Jane nodded. In the absolute silence that followed, Miles put a groping hand behind him, found his desk, and sat down hard.

"Right," he said. "I believe you. At least, I think I do."

They gaped at him. "Why?" Ringan asked bluntly.

"Because there's no way Jane or any of you could have known about Andrew Leight. The only records extant are in my muniments room, under lock and key. I've never even opened them myself. All I know are the bare bones, that he existed, and when. And I can't see any way Jane could have known that the lord of the day was called Edward, either."

"Andrew Leight? Not Leight-Arnold? I take it he's the family skeleton?" Penny, who had been stroking Jane's arm comfortingly, sat down beside Miles. She was tired, and her ear was throbbing under its plaster. "Talk to us, please. You owe us an explanation at the very least, Miles, you know you do. And we're going to want more. We're going to need access to those records."

"I want to know what happened." He was staring at Jane. "I want to know everything that happened. We've got a ghost here, I've seen her myself, but she doesn't try to touch anyone and she certainly isn't dangerous. But something obviously happened—I don't think any one of you is lying. So I want to know."

"What happened is that Jane did something insane and ridiculously brave last night," Penny told him quietly. "She let herself be drawn down into the Lady Susanna's world, and she did it even knowing she herself would likely be at extreme risk. And she managed to hold on to herself, her awareness of herself, of who she was, while she was there, to see what this was about. Incredible courage."

"It was stupid," Jane said flatly. "And I didn't start out doing that; I just held on, when I realised something was in the room with me, pulling me asleep. If I'd known about him coming at you through Ringan, I'd never have dared. Anything, anyone, who would use Ringan to damage you is a vicious, evil destroyer."

There was an appalled silence, as the three people who hadn't heard that part of the story processed the truth. Albert, looking sick, glanced at Penny's swollen mouth, at her damaged ear; it had not occurred to him that the wounds had come from Ringan. He looked at Ringan, understood what must have happened, and swallowed hard. He was very fond of these people, of Ringan, of Penny, of Jane. Outrage rose like bile in his throat.

"They're right, Miles," he said. "We've seen this now, more than once. You've got to get rid of this nasty little relation of yours. And if they—we—are going to be able to do that, we're going to need your cooperation. Questions answered, documents opened up. Otherwise, this particularly ugly genie is not going back in his bottle or gently into any good night I can think of. And it's quite probable that someone will die."

"Someone already has." Charlotte sounded fierce. "That nice woman, Sinead McCreary. That's what you were all talking about yesterday, wasn't it? All right, so she was a theatre person, she was also brilliant and lovely and funny and he adored her, her husband, I mean. I remember them together—I was sort of envious, really. You could see he was simply besotted with her. It made my throat go all tight and lumpy just watching them. And I think Penny's right, I think it was this Andrew person, this—wait. He's not actually an ancestor, is he? Because I'm already quite cross about even sharing a family name with a disgusting tick like him. And if I'm expected to call him Great-Great-Great-Grand-Uncle Seventeen Times Removed Andrew, well, bollocks to that, I damned well won't. The man was a beastly little berk."

"*Charlotte!*"

"What?" She stared at her father in honest surprise. "It's no more than the truth, Da. He was a pig."

"Will you help, Miles?" Albert patted Charlotte absent-mindedly on the hand. "Char's quite right, you know. Just from the little bit we've seen, the man was a swine while he was alive. He doesn't appear to have improved much with death—my word, he may actually have got nastier. First of all, who was he? You called him Andrew Leight, not Leight-Arnold, so I take it he was a lesser branch of the family? A poor relation?"

"Poor relation would be it—a cousin, I think, youngest child of a connection of Edward's mother. She was a Leight—Catholic family who went Anglican. I've told you, what I remember of the tale is sketchy, and likely garbled with it. He's in the 'Matty Groves' song, did you know that? Family legend says Andrew was the servant mentioned."

"The tale-bearing servant? That was a relative? I didn't know that." Charlotte blinked at her father. "Why didn't I know that? I should have—it's amazing."

Her father ignored this, and spoke to the room at large. "You'd do better to sit down in the muniments room and read the documents yourselves. I'll get the Callowen archivist out here; he always has the first few days of the festival off, but he's likely at home, just past Purbury. He'll get you what you need."

Ringan, surveying the scene in the Callowen House muniments room, reflected that of all the times he'd had to research a ghost during the past twelve months, this was the first time he'd had to ask for additional chairs.

The room, not overly spacious to begin with, was uncomfortably full. Charlotte, Jane, Penny, Albert Wychsale, and Ringan himself had been joined by Roger Searle, the Callowen family librarian and archivist. Searle, while not actually large in any physical sense, radiated the sort of energy that Ringan mentally categorised as being of the bouncy variety; certainly, with the archivist's entrance into the muniments room, the walls seemed to get somehow closer together.

"At least they don't call this the Great Muniments Room." Penny's voice, pitched very low, tickled up against Ringan's left ear. "That would be criminal, if you want truth in advertising."

"True. It's more like the Architecturally Insignificant Muniments Room." He grinned sideways at her, the grin becoming a bit fixed when he caught the dark patch of scab at the corner of her mouth.

"Or the Slightly Cramped Muniments Room." She saw his face change, and understood why. "Let it go," she said quietly. The buzz of conversation in the room left her voice inaudible to anyone more than a few inches away. Searle was talking to Albert Wychsale; even his voice seemed to bounce. Penny spoke to Ringan, and only Ringan heard her. "For now, let it go. Please?"

"I will if you want me to."

"Good." She kept her voice low. "I have the feeling this bloke feeds on anger, and all the dark emotions. Negative energy and all that. You know? Like some sort of science fiction monster. I think it makes him stronger. And frankly"—her voice wavered a bit, at last—"he's quite strong enough, ta."

Ringan swallowed. It occurred to him that what he really wanted to do was to go to the nearest decently sized town and find a book-shop with a supernatural dictionary. Albert had called this thing an incubus. Ringan himself had heard the term before. Spirits visiting sleepers in the night for a bit of slap and tickle weren't an uncommon basis for a song, but was that actually what an incubus was? The need for greater knowledge had suddenly become imperative.

Ringan bit back an upsurge of impatience and helplessness. How many people were they going to need? There weren't even likely to be that many family records that dealt with the period in question. This wasn't a matter of having to narrow down the time of the events. They'd had to do that, first with Ringan's own cot-tage and then with the Bellefield Theatre, but that wasn't the case here. They knew just who the hunter here was, they knew his prey, and that meant they knew, to within a week or so, what they needed to find. And besides, the room was warm, and too crowded . . .

Abruptly, Ringan stood. Everyone turned towards him.

"It seems to me," he told the upturned faces, "we've got an aw-ful lot of people to nail down one small bit of confirmation. If no one minds, I'm going to head into the outside world and see what I can find out about incu—what's the plural of incubus, anyway? Incubi? No matter, because, please heaven, we're not looking at plural. Is there a bookshop in Purbury, Charlotte, or do I have to go all the way to Havant, or Portsmouth?"

"There's a lovely bookshop in Purbury, really lovely. It's run by this sweet sweet man called Stanny Roche. I used to go slip off and play with the shop cat. Stanny's always had one." Charlotte tilted her head. "Also a nice little library, but I don't know what they've got about sex-ghosts and suchlike. Do you want some company? Shall I come along and help?"

"Actually, Char, you'd do better to stay here and be the Answer Lady. I mean, what with your being family, and all. You know?"

Penny got up and stretched. "I could do with a break, as well. Besides, I want to see about getting the heel of my shoe repaired; I broke it last night and they're the only high heels I brought along. Ringan, do we need a notebook? No? Right, then, we're off. We'll see everyone at dinner. Have a lovely time."

The afternoon was beautiful, a glorious summer day in the South of England. The rolling lawns were verdant, the sky a smoky, dark-casted blue hinting at a summer storm off towards France. Ringan, smelling water in the air, decided to leave the roof of the car up. They headed down the white road through the avenue of trees, went through the wrought-iron gates, waved at the gatekeeper, and headed off towards Purbury. Behind them, the treetops moved uneasily in a strengthening breeze.

Ringan, his hands relaxed on the wheel, was aware of relief, almost as if he'd just escaped from something. It was surprising, he thought. If anyone had told him three days earlier that getting out of Callowen House would be something he'd look forward to, he'd have thought they were barmy . . .

"Ringan?"

He glanced at Penny. Her voice was a bit too careful. He knew that tone; she wanted to ask him something and wasn't sure of herself. He said nothing. She'd sort it out and ask him whenever she was ready.

"Ringan—" She took a deep breath.

"It's all right, lamb." He spoke gently. "If this is about last night . . ."

"Yes, it is, but not about—oh, bugger! It just sounds so stupid. Right, here we go, then. Last night, after the show, when everyone was milling about and talking—I saw Char and Julian Cordellet go over to you. And you did not look at all chuffed to see them, and that's putting it politely. You looked absolutely warlike. So, who were you narked at? And why?"

Ringan took a moment, trying to sort it out in his mind. Penny was far too acute for her own good sometimes; actually, to be fair, she was far too acute for his own good. He remembered the moment, a tipsy Charlotte with madly flapping sleeves, charging up to him, with Julian Cordellet in her wake. Cordellet—he really was an indecently good-looking bloke—offering a hand, compliments that sounded warm and genuine, congratulations on a great performance. And he remembered, rather shockingly now, the dislike and resentment that had welled up in him, and words, something in his head, something that had spoken and accused—he couldn't remember now, just that he honestly hadn't wanted to shake Julian Cordellet's hand. And there had been something more, something about Penny, about the two of them, astride their pretty horses, heads close together . . .

He felt blood come up in his face. That reaction had been pushed aside by what had followed, but the reaction, in its own way, was almost as shocking. And Cordellet, who had done absolutely nothing to warrant it, had seen it. It made Ringan want to writhe in shame.

"It was Julian, wasn't it?" Penny had been watching the memory play itself out on his face as he considered. "Why, Ringan? He's a nice enough bloke, if a bit too talkative and self-absorbed. But the way you looked at him, that was actual hate. It stopped me in my tracks. I don't remember ever seeing that look on your face before. Why? What did he do?"

"I—I don't know." It hadn't been the first time, he thought. He'd been resentful of Cordellet from the first, disliking the sight of his smooth hair and fine bones bent so close over Penny's head at the welcoming dinner. He remembered his own too-casual questioning of Penny as they lay in bed that first night, and he flushed. Then, yesterday morning at the sound check, watching their horses canter side by side, Penny laughing up at Cordellet, something hard and ugly closing like a diseased fist around Ringan's own heart . . .

(privilege, why should he have so much, look at him swagger, a fine figure on horseback he made, your lady at his side, whispering into her ear, she rose to him, the common little jade, yours by right, yours . . .)

"Penny for them?"

Abruptly, without signalling and with no warning, he pulled the car over to one side of the road. An estate wagon, following too close for safety, swerved past the Alfa with a protesting blare of its horn.

"I wanted to kill him." The skin above the neat upper curve of Ringan's black beard was mottled with patches of red. "I wanted to wrap my hands round his throat and squeeze until something popped. My God, Pen, I was jealous. Jealous! That isn't me, is it? When have I ever been jealous? Yesterday morning, when you were riding. At dinner, and then last night. But it wasn't me. I thought I heard something, when he came up last night, after the show—something speaking, something about how easy things were for him, his privilege. It wasn't Julian Cordellet I was resenting." He turned to look at the silent Penny. "Was it?"

"I don't know." She watched him, her face betraying nothing. "I don't think so. Why did you resent him?"

"He was talking to you, at dinner—that first night. Again, yesterday, when you went riding with the family. He—the way he leaned over you, smiling, the way you were smiling back . . ."

His hands had clenched hard. She stared at him for a moment, barely breathing, watching him wrestle with himself. Finally, his hands relaxed, and she let her breath out.

"Not you, then." He jerked his head around; her voice was completely matter-of-fact. "You, jealous? Don't make me laugh, mate, you've never got jealous the whole time I've known you. You've watched me do passionate love scenes onstage with some of the dishiest men in the business, occasionally without a stitch of clothing on above the waist—remember when I did Lady Macbeth? You never batted an eye. But Julian Cordellet? Here? Now? Please." She shook her head. "That's total pants, mate, and you know it. I couldn't swallow that much coincidence if you put it through a food mill and slow-cooked it first. What about that voice in your head? How could you think it was you?"

"When did you start using slang like 'pants'?" He was grinning despite himself. "And when did I become 'mate'?"

"When I needed to make you laugh. I was saving 'naff' in case the big guns didn't do the trick, but I can put that one away for another day. 'Pants' and 'mate' seem to have worked a treat." She laid a hand lightly on his cheek. "Under the influence, Ringan. You didn't see yourself just now. Good thing, because you wouldn't have known who you were. There was a sort of residue of last night. Can I just say how glad I am that you're you, and not him?"

"Oh, *God.*"

His voice broke and his shoulders began to spasm. She held him and let him cry against her, the horror of what had happened the night before, his own reaction to what he had so nearly done, pouring out and away. It was over in a minute or two. He sat up, blew his nose rather fiercely, and restarted the engine.

"Are we clear now?" Penny rolled her window down and let a rush of wind move through the car. "Between us, I mean—about last night? Clear?"

"Clear, lamb." Ringan cracked his own window. It felt as though, between them, the summer breeze and Penny's extraordinary generosity had blown the miasma of Andrew Leight out, and away. The sky was a darker blue now, clouds edging past at a higher speed. It was time to move on.

Char had been right; the bookshop in Purbury, with its Georgian façade, was a gem of a place. It was narrow but deep, very well ordered, with overstuffed shelves and one glass-topped case of rare editions. An enormous tabby cat dozed in a splash of sunlight on the proprietor's wooden desk.

Stanny Roche himself proved to be a seventyish man with a shock of beautiful white hair. He stood as they entered, sliding a marker between the pages of the book he'd been reading.

"Afternoon. Help you?"

There was something austere about him. He seemed detached, a bit remote and ever so slightly offputting; whatever the quality was, it tied Ringan's tongue for him. Penny, apparently either oblivious or unaffected, introduced herself and Ringan, dropped Charlotte's name, and without an unnecessary word, told Stanny Roche what they needed, although not why they needed it. She was so unusually concise that it occurred to Ringan she might not be as unaffected as he'd first thought. Roche nodded at them.

"You want a demonic reference book, then?" Spoken in that clear, pedantic voice, the words were surreal. "Something that gives you a detailed look at incubi and succubi, and that specific sort of demon?"

Ringan opened his mouth, but Penny trod on his foot. Bewildered, he stayed silent as Roche led them to a section of shelves near the back, ran one parchment-coloured finger along a series of leather-bound spines, and pulled the one he wanted free of the rest.

"Here y'are," he said calmly, "*Defining Devils,* 1938, Hannock and Bridge. Let me know if this isn't what you need."

He went back to his book, his chair, and his cat. Penny stared after him for a moment.

"Spooky," she said in a very low voice. "He reminds me of the deacon of the church at Whistler's Croft, when I was small."

"Penny, why did you nod and smile and say this was what we needed?" Ringan was mildly irritated. "Why did you stamp on my foot? We're not looking for a demon—I don't even believe in demons. It's ghosts we're after."

"Well, he said incubi, and he went straight for this book. It's his shop, after all. I was just assuming he'd know." She looked at him out of the corner of her eye, bit her lip, and dropped her voice even lower. "I never argued with the deacon, either," she confessed. "He frightened me half to death. It was that sort of distant, donnish I-know-all effect. Scared the life out of me. Here, come on, let's look this up."

Heads close together, they found the information almost at once; as might have been expected, the book had an extensive index. Ringan was conscious of a small upsurge of triumph. Research, in his experience, was not usually so easily completed.

As they read the definition, however, any remnant of gratification vanished. He looked at Penny and saw bewilderment in her face.

"What in hell?" Her mouth was half-open. "This can't be right. There must be more than one sort of incubus out there."

"Twenty-eight flavours? I doubt it. We're talking about things that go belly-bumping in the night, not about ice cream." Ringan didn't sound sarcastic, he sounded grim. "Penny, if there's any chance this is right, we're in deep, dirty water here. Let's see that again."

Heads together, they read the entry:

Incubus (succubus, female): *n,* a demon or evil spirit who supposedly seeks to have sexual intercourse with the living, in the case of the incubus, with a living woman as she sleeps. In medieval Europe, reports of these nocturnal visitations were prevalent; it was generally believed that these spirits were responsible for the birth of witches, as well as deformed children. From the Latin *incubo,* from *incubare,* to lie down upon.

This unpleasant blurb was accompanied by a reproduction of a cheesy bit of mildly pornographic art, done in the Pre-Raphaelite style. It depicted a dark, amorphous, and hideously malformed shape, swooping down upon a buxom sleeping woman with an improbable mane of strawberry-blonde curls, and a faint anticipatory smile on her face. They regarded the drawing with distaste. Penny shook her head.

"Demon. Demon? Rubbish. That's beyond bizarre. And I'm with you, I don't believe in demons, either." Penny scanned the definition again. "Well, it does also say 'evil spirit,'" she said doubtfully. "I suppose a ghost might be considered an evil spirit, especially one who goes around attacking people while they're snoring."

"Damn." Ringan closed the book. "Look, this doesn't make any sense, does it? I mean, we *know* who this bloke was, right? There's no mystery here. If this is—was—Andrew Leight, then he's not an evil spirit and he's not a demon, or any of that rot. He's a dead bloke who won't vacate the premises, and that makes him a ghost, full stop, end of puzzle. So if this definition is right, he doesn't fit. He's not an incubus. What are you doing?"

"Seeing if there's anything else on these shelves, that's what." Penny was moving along the well-ordered rows, reading the lettering on the leather and buckram spines. "There's all sorts of books on ghosts—maybe some are indexed?"

They were interrupted by a cough from behind them. Penny, startled, swung around and found herself staring at the proprietor. He had the tabby cat draped over his neck and shoulders, like a huge soft shawl with claws. It was asleep, and purring loudly.

"Problem?" Stanny Roche asked mildly. The cat opened its eyes, trilled, and stretched a paw towards Penny, all without so much as wrinkling the cloth of Roche's jacket.

As Penny would later tell Ringan, it was probably the presence and position of the cat that had done it. Whatever the cause, she suddenly—and as Ringan pointed out, unilaterally—decided to abandon secrecy, and proceeded to tell the bookshop owner the entire story. He heard her out with an air of imperturbable calm.

"Not surprised, really. Always suspected there was more up at Callowen than just poor little Lady Susanna. Had a few odd moments there myself, at festival time." He moved his shoulders, slightly shifting the cat, who was now kneading and purring. "Ouch, Pye, stop making bread on my shoulder. Not the sort of unpleasantness you're having, of course. More like mood swings. Not usual to me, at all. Strong feelings, also very much not mine. Reactions." He touched the cat's tail. "You know?"

"Really? Strong feelings, like, jealousy, maybe?" Ringan reached a finger out towards the cat, stiffened, and narrowly missed crashing into a set of shelves as the cat Pye suddenly leaped from Roche's shoulder to Ringan's and settled there. Ringan staggered back and steadied himself. "Oi! Hello, cat. You weigh as much as a small telly, you know that?"

Penny was grinning. Roche casually brushed some loose soft fur off his shoulders.

"Not jealousy in my case. More like sudden fits of anger. Didn't make sense to me; I was seated next to a woman from a German newspaper and we were chatting. She said something I didn't agree with and I had to get up and walk away. Otherwise? Might have done something I regretted later. And the question we disagreed on, just a book, or something of that sort. Nothing to call for anger—not politics or history or any of that."

"But you got angry." Ringan was nodding. "If you don't mind my asking, what year was that? How long ago?"

"Oh, twenty years at least. I remember Miles had an American banjo and fiddle group here, and it was quite amusing, watching everyone dancing on the chairs." Roche moved over to the shelves. "Anyway, your little problem. Have to say, I don't think you have a conventional incubus up there, not if you know he was actually someone at some point. Did I say something amusing?"

"'Conventional incubus,'" Penny told him. "That's not a phrase one hears every day." She sighed. "In a way, it's comforting to know I'm not suddenly expected to have to try and believe in demons. Because, well, I simply don't."

"Nor do I. Ow! Right, cat, I've got a crick in my neck. Down you go." Ringan moved his shoulders, and the cat Pye slithered down his front, landed on the floor, and promptly fell asleep again. "So we have a randy ghost, with psychotic tendencies, and he has a definite attraction to my bandmate, Jane Castle . . ."

"Who, by the way, looks very much like that Mytens painting of the Lady Susanna," Penny finished for him. "So we're back where we started. Ring a ring of roses. Except for one thing. Mr. Roche, did you mention your reactions to Miles?"

"I did not." Roche seemed surprised at the question. "How would I have put it? 'Miles, dear man, I'm having strong feelings about things I normally wouldn't even notice, and do you have a nasty of some sort on the premises?' I assumed he already knew there was something floating about the baronial halls, but didn't want it known. I just declined my invite to the next festival. Went fishing instead."

"I wonder," Penny said slowly.

Ringan looked at her. "Penny for them?"

She met his gaze. "I wonder how many other of the Leight-Arnold guests have had similar reactions, and never mentioned it to Miles for just that reason. Because Miles told us he'd never heard of anything, and I think that's no more than the truth. But if a lot of people had things happen, and didn't want to bring it up to their admittedly terrifying host—I certainly wouldn't want that falcon of his being turned loose in my vicinity—then Andrew Leight, if this is the ghost of Andrew Leight, could have been infesting Callowen House for a very long time indeed."

Six

The servant who was standing by
And hearing what was said
He swore Lord Arnold he would know
Before the sun was set

The four remaining researchers in the muniments room were taking a break. In all honesty, they'd barely begun; the archivist, Roger Searle, had been frighteningly efficient, listening to a babble of input and second-hand information, and extracting core questions as easily as a mother dealing with a splinter in a child's palm. He'd pulled three bound registers from behind glass cases and set them carefully on the table. Charlotte flipped one open casually, blinked rapidly at the minuscule script, slammed the leather cover back into place, and snorted. "Oh, damn it all. Was all this written using someone's eyelash for a quill, or something? Gah. It's tiny. I predict migraines for everyone."

Searle winced. "Lady Charlotte, please! Do be careful. The books are four hundred years old and they need to be handled with delicacy." He removed the volume she'd been looking at and opened it gently. "Now. We're looking for information about one Andrew Leight. Cousin of some sort to Lord Edward Leight-Arnold on his mother's side? Ms. Castle, could you venture a guess as to his age? That would really help place where we ought to start our note taking. Lord Edward surprised his wife and Matthew Groves together on 2 September 1629."

"He looked to be in his late twenties, or maybe a bit older. Not much older, though. Early thirties at the most." There were blue circles under Jane's eyes, and a certain eggshell quality to her skin that was unusual for her. Albert, watching her uneasily, found her watching him, and offered a reassuring smile. She blinked at him for a moment, as though she wasn't certain quite who he might be, and then managed to smile back. The effort required by that simple act was obvious enough to be unsettling.

Albert got abruptly to his feet and pushed his chair away.

"Searle, can I leave you and Charlotte to it for a little while? You're looking for anything in the family records on the subject of Andrew Leight, born somewhere at the end of the sixteenth century. It's a pity no one's thought to enter everything in the family archives onto a computer—you'd save poor Char's eyesight then."

He slid a hand under Jane's elbow. Even the flesh of her arms looked different. Surely those veins, seemingly thousands of angry indigo lines, hadn't been visible yesterday? And was it possible to somehow lose enough flesh to be noticeable in the space of a single day?

"I think Jane needs some air," he said firmly. "Come on, Jane, up you get. Let's take a turn in the garden, shall we? It's awfully stuffy in here. Carry on, if you would, you two."

Jane came up limply, nearly a dead weight on his arm. She seemed to be fading as he watched. He supported her to the door and out onto the lawn, hearing with one ear a discussion on Andrew Leight's probable parentage start up behind him, and wishing either Ringan or Penny had stayed behind. For some reason, Albert was suddenly feeling helpless and overwhelmed.

"Albert? Can you loosen the grip a bit, please?"

He started. Shifting his fingers, he saw with horror that even the light hold had left an imprint of his fingers, and a spreading bruise.

"This is preposterous." He stopped, and stared down at her. He was small and compact, but she seemed tiny, birdlike. "You look like Dracula's been at you, for a week running."

"Do I? That's how I feel as well. Elevenses for a vampire." She looked sluggishly down at her elbow and forearm. The bruise, non-existent moments before, was now purple-black. She managed another of those faint smiles; it looked as if even lifting the corners of her mouth was an effort, impossible to sustain. "I wonder if garlic and holy water would do the trick?"

"Jane, listen to me." He slipped an arm around her waist, a completely platonic gesture, exerting no pressure at all. He led her away from the beautiful towering elegance of the house. There were high hedges to the west, not far, most probably the outer edge of one of the estate's many lovely little rose gardens. Albert headed for them; it was almost as if he sensed she might recover once she could no longer see the building. Besides, if there was a garden, there would also be a bench, and she looked as though she needed to sit. He said, very flatly, "You have to leave here. You have to clear out. I don't think you're safe anywhere at Callowen."

"Well, Penny and Ringan are going to stay up with me tonight. Take turns watching to make sure—"

"No. I mean I don't think you're safe here, full stop. Not in broad daylight, not within sight of the house, and especially not within sight or influence of this creature, this—whatever he is now. Not a basic ghost, I'd say."

"You said it was called an incubus, didn't you?" They'd reached the opening in the trimmed privet hedge, following the garden path. In the centre of a riot of lovely roses was a curving stone bench. "The word sounded very familiar," Jane added. "I know I've come across it, and I seem to know vaguely what it is, but I can't pin down how. I don't read ghost stories. Maybe in a song? My brain's not working properly, I'm afraid."

"I've no idea how I know it, either. Some piece of scary lit read too young, perhaps. I expect it's one of those bits of general information that float in and out and people pick up on, or not. Besides, I could so easily be wrong. Here, sit down, Jane, do."

They reached the bench and he watched her sink limply onto it. There was rain coming, Albert thought, a bit of electricity, a summer storm on its way in from the south coast. The air was oppressively close. "And now, child, I'm afraid I'm going to be quite rude and say just what's on my mind. You look watered-down. You look like *eau de Jane Castle,* rather than the full perfume. And I think you need—Jane! What is it?"

She had raised her head and was looking around her, at the roses, the hedges, the path, the stone bench. She lifted one foot, staring at her sensible espadrille as if she saw something else. There were wonder and awareness in her face.

"It was here." She lifted her face to Albert, and he saw a cold blind horror there. Her voice was thin. "This bench. Here."

"What do you—"

"Susanna." Her voice was shaking. "Here, in my dream. This was the garden. Those hedges, this bench. Edward came—Ned, I mean—she was doing some sort of needlework, and then he left and Andrew—he—came in; there was another path, behind her, and he came in, and he pulled her down off the bench . . ."

She was swaying in her seat. For a moment, an odd dislocated fracture in the humid summer afternoon, Albert saw a rough form in her hands, a soft summery gown instead of tailored trousers, dainty satin shoes. Dizzy, fighting dislocation and nausea, he looked beyond her and saw the second path, partially obscured by the angle of the curving bench.

And for a moment, while that fracture held, there was more: a darkness, an interloper. Hunger, and anger, and a kind of menace beyond Albert Wychsale's experience. There was sound as well, ragged and excited, a patch of scratchy breathing. And there was a shadow, with depth to it, and something more . . .

The present and the past seemed to merge, to shimmer in the oppressive heat of the day. Suddenly, Albert was back in the tithe barn at Lumbe's cottage, a year in the past, with Ringan and the rest of the band trying to put to rest a pair of ghosts of a very different flavour, and the dim shapes came and went during the exorcism of Will Corby and Elizabeth Roper . . .

"Matty? Matthew Groves?"

Jane's voice wavered. The wind had picked up; it caught stray tendrils of her pale hair and whipped them around her cheeks. "Is that you, Matty? No, I'm not harmed, there's nothing to be done—only, please, say nothing to my lord of this. He'll believe no ill of Andrew, his own kin. I'd be cast off, sent away, my sons taken from me. I'd have no wish to live, then. Swear you won't tell him. Swear to me. Please?"

"Jane?" The urge to do something, anything, was almost unbearable. Albert reached out to her, his heart racing erratically, its rhythms spiralling and frightening. "Get up. Hurry! We can't stay here, it's not safe—"

A crack of thunder, a moment of static, sharp and talkative. The clouds that had been massing on the horizon were suddenly directly overhead. The first drops of rain hit Albert, smearing his glasses.

"Swear it." She was clutching his sleeve, not seeing him, babbling now. "Please, please, swear you'll not tell my lord."

Albert, sixtyish, portly and unathletic, tensed his back muscles and picked Jane up in both arms. She was limp and unresisting, her eyes half-open, her cheekbones pointed with scarlet. His muscles, unaccustomed to such use, protested ominously.

His feet wanted to break into a run, but he held them in check, stepping carefully. It would be easy, too easy, to slip and fall, hurting himself, hurting Jane.

One step forward, another, through the hedge and onto the lawn. The rain, hard clear drops at first, was becoming a knifelike curtain of water, hitting earth and flesh too hard for comfort. He was sweating with effort and fright and urgency. Heat lightning rippled ahead of him, flashing in a ragged white plume on the hedges and the mansard roofs.

Don't tell my lord, you mustn't tell my lord.

Had he heard the words? Jane seemed to be asleep in his arms, eyes closed, lips not moving. Who had spoken? And how could he have heard anything at all, above the din of the falling water and the thunder echoing across the Callowen land?

Please, Matty, swear to me, please, please.

His legs felt heavy, sodden, old. One step, another. The white stone of the path was slippery with running water, but the lawn would be worse. He mustn't drop Jane. He mustn't set her down, either. There was something watching him, something dark, angry, something with a taste of bitterness hanging in the electrically charged air like a bad memory . . .

"*Albert!*"

The voice, masculine and urgent, cut through the noise of the weather, and overpowered it. Jerked back to reality, Albert looked up.

Miles Leight-Arnold, astride his enormous silver gelding, came across the lawn at a hard canter. The horse wanted to gallop; even at a distance, Albert could sense the iron control Callowen was exerting to keep his mount at a slower pace as the animal strained forward.

Horse and rider skidded to a halt, and Albert understood why the enforced canter was needed. The wet grass was treacherous.

"Stand, Lothian. Steady, you fool, it's only water. We'll get you indoors in a bit. You've been out in wet before—what in hell's wrong with you?" Callowen was soaked through. His voice was as controlled as his horse. He braced himself in the saddle, his boot heels hard against the stirrups, leaning as far down as he could. "Hand her up to me, Albert. Hurry now."

The gelding's superb muscles moved uneasily below a coat made even glossier by the rain. Lothian, obedient to his rider's pressure, held still, but his uneasiness was apparent in his rolling eyes and flaring nostrils. He whickered slightly, but was otherwise still as Callowen reached down to receive Jane. She seemed to be waking, and reviving a bit.

"What . . . ?"

"Hold on." Callowen's voice was imperative, the tone past arguing with. "Lothian'll take us both, he's up to our weight. Up you get, lady."

Jane was set down between Callowen and the nape of Lothian's crested neck. Eyes widening, she settled herself, draping her legs loosely just behind the horse's powerful shoulders, leaning the small of her back against the cantle, and bracing.

Holding the reins, keeping the pace slow, Callowen turned his mount towards the house.

"She mustn't go inside." Walking alongside, his shoes squelching with every step, Albert had to raise his voice above the downpour. The wind wanted to carry his voice away. There was a sense of urgency thrumming in his veins, something that seemed to have communicated itself to him as he carried Jane Castle in his arms. "It's not safe for her, Miles. She's not even safe within sight of the place."

"She's not going to sleep here tonight." Miles pitched his own reply to be heard. "We'll phone down to the B&B in Purbury. Annie Whitlaw runs the place, nice woman, very capable, doesn't ask a lot of questions. She'll put Jane up for the duration. Jane just needs to pack a bag."

"She shouldn't go inside at all."

Albert's tone was so flat, so exasperated, so completely unwilling to admit the possibility of disagreement, it cut through everything else. Both Jane and Miles turned their heads and stared down at him.

"Why in hell not?" Miles demanded. "It's the middle of the afternoon and she's surrounded by stalwart gents."

"Because Andrew was there. Just now—in the rose garden."

Lothian reared suddenly, a small jumpy motion, as Jane unconsciously tightened her fingers in his silver mane. Miles swore, and gentled the horse.

"Steady, boy. You'll have us both in the mud if you do that. Are you serious, Albert? Yes, I can see you are." Miles turned Lothian's head away from the house and towards the stables. "We'll call up to the house, have one of the maids pack Jane's things. Talk to me, Albert. He—was there? You saw him?"

"Saw him, or at least his shadow. And I smelled him, felt him— something. He was there, Miles, that's all I can tell you. It was just for a minute or two, but out of nowhere, Jane was wearing different clothing, a gown, little slipper things on her feet, and I could—" He stopped suddenly, his round pleasant face closing down hard.

"You could what?" Miles asked.

"I could hear him." The rain had eased. Albert's voice was clear, and very quiet. "I could hear him breathing."

". . . or, supposing it's some sort of evolution. Suppose everything everyone ever thought of as being a demon or a devil, suppose they're all just ghosts who've gone sour and tight-arsed and had their souls shrivel up on them?"

"What? What are you talking about?"

Ringan, his concentration divided between the road and the rapidly worsening weather, spared a puzzled look at Penny before bringing his attention back to keeping his car on the road. She'd been speculating aloud, and at a record clip, since they'd thanked Stanny Roche, petted the cat Pye, and run for the car. The storm had hit Purbury as they were belting themselves in. In the ten minutes since pulling away, the afternoon sun had disappeared behind a wall of moisture, and the drains were already clogged, sending the beginnings of small floods eddying out across the road.

"No, I'm serious. Listen, Ringan—I have this idea, something that just sort of popped into my head, back at the bookshop."

Penny's voice was edged and intent; Ringan, unpleasantly jolted, realised he hadn't heard her sound this way since coming to Callowen. "Think about it. What if there really were demons and devils and evil spirits, but not really, because they'd all begun the day as ghosts, and then just gone bad?"

"I don't know. Penny, could we—"

He broke off, swearing, just missing a fallen tree branch floating in the road. They'd left Purbury behind, and the quiet country roads were rapidly becoming rivers of rainwater and debris. The air was charged with static, and the sky behind them to the south was a leaden angry grey, shot through with yellow. Noise, the crash of water-laden clouds banging off each other, echoed around the car. Ringan winced, and tightened his hands on the wheel. The windscreen wipers were already hard at work.

Penny's eyes were wide and fixed. "What if Andrew Leight actually is an incubus, and it's the entire concept of incubus as evil spirit or demon that's wrong?" She seemed oblivious to anything other than the idea, oblivious to the storm around them, to his tension, to anything else at all.

He shook his head, and managed a reply. "The theologians would flay you alive if you pushed that, love."

"Why?"

"I haven't got a clue, Pen." The sky was a brutal colour; the clouds in his driving mirror looked apocalyptic. "Original sin, or something. I suspect that concept you're proposing tramples on a lot of what the old Church holds dear."

"Well, can you think of anything else that makes even the slightest bit of sense? I can't." She seemed unaffected by the storm, which was now ramping up in both power and violence. Water smacked hard into the Alfa's fabric roof, shards of angry noise. "Ringan, look at it, will you? I mean, just look at it. Item one, dead bloke called Andrew Leight. Item two, formerly alive bloke Andrew Leight was a rapist at the very least and probably other things just as bad Item three—" She broke off and stared at Ringan, seeming for the first time to notice his rigidity. "Is something the matter? Am I boring you?"

"You're not boring me, dear, no. You're scaring me a bit, though. Did you happen to notice this storm?"

"It's just weather, isn't it?" She shrugged and returned to her idea. "Where was I? Right, third thing: Andrew's been dead going on four centuries but he's not only still around, he's randy. Frisky and randy and quite the wicked twisty ghost. And item four," she added triumphantly, "the only known definition of a frisky randy twisty ghost is as an incubus, but an incubus isn't a ghost, according to the books, it's a demon or an evil spirit. So what is he?"

"How in hell do I know!" His nerve and patience snapped suddenly. "I just let him use my body to try to kill you with, remember? I didn't invite him out for a quick pint down the pub, so that he could give me all the gen on what he was and how he got that way. Why in hell are we having this discussion right this moment?"

"Because it's important." Her voice brought his head around; the car swerved and skidded in a gust of wind, and he looked back at the road. There was a disturbance in Ringan's chest, a recognition of something, a memory of Penny as she had been during an encounter with another dangerous ghost. They were approaching Callowen, the wrought-iron gates with their intricate family crest glittering and black in the wet. "Because it's vital. Because knowing what he is—Ringan?"

"What?" He heard his own voice shake, and clamped down hard on his nerves. She was peering through the foggy windscreen. "What's up?"

"Isn't that Albert's car?"

Albert Wychsale's Volvo estate wagon, travelling towards them too fast for safety, pulled up just inside the wrought-iron gates. Ringan brought the Alfa abreast of Albert's car, stopped, and lowered his driver's side window, wincing as rain blew sideways into his eyes.

"Albert! What's wrong? What's happened?" As Wychsale brought his own window down, Ringan got a look at the Volvo's other occupants. "What in hell? Are you kidnapping my entire band?"

"Follow us, Ringan, will you? Number Twelve, Swan Close, Purbury. That way, in case one of us washes off the road in this muck, someone can swim back to civilisation and get help. We'll explain once we've got Jane delivered, and we're indoors."

Ringan turned the Alfa back in the direction from which they'd just come, and followed Albert's car. Half an hour of careful driving later, he nosed into the space behind the Volvo and followed the others up the shallow front steps of a picture-postcard cottage, covered in ivy and rambling tea roses. The rain had stopped.

A middle-aged woman, plump and cheerful, opened the front door before Albert had even had time to ring.

"Hello. You'll be Miss Castle and her friends, then? Come in, come in, do."

There was something very calming about Annie Whitlaw. She

was soft, somehow, the kind of softness that brought to mind images of beloved childhood nannies and grandmothers wearing aprons. One almost expected the house to smell of newly baked bread, or hot fruit pie. And surely, Penny thought, there must be a fat tabby cat or an elderly spaniel curled up on a cushion somewhere in this Beatrix Potter tableau?

Annie Whitlaw fluttered her hands and smiled generally around. "Have you got bags to bring in, then?"

"Two—one bag, and there's her flute. In the boot. I'll get them." Liam took the keys from Albert and ran back down the steps. Water dripped off the ivy and roses, and splashed down his collar. Swearing under his breath in Gaelic, he retrieved Jane's things from the car and hurried back indoors.

Annie Whitlaw ushered her guests into an overfurnished front room, took their coats, excused herself, and after a brief absence, came back, rather surprisingly, with beer. Once seated, she smiled comfortably around at her guests.

"Well, now," she said cheerfully, "Lord Callowen rang me up. He asked if I could oblige with a room for a Miss Castle—and I can, no question, but he only made mention of Miss Castle, and were all of you needing a room? Because if I need to find rooms for all of you, we're likely to be a bit cramped. I've only got the three guest rooms, you see, and one's all piled up with my grandmother's things from her cottage, that she left me."

"No, thank you, Mrs. Whitlaw. It's only Jane who needs a bed." Albert cleared his throat. "We're not certain how long for, but it's likely for the duration of the festival. Lord Callowen says, let him know the cost, and he'll cover it, and he asked me to see if you needed anything now, up front. If you do, I'll be more than happy to—"

"No, nothing at the moment, thank you, sir. But if you'd tell Lord Callowen I'll let him know? I'd be obliged to you."

Jane was looking more relaxed by the moment. Penny, closing her eyes, let herself drift off. The cottage was warm, and smelled pleasant, and safe. It had been a very tense few days; her sore mouth and painful ear were constant reminders of just how wrong things could go. It was nice to relax, to doze off, without having to wonder what was waiting in the shadows. . . .

"Penny?" Ringan touched her shoulder. "Wake up and come along, lamb. We're all going to have some nosh at the local tearoom before we head back to Callowen."

She jerked her head. While she'd gone off into a reverie, the others had concluded what remained of their arrangements for Jane's stay. Everyone else was standing; Jane had picked up her bag and her flute case, and was getting ready to follow her hostess upstairs. As they headed down the front steps, Penny noticed an enormous tiger cat, stretching itself in the garden, and grinned to herself.

The proprietors of the tearoom, a bow-windowed delight in Purbury's alternately Georgian and Regency period town centre, obliged the group with a large round table in one corner of the room. They were given sandwiches, fruit scones, ginger snaps, toast and clotted cream, and a huge silver pot full of fragrant tea. Between bites and sips, a round-robin discussion took place in lowered voices.

(". . . so, are we cancelled? The rest of the shows, I mean?")

(". . . depends on whether Miles can juggle the schedule.")

(". . . about the fee, do we have to return that?")

(". . . supposing Jane came back just for gigs—would that be so dangerous? If we brought her back to Purbury afterwards, and never left her alone in the house?")

(". . . not sure it's fair to even ask Jane if she'd consider doing that, or whether . . .")

The conversation, a quiet, intense spiral of what-ifs and maybe-nots, washed over Penny. Her mind had returned to the question she'd been worrying on the way back from Stanny Roche's bookshop. Her sensitivity to the unseen world, oddly dormant in the face of Andrew Leight's onslaught, was beginning to tingle to life at last.

What, exactly, was Andrew Leight? If the Callowen archivist had done his job, they'd know all about Andrew Leight's life once they got back. But it wasn't going to be enough; something in Penny was convinced of that. It was understanding what he had become that was going to be the key to getting rid of him, to casting him out into darkness, to Heaven, to Hell.

Penny thought back to the haunting of her own theatre, the Bellefield. The spirit there, Agnès de Belleville, had been virulent. She had been dangerous. She had been fire, and smoke, and torment. But her tortured spirit had meant no one special ill. Her unshriven death by fire had shaped her actions, her reactions, the sense memory that had outlasted her burnt body, when the flames set by Wat Tyler's peasants brought her down with her darkest sin unconfessed.

Andrew Leight, though—he was different. She didn't know why her certainty was so strong, that he was an entirely new thing from what she'd dealt with before, but know it she did. Was he merely a ghost, merely the need left behind, as had been the case at Lumbe's cottage, and again at the Bellefield? Her rejection of that idea was absolute. Whatever Leight was, he was not a sense memory shaped by need. Something in him, or about him, wanted to hurt, to take what was not and never had been his, and perhaps her resemblance to the Lady Susanna, whom he had hurt so badly, meant danger to Jane Castle.

The voice in her head, small and clear, was her own. As voices from inside are wont to do, it forced her to look squarely at what she'd been ducking away from.

Evil. Why don't you want to use the word, Penny? You picked up the smell of evil.

Waking late in the afternoon from a light nap, Jane Castle found herself restless.

The sleep had been needed, and had left her refreshed. It was amazing, she thought, how she'd not understood just how tense and unnatural the atmosphere at Callowen House was until she was free of it. The reaction, the sense of safety and escape, of disaster averted by the barest intake of breath, was visceral. She could feel it in every muscle.

That same feeling of relief was keeping her from trying to remember what had actually happened in the rose garden a few hours past. There was a gap in her memory, a maddening little dark space, behind which something enormous and heart-shaking awaited discovery. She remembered feeling dizzy, detached, sitting in the muniments room with the others. She remembered the sense of dislocation from her own body, the loss of energy, of determination, of will. Albert had taken her out of the house; she had filled her lungs with heavy humid air, tasting the water that would ride in on the storm clouds. They had made for a bench, a stone bench, curved and weathered. There had been roses.

Thunder in the distance, her eyes meeting Albert's own. That much, Jane remembered. Beyond that, there was nothing. From the disturbance in the atmosphere, and in Albert Wychsale's eyes, to coming slowly back to find herself astride Lothian with Miles Leight-Arnold up behind her, she could remember not one moment.

Jane lay on the single bed in the comfortable room at Annie Whitlaw's bed and breakfast, staring at flowered wallpaper and lacy curtains, not seeing them. The rain had stopped, started up again, stopped. Weak sunlight dappled her trouser legs with airy patterns of late afternoon.

Jane turned her head and looked at the clock on the table beside the bed. It was half past six.

She swung her legs to the floor, stood, and stretched. She was damned if she'd lounge about in this dainty little room for the entire evening. She was hungry, she was bored, and she was away from whatever watched from the high places of Callowen. She wondered idly how the rest of the festival would play out; if she herself was no longer there to act as some sort of lightning rod for Andrew Leight's malevolence, perhaps the festival could go on with no further disturbances. But suppose Miles Leight-Arnold refused to release Broomfield Hill from the contract? She'd have to go back to Callowen, flute in hand, ready to entertain.

Involuntarily, she shivered. Something had flashed in the darkness of that gapped memory.

A curious blankness moved over Jane's mind, bringing the dark shadowy unremembered thing closer. She pushed it away. No, she thought. I'm not looking in there. I'm not going to look. Not tonight. I won't. I can't. Come on, Jane, think of something else, think of someone else, anything or anyone. Harmless. Make this be harmless.

Charlotte? Yes, that was good. What would Charlotte be doing, now the storm was done?

The curtain in Jane's mind shivered.

She might be out riding with her father, the falcon Gaheris slamming into the earth, coming up with something struggling in its talons, begging for mercy, no air, there was no air, please, let go of . . .

Jane sat back down on the edge of the bed. Her eyes were wide, and her gaze was fixed, staring but seeing nothing. Something behind that protective curtain over the gap in her memory was pushing hard against it, wanting out.

She was breathing like a horse, air whistling through her nostrils. Sickness rose up in her stomach, flooding the back of her throat.

Eyes. There were eyes within an inch of her own, the full weight of a body holding her down, but not in lust, this wasn't even as sane or clean as lust, this was different, darker, this was an evil, dangerous game, and she was the game piece, she was the rag doll, and something was happening, something, there was no light no help but there was a man's voice, a boy's voice, a taste of something at the back of her own throat.

The boy's voice came out from behind the fragile veil that protected her from a dead woman's memory. It rang out in her head, slightly shrill, shaky and frightened, yet defiant.

. . . you leave my lady alone I'll fetch Lord Edward and then it's you who'll be cast out—

Jane whimpered. She forced herself to think, to consider.

A man's voice. A boy's voice.

The boy's voice, now, was it the voice of a child, perhaps one of Lady Susanna's own sons? No. Jane didn't know why she was so sure, but her certainty was absolute. The Leight-Arnold boys were children, no more than that. Richard, the elder, was a tousle-haired child of four, and Charles was scarcely out of swaddling. Jane had heard anger, panic, awareness. The boy's voice had, perhaps, been the voice of a teenager . . .

The light rap on the bedroom door shocked Jane back to awareness of herself. She bit back a cry of something primal, feeling her fingers spasm and clutch, clawing hard into the pretty quilted coverlet.

"Miss Castle?" Annie Whitlaw's voice was comfortable and placid and blessedly real. "I was wondering if you'd fancy a bit of supper?"

"Yes. Yes, I would. Thank you." Was that her own voice? Jane had no idea how she had produced a sound. Sweat poured down her back; in the soft summer warmth, she was clammy and shaking. "I'll come down in a minute."

She forced herself upright, and stood for a few moments, silently commanding her shaking legs to steady themselves. It was a damned good thing, Jane thought, that her room came complete with its own loo and bath. If she'd had to wander about the place in this condition, she'd send anyone she met in the hallway screaming for cover.

She ran the water in the tiny bathroom sink as cold as she could get it, held a monogrammed bit of terrycloth under the tap, and covered her face with the cloth, bits of what she'd just remembered dancing maddeningly behind her eyes, just beyond her mind's full reach.

A man's voice. A boy's voice.

She had known both voices. It made no difference, in the end, that she couldn't put a face or a name or an identity to either one. All that mattered was that neither of them had belonged to the monster, to the chimera who stalked her memory and her dreams, the incubus, the stealer of life and sanity and sweet sweet sleep that had been, that was, Andrew Leight.

take your filthy hands away from her you nameless thankless whelp, Susanna, Sue, oh Christ have mercy no—

Jane's hands jerked, and the towel slid to the tiled floor. The voice had been loud, resonant, literally at her shoulder. But there was no one in the cosy bathroom with her, nothing but the fluttering curtains, the faded monogrammed towels, the first onset of evening shadows, beginning to lengthen.

She stood for a long time, her palms pressed to her face, tears pooling unshed behind her eyes. The Lady Susanna had known that voice, and known it well. It was the voice of a protector; it was the voice of a friend. Jane didn't know how she knew this. She only knew it was the truth.

She went downstairs in search of supper. As she made small talk with Mrs. Whitlaw, and listened to her hostess's chatter, her mind was ramping up its defences, pushing away the growing belief that physical distance from the rose garden and whatever had happened there would not release her from needing to see this thing through to its finish.

Seven

And in his hurry to carry the news
He bent his breast and ran
And when he came to the broad mill stream
He took off his shoes and swam

"Ringan?"

He was fathoms down, as deep into sleep as he could go, his face buried in the depths of his pillow. His breath came in comfortable little snores. He was dreaming about fishing, of all things. He didn't even like fishing, so why this dream, in which he was a child again in Scotland, except he'd never once gone fishing as a wee boy, so what was he doing dreaming about fishing, and someone was calling him, a voice filtering through the layers. Was it his mother? No, she always yelled, never whispered, so why would she whisper now, and would someone let that bird out of doors, it was piping and crying—

"Ringan, wake up. Please?"

The whisper was urgent, cutting through the mists of sleep. He snorted, rolled over, and opened his eyes blearily.

Penny's face was a white smear in the darkness of Callowen House. Her lips were shaking; in the diminished light, he didn't know whether he saw her fear, or sensed it.

"Pen? What—" He knuckled his eyes and pulled himself upright. "What is it? What time is it?"

"It's just gone four. Ringan, wake up, will you? Please? There's—there's something wrong." She swallowed. "Listen."

"What do you—" The words died in his throat, as his conscious mind suddenly registered what his ears had been hearing, even in sleep.

The sound raised all the hair on the backs of his arms, and tightened his spine. It seemed to come from everywhere at once, now swelling, now sinking. It was not a bird.

"Jesus," he whispered. "What . . . who . . . ?"

"Someone's crying. A woman." Penny's voice was very quiet. She was very still, her body a concentrated slash of attention against the night-shadowed room. "It's coming out of the walls."

The weeping—it was extraordinary how distressing the sound was, a thin wailing that induced a nearly unbearable desire to find and comfort whoever it was in such pain—swelled to a heartbroken crescendo, and stopped. Penny shuddered, reaching out a hand to touch nothing. She then went perfectly quiet again, sitting motionless as the weeping spiralled upwards once more, leaking through the solid walls of Callowen House.

Ringan, cold to the bone, reached for Penny's hand, and gripped it.

"Susanna," she said, and sounded almost normal. Her voice held unarguable certainty. "It's the Lady Susanna. She's—it's—God, Ringan, I've never heard anything so desolate."

"No," he agreed, and felt something splash on the back of the hand that clutched hers for dear life. Tears; Penny, unaware, was weeping herself. "Penny, my lamb, don't. Don't cry. We'll—we'll find her, help her. We'll do something."

"I'm sorry." Her whisper was tremulous, and she lifted her free hand to her wet cheeks. "She's in pain. I can't help it."

The walls seemed to shimmer with the strength of Susanna Leight-Arnold's grief.

Penny flung the duvet away and stumbled towards the door. Ringan caught her up at the bedroom door.

"Wait," he told her, and ran back to the nightstand, narrowly missing jamming his bare toes against the heavy bed leg. He'd remembered that the official "Welcome to Callowen" packets had mentioned a torch, one in the nightstand in every room, in case of summer storm outages. The torch, reassuringly heavy and solid, was there. He clicked it once, and found it was working perfectly. Penny already had the door unlocked and was half in, half out of the bedroom, straining into the darkness of the ancient manor. "Right," he said. "Let's go."

They went quietly down the carpeted hallway, Ringan leading with the torch pointed straight ahead, Penny at his heels. As they got closer to the top of the Great Staircase, they became aware of other sounds during the brief, rhythmic lulls in that supernatural lamenting; behind various doors, voices murmured, sleepers woke, people questioned each other in frightened tones.

"We're not the only ones hearing this." Penny, her voice pitched low, sounded relieved. "I did wonder."

"They may be hearing it," Ringan told her quietly, "but they're not exactly rushing out to investigate."

Down the long hallway, past tall windows where the heavy draperies had been pulled back. The lawns were lovely, covered in the last knife-edged vestige of moonlight that glittered and reflected off the leftover moisture of that afternoon's storm.

At the final turn leading to the top of the Great Staircase, Ringan stopped. Penny, nearly overrunning him, heard him swallow an exclamation.

There was a woman at the foot of the stairs, looking small and unnervingly faraway. Her white gauzy nightdress fell in a pool to her bare feet. She was somehow insubstantial in the vast dim recesses of Callowen's entryway. Before Penny's wobbling knees could betray her and give out entirely, the woman looked up and saw them. She started up the stairs, and Penny recognised the cloud of flaming red-gold hair, unbound for the night.

"It's Char." Ringan started forward. "She must have heard the crying and come down to—"

The new noise came out of the night like the growl of a wolf in a place where no wolf should be. It started low, a rumble that might have once been a voice. Something in it was wrong, the suggestion of broken glass that slid and cut, a vicious cascade of rage. It rose, growing sicker and sharper in pitch, becoming a horrifying feral snarl, the call of the hunter, thwarted.

Penny cried out, and covered her ears. *No place to run,* she thought madly, *nowhere to hide.* Thoughts flooded her mind, realisation, understanding, the knowledge that he was watching them, with his odd eyes, so like Charlotte's. *He's all over the house,* she thought, *the lands, anything that belonged to Callowen. The place isn't haunted, it's infected. He's like an infection. No place to run, nowhere to hide . . .*

It was everywhere, a black filthy wind that was cold and hate and sound that turned the bones to water. Angry and malevolent, it slammed down the staircase, coursing over Charlotte where she had stopped, halfway up, lifting her hair behind her. She planted her bare feet; the suggestion of mulishness was unmistakable, even in the uncertain light and with half the Great Staircase between them.

Ringan heard glass rattling in window casings, the chatter of porcelain in cabinets all over the house. The thin high wailing stopped abruptly and with it went the wind; left behind was a terrifying hush, the sense that Callowen House was holding its breath.

"No."

Charlotte had both hands out in front of her. There was a high note in her voice, but no fear at all. Her cheeks were flying spots of furious colour. "You just damned well leave her alone, Andrew Leight!"

Ringan, immobile at the top of the stairs, had forgotten about Penny, about the rest of the festival guests, about anything in the world except the scene before him. As he stared, the torch gripped in one hand, the Mytens painting shimmered. A soft glow lit the lush carpet and spread like the landing lights of a UFO, pouring down the stairs to the hall below.

Lady Susanna came out of her painting.

She was nothing, nothing at all—wraithlike, a pale painted butterfly of a girl, gone too young. She was barely a ghost at all, merely a sense memory of herself, unable to let go. She went down the stairs, her once-pretty face a pale tattered sail, devoid of expression.

Charlotte, directly in her path, stood her ground as the ghost moved straight through her chest. Lady Susanna's living descendant said something, words, but she was too far down the stairs for Ringan to hear them clearly.

At the foot of the stairs, Lady Susanna turned left and faded to smoke. Then the ghostlight was gone, and the painting was merely a painting once more.

Quiet settled on Callowen House.

From out of doors, deep inside the mews somewhere on the estate, came the wild muffled scream of an enraged falcon. Gaheris, Ringan thought hazily, the bird. Miles Leight-Arnold's pampered feathery killing machine, pulling against the jesses that bound it to the block, maddened by—what? The hawk must have picked up on something. They say animals sense things, don't they? They say . . .

Somewhere in the recesses of the family's quarters, a door slammed heavily. Ringan heard a deep peremptory voice, calling out: Miles Leight-Arnold.

Ringan became aware of something, a dead weight, leaning heavily against the back of his ankles. He turned around and saw Penny, limp on the carpeted floor at his feet. She had fainted.

"Mr. Laine? Might I have a word with you, when you've finished your breakfast?"

Ringan, who had been pushing buttered egg around on his plate, set his fork down, looked up, and found himself staring at Roger Searle, the Callowen family archivist.

Ringan had already decided that this was the oddest meal he'd ever sat down to. All around him, the festival guests and his fellow performers were either locked in whispered, feverish conversations in far corners of the elegant dining room, or else they were studiously pretending that no whispered feverish conversations in far corners were called for. Under the circumstances, denial struck him as a lost cause, but to each his own. The one thing that no one seemed actually to be interested in doing in the elegant dining room was eating breakfast.

"Yes, of course. In fact"—Ringan set his fork down and pushed his chair back—"I haven't got much appetite this morning, anyway. What's going on?"

"Something I think you ought to see. In, er, regard to that family matter we've been researching." Searle lowered his voice slightly. "Information. In the muniments room."

"Something about Andrew Leight?"

"Not precisely, no." There was an odd, guarded note in Searle's voice. "Something about the Lady Susanna."

"Sounds interesting." Ringan followed him out. "We ought to have Charlotte and Penny in on this, as well, don't you think?"

"They're already there. I ran into Ms. Wintercraft-Hawkes coming downstairs and, er, well, I hijacked her away from breakfast, I'm afraid, though she said she'd send for coffee. Charlotte—Lady Charlotte—was already up and about."

Searle opened the door to the small room where the family records were stored. Penny, her chin propped in her left palm, was using her right hand to sip what smelled like a dangerously strong cup of coffee. Breakfast—a scone with a dollop of jam—she was resolutely ignoring.

Ringan, catching her eye for a fleeting moment, felt a wash of familiar unease. There was a wilt to her upper body, a sag to her general posture, that spoke eloquently to his eye of something darker than simple lack of sleep.

Something unpleasant moved down Ringan's spine, planting a barb in his conscious mind. Twenty-four hours ago, Jane had looked just this way, but now Jane was safe away in a cottage in Purbury. Instead, here was Penny, his Penny, the sensitive who had shown no signs of her customary weakness in the presence of the Callowen ghosts until now, looking as frail and tired and vulnerable as Jane had done, sitting in that very chair.

"Ringan! I was *ghosted* last night, did you see? You did see, didn't you?" Charlotte, dressed for riding, showed no adverse signs of the family's more respectable phantom having flown through her rib cage not five hours earlier. In fact, Ringan thought, she looked indecently pleased with herself. "My however many times grandmum! She went straight through me and whoosh, off to the left, and out. Wasn't it spectacular?"

A strand of bright hair, escaping as usual from the unsteady chignon beneath her riding cap, caught her attention. She twirled it round her index finger. "Roger says he's found something," she added. "We're just waiting for Penny to finish her coffee so that it won't get spilt all over the family doodahs."

"Sorry." Penny's voice dragged, and the burgeoning knot in Ringan's stomach tightened to pain. She set the china cup down in its saucer. "I'm finished. What is it you found?"

"It's here. Or rather, they're here." Searle unlocked one of the glass-fronted bookshelves on the wall. Removing two leather registers, he set them down at his end of the long table, and opened each to a page, bookmarked with a strip of acid-free paper. "It's actually two mentions of the same thing, made by two different people, two centuries apart. And I hope—in fact, having been told about what happened this morning, I pray—that this will be useful."

The others gathered round the table, Penny moving slowly. Ringan, peering at the precise faded lettering in what was obviously the older of the volumes, muttered under his breath.

Unexpectedly, Penny stood up, and leaned against Ringan's back. "Hang on, Ringan. Let me have a butcher's, will you? I'm probably more used to this sort of calligraphy than you are."

She peered over his shoulder, and began to read aloud:

14 September 1629. By the request of Lord Edward, who in his inconsolable grief is desirous of ridding his house of all manner of effects that might bring the events of 2 September more freshly to his mind, I today gave a great bundle of the Lady Susanna's effects into the care of the poor Lady's mother, at her grandmother's house in Purbury. This was an exceeding sorry task for me to have to perform, and I did have some

small time when I most nearly could not make myself stay in that house, for to see how Dame Gedlington held fast to her slain child's treasures will weigh heavily on my memory. Touching was the sight of her tears, staining those pages of her daughter's written accounts of her life as Lady of Callowen. Having been forbidden to do so, I could not speak to the Dame's questions, though she did plead most piteously with me, that I should tell her how her daughter had come to such an end, and whether those rumours and whispers of the Lady's infidelity might be true or no. . . .

Penny's voice trailed off. For a moment they were all quiet.

"A diary." Charlotte looked up at her family's archivist. "That's what this bloke means, isn't it? Susanna kept a diary."

"Not necessarily," Ringan objected. "He says it was accounts. Maybe it was just one of those housekeeping books well-born wives always seemed to keep for posterity. You know the sort of thing—how to kill bugs, quince and neat's-foot jelly recipes, ordering new curtains."

"What in sweet hell is neat's-foot jelly?"

Startled, they looked up to see Lord Callowen leaning against the door-frame. His deep voice was rough around the edges, and his dark eyes seemed even darker with lost sleep.

"I have no idea," Ringan told him. "I'm sure it's something, though."

"Da, Susanna kept a journal." Char came round the table and pulled at her father's sleeve. "Come and look, will you? Who was the bloke who wrote this?"

"Lord, Charlotte, how in the world would I know? And stop trying to rip my arm off." He followed his daughter to the table. "Good morning, everyone. Roger, is this the register that talks about Andrew Leight?"

"No, My Lord. We're going to have to go back a couple of years to find out how Andrew came to Callowen, I think. He's mentioned, of course, but there isn't much here."

"Find those, Roger, will you, when you get a moment? I want to see those mentions." Callowen's gaze was on Penny. He reached out and, with surprising gentleness, touched her shoulder. "Sit down, child, do. You look nearly as played out as Jane did when we took her to town. I'm afraid the house ghosts are making this visit one you'll want to forget."

He pulled out a chair, and Penny sank into it.

Ringan's jaw was tight. "Pen—"

"Later, darling, all right? We'll talk." Whatever thoughts had come to Penny after the events of the early morning, she had no intention of sharing them with the others.

"In the meantime," Callowen said, "what's all this about a diary? "No Char, let Roger tell me. He does this better than anyone."

Searle promptly justified Callowen's faith in him by reciting the diary passage in question without so much as glancing at the register. Miles took a moment to absorb it.

"Gedlington," he grunted. "The name's familiar, but not from the here and now. I've seen it somewhere, but—damn. Where would I have seen it, Roger?"

"In the Purbury churchyard." Surprisingly, it was Charlotte who spoke up. "There's a few graves, and a small mausoleum, near the east wall of the church, kept all locked up. I used to sneak out after services, and take rubbings of the headstones."

"She's quite right, Lord Callowen. The family died out sometime during the seventeenth century, I believe. I'd have to take a look at the actual registers at St. Giles for the date."

"We'll do that," Ringan said. "High time we did something. We've been worse than useless. We skipped out on the research here yesterday. I'll take Penny and we'll go to—did you say St. Giles?"

"St. Giles in the Green, yes." Callowen spoke absently; he was scanning the older register, reading quickly. His brows were furrowed, lines taut around his mouth. Penny, watching him, thought that his resemblance to his own falcon was too pronounced for comfort. "Roger, ring up the rector, will you, and ask him to have any of the period church documents that mention the family ready for Ringan and Penny. Assuming Penny's up to it, that is."

"Oh yes. Absolutely. In fact, the sooner the better." Penny had caught at Ringan's impatience, and was responding to it. She wanted to be out and away from Callowen. She wanted, needed, to be doing something, anything at all, to find the truth and put an end to all this.

"Good." If Penny's eagerness to get away from Callowen had hurt Char's feelings, Miles seemed unmoved. "Why don't you plan on getting there in an hour or so? The rector should have what you need ready for you."

"There's one thing—" Searle said diffidently. "I should be clear, we aren't talking about the actual registers of church business. Those are all kept at the County Archives in Winchester. These would be the personal notes and journals kept by St. Giles's incumbents over the centuries. I'll let Walter Hibbert—he's the rector—know what's needed."

"Ta. We're on our way, then—oh! Half a minute." Ringan turned back to the table. "Didn't you say there was a second entry? We haven't heard about that one yet. When's it from?"

"Right." Searle read down the page of the second register. "It's dated 20 June 1824. I haven't done much with the family archives from that period, so I don't know who the steward was. Here—it says, 'Spoke with John Anderley's widow, Annie, this morning. In her clearing of his effects, she was most surprised to discover several items of some antiquity, in her belief the item of greatest interest to the House being some pages which, if the note atop their binding is to be believed, are writ in the hand of Lady Susanna Leight-Arnold, who is said to emerge as a spectre from the painting that graces the head of the Great Staircase. I conferred with Lord Callowen, saying that the Widow Anderley had offered these items to us, but was told, rather brusquely, that he had no interest and would not bespeak them.'"

"Gah! Short-sighted rubbish. You don't turn away family documents," Miles snapped. "1824—that would have been George.

Only Tory this family ever had. That's some research that will certainly need doing. If you happen to run into Jane while you're in town, tell her I hope she's feeling better."

Ringan drove barely a hundred yards beyond the gates of Callowen House, just far enough to ensure that the Alfa was no longer on Leight-Arnold land. Then he pulled the car into a cul-de-sac beside a padlocked lychgate and killed the motor.

"Talk to me." His voice was controlled, quiet. "What happened to you this morning?"

Penny turned her head to regard him. She was well aware of just how close to the edge of panic he was. She knew, too, how difficult it must be for him to stay quiet. While his voice was calm and under control, the muscles of his jaw betrayed him; the edges of his black beard kept wanting to jut and bristle as he forced himself to relax, only to tense once more.

"It's all right, Ringan. For the moment, I'm all right."

"It came back." He watched her face. "The sensitivity, the same thing you had both times before, with the other hauntings. Didn't it? After what happened this morning? It came back."

"Yes—well, no, not precisely the same thing." She closed her eyes, remembering the pitiful weeping of the Lady Susanna, the balked hungry snarl of Andrew Leight, the knowledge that had flashed in her when Susanna had passed through Charlotte on the stairs, a knowledge and understanding that had hit her hard enough to knock her unconscious. . . .

"This morning was different, then." He watched her. "How?"

"Well, for one thing? No pictures, no images. Not visual. It was . . ." Her voice died. Ringan opened his mouth, then bit back whatever he'd planned to say. He knew that prompting would hinder rather than help; that even their longtime phrase inviting communication, "Penny for them," must remain unsaid. Finally, she spoke again.

"Ringan, you know how, at Lumbe's and then at the Bellefield, I saw things? Visions of people, of what they were doing, what they'd done, of things around them?" Ringan nodded.

"Right," she said. "This morning—I didn't see anything, nothing that you didn't see, I mean, but, it's going to be tricky, trying to describe it." She took a deep breath, and spoke slowly. "When Susanna came out of her painting—there was that pool of light, spilling out of it, all over the carpeting. Remember?"

"I do." Ringan thought back, seeing the bizarre luminous glow that had seemed like a river of starlight. "It actually touched my feet," he said aloud. "I remember I expected it to be very hot, or very cool. But it wasn't. It just felt like plain old air."

"I was barefoot as well. And it touched my feet. And when it did—oh, *hell*."

Her face suddenly crumpled. Ringan twisted his body round and gathered her in. She shook for a minute or two, transmitting warm terrifying shocks down his nervous system. As he held her, a very clear thought came up in his mind: *I hate Andrew Leight*.

When the shakes had passed, she pulled lightly against him. He released her at once, and saw that her eyes were dry. The nerve storm had produced no tears.

"Right." Her hands now lay, relaxed, in her lap. "This is tricky—describing it, I mean. It was a bit like the way I imagine those light shows were, the ones they used to have at rock concerts back in the sixties, all wavy odd lines and patterns that seem random but aren't, and then everything slipping around like ripples in a lake, then shifting into a real thing, but distorted. You know? The light touched my feet and something happened in my head—the way I see things, understand things, it all sort of phase-shifted into a slightly new way of seeing and knowing."

"Wow."

She smiled at him, a small grin, strained but real. "Wow it is, love. I knew her—Susanna. That light touched me and I *got* her. I couldn't see her, but I could remember things, things in her heart and her soul and in her memory. And they were horrid, awful things. Andrew Leight holding her down—he bit her, Ringan. Just hard enough to hurt, not enough to break the skin, because I could also get him, and I knew he wanted her to feel it under the flesh, it was about power, not sex, remembering some of the beastly wretched things he'd whispered to her, telling her she was a whore and scum and not worthy to be——"

"Hang on, love." Ringan's own mouth was dry. "Take a breath. You're the colour of old cheese right now. Take a breath."

Penny shook her head. "No. While it's this close to the surface, I'm telling you. Because I don't know how long I'm going to remember it, in quite this way. It's already beginning to fade out."

"All right, Pen. Tell me, then. I'm listening."

"It was his main weapon over her." There was a driving urgency to her voice now. "She came from a lower rank entirely—she'd married well above her. It was a love match, a much older peer falling for a girl less than half his age. She was smart, she was pretty, she was educated beyond her own station in life, really, but she was barely yeoman class, and here he was, a peer of the realm. Memories, I got snippets, things she forced herself to think of when she was being pinned down and brutalised by her husband's poor relation. He was still light-years ahead of her socially, you know? So he could use that to beat her down, frighten her, keep her silent about what he was doing to her. She lay there and took it, just took it, from Andrew, and she thought about Edward the whole time. It was systematic, Ringan, an old, old story. Andrew raped her, he'd twist flesh so he could listen to her scream and she never did scream, Ringan. Instead, she—she went away. Went to a place in her head, to a memory where she was remembering times with her husband. Sometimes she thought about her two boys, but mostly, it was all about Edward."

Ringan's eyes were damp. Tears leaked down Penny's face. Unaware, she went on.

"And Andrew—he hated Susanna because he hated Edward. Ringan, the depth and sickness of his hate for his cousin were like nothing I've ever felt. He was hungry with it. He was deformed with hate. I couldn't see him, at least I thought I couldn't, but——"

She stopped, her cheeks mottled, her mouth unsteady.

"Was there more, Pen?" Ringan had given up any attempt to keep his jaw muscles in line. His beard was twitching and electric. "Susanna's memories, Andrew's total nastiness. Was there something else? There was, I think."

"Oh, yes. Something else." She clenched her hands together. "Lady Susanna came out of that light in her painting. She went down the stairs. There wasn't much of her, was there? She was basically a soft breath on the air. That's because I was remembering for her—her essence, whatever it is that makes or made her Susanna, had got itself totally separated from her actual ghost. And Andrew Leight came out of the dark and he went after her."

"Right. When we heard him making that filthy noise."

"No—that was a bit later." Penny shook her head. "Ringan, I saw him. And he wasn't human; he didn't even begin to look human. He was leathery and twisted and it's as I said before, deformed with his hate. He looked very much like that medieval woodcut we saw, the one in the book in Stanny Roche's shop. And this morning, Andrew went after Susanna. And then—"

Ringan's eyes had narrowed to slits. "What then?"

"She went straight through Charlotte." Penny licked her lips, which had gone very dry. "And Andrew chased her, right up to the point where he got to Char. And he stopped. He had to stop. There was something about Charlotte, I don't know what, that kept him from following after Susanna. I think he was afraid of her. Of Charlotte."

Ringan nodded slowly. "Penny, listen. There's something missing in all this. All those memories of Susanna's you said you felt— it was all about Andrew and Edward?"

"Well, Edward mostly. And her two sons, a bit." Her brows were knitted. "Ringan, what do you mean, something's missing? What are you getting at? What do you—*oh!*"

"Yes." He saw the realisation of what he himself had already seen come up on her face. "Got it now?"

"Matty Groves himself." She stared at Ringan. "He never even entered her head. There was no Matty, not in her mind!"

"No Matty," Ringan agreed. "Despite the family legend, and the famous song, and all the rest of it, clearly stating that Edward Leight-Arnold surprised his wife and her lover in bed and killed them together. No mention of the man the song claims was her lover. It makes me wonder just how big a cover-up we're dealing with here."

Eight

Little Matty Groves, he lay down
And took a little sleep
When he awoke Lord Arnold
Was standing at his feet

St. Giles in the Green, parish church for the diocese of Purbury, Sellingstone, and Micklesdene, had stood on its slight grassy hill in one form or another for a thousand years. Behind it was a rise of green, covered at different seasons with bluebell and campion and rare falls of soft Hampshire snow. Gently encircling it, in a curve of flatter ground, was the St. Giles churchyard.

"Pretty." Penny stopped just inside the lychgate. She rested her hand on the carved oak, polished smooth by centuries of parishioners in search of heavenly comfort. Before them was a pebbled path that led to the porch doors. "Ringan—this place is *old*."

"Not that old, Pen, at least not the parts I'm looking at." Ringan ran an expert glance over St. Giles, taking in its comfortably mottled stonework, its hideous and unabashedly Victorian stained-glass windows, its square, imposing bell tower. "It looks to have bits that go back a good long way—I'd put that belfry at early fourteenth century or thereabouts. But mostly, I'd say a lot of restoration work."

"That's not what I mean. Not the church building. I mean the grounds, the place, the—oh, hell, I don't know what I mean." She suddenly shook herself, as if trying to shed a memory or thought.

"It just feels—I just think there was something here a good long time before there was a church." She added, with complete irrelevance, "Cookpots. And bears. And people with dirty chilly feet."

Ringan felt a prickle between his shoulder blades. Someday, he thought, he might grow accustomed to Penny's moments of ghost-induced oddity. He wasn't betting on it; the lurch in the pit of his stomach didn't seem to be less now than it had been a year ago.

The arched doors, carved of the same forest oak as the gate, swung open, and a man in a cassock emerged. He stood, nearly invisible in his black clothes, and waited for them to join him.

Penny and Ringan made their way up the path. Penny stopped once, opened her mouth, then shut it again. She blinked, looked around her, and hurried to catch up.

The Reverend Walter Hibbert was not what Ringan had been expecting. He was a young man, barely thirty, with enormous brown eyes and a shock of unruly chestnut hair. Whether because of Penny's comments or because of the quiet village setting, Ringan had been expecting the ecclesiastical counterpart for Stanny Roche, an elderly, austere man in his seventies.

"Good morning. I'm Walter Hibbert, Rector of St. Giles. Welcome." If Hibbert had caught Ringan's surprise, he was too well mannered to comment on it. "Mr. Laine? Ms. Wintercraft-Hawkes? Welcome to St. Giles in the Green. Roger Searle rang up from the house. If you'd like to come in, I've got a few things over at the rectory that you may find useful."

They followed him indoors. Ringan stopped just inside, looking around appreciatively.

St. Giles was beautiful. It had triumphed over patchwork restoration attempts, over a nearby military presence during two world wars, over devout Victorians with more money than taste. The chancel was broad and gracious, the roof above it soaring like a cathedral's interior, arched and broad-beamed. Wide steps led to the altar, behind which one of the building's remaining original windows scattered diffused light in as many colours as Joseph's coat. Ringan heard Penny, at his right shoulder, murmur an appreciative noise.

"Oh," she said, "this is lovely. So calm, so—I don't know. Very different from the churchyard. No fear. Or despair."

"Fear?" Hibbert was startled into speech. "Despair? I'm sorry, but—you said the churchyard frightened you? I find it remarkably soothing, myself. There's something very calming to my soul, to contemplate sleeping away the ages in such a setting. But I know graves don't appeal to everyone."

"No, no." Penny shook her head vigorously. "I'm not frightened of graves—the fear I was talking about isn't mine. I meant, there was fear coming up from the ground. Just where the path starts its rise—I could feel it. Misery, too. A group of people, with weapons, and dirty bare feet."

"You actually felt that? Coming from the earth itself?" Hibbert stared at her. "You're a sensitive, then?"

"Reverend." Ringan had finally caught up, and understood what Penny must have sensed. The old building, the curve on which it was built, the ancient gate of oak from the dark English forests, now long vanished . . . "This hill, the one the church is built on—"

"Ah." Hibbert apparently understood as well. "Yes. Well, if you happened to be a sensitive, I can see how uncomfortable it would be. Yes, St. Giles is built on a prehistoric site. I don't believe the experts ever decided whether it was a long barrow or a burial mound, but certainly, bones were found here."

"Would that have been during the construction of the original church?" The historian in Ringan had been roused. "Twelfth century or thereabouts is what I guessed."

"Towards the end of the twelfth century, yes."

"It was a long barrow." Penny's voice was flat with certainty, and the irises of her eyes were enormous. "There was some kind of plague. All those people, curled up together, making each other sicker. They mostly died—all the livestock, most of the people. So actually, I suppose you'd have to say it was both, wouldn't you? Barrow and grave, all together."

Ringan heard Hibbert catch his breath. For a long moment the ancient building was absolutely quiet. Then Penny sighed, a long exhale, and her eyes cleared.

"Oh, lord. I did it again, didn't I? You must think I'm a complete nutter." Penny, back to her usual self, turned an enchanting smile on Hibbert, and offered a hand. "I'm awfully sorry, Reverend. What a way to introduce ourselves! I'm Penny, by the way. And this is Ringan. And I promise, we honestly don't swan round the place, dripping ectoplasm and holding séances, or anything like that. We're really quite normal."

"Walter." Hibbert shook hands, smiling. "And honestly, don't worry about it. If I could feel what you obviously felt, I suspect I'd have reacted that way myself."

Penny, cheerful and completely in the moment once more, chatted happily with Hibbert about Callowen House, Purbury, the beauties of Hampshire. The rector did indeed have good manners; it was obvious to Ringan that he was dying to ask Penny questions about her sixth sense, but she wasn't providing any openings and, that being the case, he wasn't going to push the issue. Accepting the situation, he came straight to the point.

"Searle asked me to see if we had any documents in the rectory library from two very specific periods. Actually, it was really for one period leading into the next, but he sounded very definite in naming them as two distinct sets of documents. I checked and yes, as it happens, there's rather a lot from both points in time. The first period he asked for, I assume would concern Callowen's poor ghostly murder victim, since he specified the autumn of 1629. But he also asked if we had anything by any of the incumbents of the previous six years, from 1623 forward." He shot them an apologetic look and smiled disarmingly. "Now, that puzzled me. I'll confess to being nosy, a terrible character fault for someone wearing this particular collar and coat. Part of it is being a relative newcomer to the parish; I haven't got to know all the back history of Purbury, or of the Leight-Arnolds. I do know about Lady Susanna's ghost, of course. I'd love to know more about her, beside the legend and the song. But Lady Susanna isn't buried in the Callowen vault, under St. Giles, she's buried in a special mausoleum in the Callowen grounds, and I haven't been to look at her tomb yet. It's not open to the public—you have to request a special viewing."

"I think Searle split the request into two periods because we're hunting down two very different bits of information, and they may or may not overlap." Penny touched a polished pew back with a fingertip. "At least, wouldn't you say so, Ringan?"

"Yes, I would. Anything you've got from 1629—we're hoping to find a mention of Lady Arnold keeping a sort of journal, an accounts book or a household book, or something. There's a mention of it, twice, in the Callowen family documents. But the earlier records, that's something else. We really want to find as much information as possible about a particular relative of the Arnold family. Specifically, we're looking for information about a cousin, Andrew Leight, who came to live at Callowen, we're not sure when."

"That's going to make the research a bit tricky," Hibbert said thoughtfully. "And about Andrew Leight. You say there are documents from both periods?"

"There certainly are. The notes from the Reverend Charles Lockereigh, from autumn of 1629—he was still the rector of St. Giles at the time of the actual murder, or that month at least, and had been for decades—are strange, and rather guarded. Lockereigh was replaced the month of the murder itself, very abruptly. But I didn't really read too much in depth of the earlier entries, since I didn't know what I was—"

"Replaced?" Penny spoke sharply. "Before or after the murder, do you know? And would that have been at the request of Lord Edward, or was that sort of decision left up to the local bishop?"

"I'm betting after. I'm betting days or maybe hours after, in fact." Ringan stared at Penny. His beard was bristling. "And once I win that bet, I'll take the kitty and put the whole thing on Lord Edward being responsible for the change—Purbury and the rectory here, they're all part of the Leight-Arnold demesne. You know how you said you couldn't find any hint of Matty Groves in Susanna's thoughts, Pen? I'm beginning to believe that either

Matty Groves had nothing to do with Lady Susanna, or else didn't exist at all."

"He existed, all right."

They all turned. Jane, in soft cotton trousers and a sun-hat, stood framed in the doorway.

"Hello, Ringan. Hello, Penny. Hello, Rector—I don't know your name, I'm afraid."

"Jane!" Ringan went to her. "Are you feeling better? And what in the world brings you down here?"

"This is Jane Castle, Walter." Penny, watching Jane with a faint crease between her brows, made the introduction. "Jane is the flautist in Ringan's band, Broomfield Hill. She's staying here in town, at Annie Whitlaw's bed and breakfast—things got a bit iffy up at the manor. Jane, this is the Reverend Walter Hibbert. What's up? Did something happen? You haven't been back up to Callowen, have you?"

"Something happened, yes. Not much of a something, not after all the rave-up stuff with Andrew up at Callowen, but something. Voices. Last night, or rather, early evening, upstairs at Annie Whitlaw's. And no, I haven't been back to the manor. I'm likely going to go, though. There doesn't seem to be much point in staying clear, and I think—I have a feeling—that I ought to go back."

Jane came all the way in. She looked reasonably well rested, but her steps were slow, and she kept glancing around, as if expecting something to come out of the woodwork. "I just came down to see about a grave. Matty's, in fact. I wanted to see if there is one. I want to know where he's buried."

There was a moment of silence. Her words, chilling in and of themselves, had been spoken prosaically, almost casually. Whatever had happened the night before, whatever had sent Jane looking for a headstone, didn't seem to have worried her much.

"You heard voices?" Ringan caught Penny's eye. "Whose, Jane? Do you know?"

"Edward's. And Matty's." She turned her head and looked at them. "It's all a lie, Ringan. I'm beginning to piece together what must have happened that day—I've been getting echoes, bits and pieces. The song? Nothing but PR. One big damned filthy lie, designed to cover something up. I don't know what really happened yet, not all of it, but I am sure about one thing. Susanna never betrayed Edward."

"We'd already sussed that much out for ourselves, ta. We made Lady Susanna's acquaintance on the Great Staircase this morning, and the light from her painting lit Penny up, as well as the carpets." Ringan walked forward and touched Jane's shoulder, lightly. "I'm a little more worried about the fact that getting out of Callowen doesn't seem to have kept whatever is going on up there away from you. And we're going to talk about that, make no mistake." He looked at Walter. "Could we impose on you for a chair? I think Jane ought to sit down."

"Certainly. If you'd like to come across the churchyard to the rectory? There's plenty of chairs, and besides, there are some journals I believe you wanted to look at. I'll bring them back over with us."

At about the same time Jane Castle was making up her mind whether or not she wanted to visit the church, Charlotte Leight-Arnold was deciding to visit a grave or two herself.

The encounter on the stairs in the cold pre-dawn light had left her in a very strange state of mind. She was edgy yet focussed, adrift yet determined. Above all, she was astonished at herself, and at her fierce sense of protectiveness towards an ancestress, a wanton who had died at the end of her husband's sword nearly four centuries ago.

She had understood Penny's desire to get out and away from Callowen. Charlotte's own feelings were unbalanced and in need of sorting, but the most immediate and easily identified was an intolerable restlessness. After Penny and Ringan left, she turned to her father.

"Da? Can I talk to you?"

Miles said nothing. He didn't seem to have heard her; he was reading, one fingertip held just above the open page, eyes and finger alike moving quickly down the tiny script. His brows had drawn down and together, tightening the skin of his face, thinning his lips and throwing the hawk's nose into stark relief.

"Da—"

"Wait a bit, Char, will you?" He read to the end of the section, and looked up. Roger Searle, courteously silent, heard Charlotte catch her breath, saw the expression on Callowen's face, and bit back an exclamation of his own.

"Da! What is it?"

"Nothing." This was so obviously a falsehood that even Charlotte was speechless. Her disbelief, however, showed clear enough on her face, and her father coloured slightly.

"I'm curious, that's all. There's a note in there, a personal note from Edward's steward, that surprised me. Something about a visit from the Bishop to Callowen, an unexpected visit. It was a day or so before Susanna was killed. I want to think about it for a bit. Right. What is it, Char?"

"Nothing." Something in Callowen's face was making his daughter obscurely uneasy. Was that doubt she was seeing? No, surely not. Yet he looked, at the very least, distracted and thoughtful. What on earth? "It's only—I haven't been to the family crypt since before I left school, and I was thinking a visit might be useful. Also, I want to visit the Folly. I've not been there in donkey's years. Is it locked?"

"What, Lady Susanna's tomb? Of course it's locked. When have we ever left it open during festival?" He jerked his head at Searle. "Roger, can you arrange to let Char into the Folly, please? When did you want to go?"

"Now." Char, a Leight-Arnold to her boot heels, made a quick decision. "I'll get that done first, and do Purbury later on. With any luck at all, Penny and Ringan will have found something out—I'll see about catching them up at St. Giles. And I can check on Jane, as well."

Ten minutes later, with the key to the peristyle mausoleum known as Lord Edward's Folly tucked into the pocket of her riding jacket, Charlotte had saddled and mounted Dagmar, her favourite chestnut mare, and was cantering easily across the lawns behind Callowen House towards the north-eastern boundary of the Leight-Arnold land. Her mind was working, and working hard.

All her concentration was focussed on the question teasing her brain: why on earth had her father gone silent and evasive on the subject of whatever he'd found in the family register?

An unexpected visit from the Bishop to Lord Edward might be a bit odd—if the official state visits during her own lifetime were anything to go by, such events were traditionally arranged well in advance, and full of planning, menu consultation, scheduling, and the like.

Still, she thought, it might have been likelier, or even necessary, in Edward Leight-Arnold's day. Miles's voice moved through her mind . . . *a day or so before Susanna was killed.* . . .

Charlotte slowed the mare to a walk. Of course, that was it. Her father hadn't just been worried by the unexpectedness of the prelate's visit; the timing of the visit had upset him, as well. Something just before the killing must have fluttered the upper echelons.

But what? Had the visit come shortly after, there might have been some sense to be made of it, but as it was? Char, lost in thought, held Dagmar still and considered the question. What had brought a high prelate of the Church pelting down to Hampshire with no warning? There was secrecy implied in all this, and a mystery somewhere.

Charlotte, turning it over in her mind, turned the mare's head to the north. Lord Edward's Folly—odd, she thought, that she had always just taken that name on trust, and never stopped to consider it—stood alone on a small hill, cut off from the lawns by a trout stream. The mausoleum was approached over a small stone bridge. The building itself, a round affair of colonnades and creamy stone and a gently domed roof, lay in a pool of sunlight. It looked tranquil, and welcoming.

Charlotte, glancing up, edged her mare towards the first coping stones. Dagmar was balking, uneasy, swerving her head a bit. Charlotte became aware that the mare was sweating, sweating far more profusely than a light canter on a warm morning could account for. Her coat was heavily streaked.

"What's up, darling? Come on, then, it's only a bridge." Charlotte leaned forward, keeping her voice normal. It was an effort, and it shouldn't have been. Something was badly wrong; she knew it, understood it just as the horse apparently knew it, in a way that was as instinctive as it was bone-deep. It was too quiet: No birds sang, no insects took wing. The warm summer air was silent, thick with an intangible expectancy.

Charlotte straightened abruptly in the saddle, and pulled Dagmar to a halt. She felt the animal, over sixteen hands tall, shiver beneath her. Off to her right, in the far distance, another horseman cantered under a glimmer of hazy summer heat. Odd, Charlotte thought, Da hadn't mentioned he'd be riding. And what was that smell? . . .

so high and mighty you'll not be rid of me so easily, oh no, what rights you had here, mine, they ought to have been mine, your house and your land and your lady gay, at least I've had the one and that's the one you'll be minding most, I'm thinking

The voice came out of the ground, the stream, the soft placid sweep of Hampshire sky itself. This was no whisper, no ghostly echo; it rang with rage, dark with glee and hate. There were viciousness and violence, bringing with them a reek of death and putrefaction. It slammed into Charlotte's skull like an invisible jackhammer.

Dagmar screamed, a noise almost as unearthly as the dark wind of a voice pummelling her rider. The mare reared wildly, plunging backward, reacting too quickly to allow Charlotte enough time to react herself. The reins slipped from her fingers as she cried out, hands flying to cover her ears, trying vainly to fend off the evil laughing cascade of verbal blackness. She was aware of nothing else.

Dagmar turned, her powerful legs bearing the weight of a nearly impossible pivot. She jumped for the near side of the bridge as if the stones beneath her hooves were the gateway to some unseen hell, and hit the soft turf of lawn in full careening gallop. Charlotte, only half-conscious of her own danger, came off, landing with a sickening impact on her left hip.

Dagmar never slowed down. White foam streaming from the bit, her enormous eyes rolling and deranged, she thundered back towards the safety of her stable, leaving Charlotte motionless in the soft grass at the edge of the stone bridge that led to Lord Edward's Folly.

"Charlotte? Miss Leight-Arnold? *Char!*"

The voice came through a lovely curtain of mist. Charlotte, lying on her left side, felt her hip throbbing like a heartbeat. It hurt; so did a few other spots. And someone was calling her. Not only calling her, shaking her lightly by the shoulder, gently, taking care not to . . .

"Char?"

It was a pleasant voice, a beautiful voice, in fact. Deep, modulated, very musical. Nothing like that, that *thing,* that had been screaming and reeking and—

"Stand."

The word, spoken as a sort of casual command, was odd enough to complete the transition from semi-consciousness to full awareness. Charlotte opened her eyes.

Julian Cordellet, on his knees in the grass beside her, let out his breath.

"Thank Christ." He let go of her shoulder. "What happened?"

"My horse. Dagmar. She got spooked and threw me." Her mouth tasted like bile and old blood. Damn, she thought, my hip, damn, is the damned thing broken? "Be quiet a minute, will you? I really want to see what's cocked up."

Cordellet nodded and settled back, waiting in silence. Char closed her eyes, listening to various bits of her anatomy complaining. Hip, shoulder, wrist, all on the side she'd landed on. Nothing seemed broken, although the wrist might be.

"Bruises," she said aloud. "Maybe a cracked wrist. Damn! Sore mouth, too. Oh well. I suppose it's a bit of luck that I didn't break a rib or even my fool neck. My hair's a mess, too. Oh—hello, Julian. Why were you ordering me to stand? Bit bossy, don't you think?"

"Why was I—oh, for heaven's sake. I was talking to my horse! Can you sit up?" Cordellet sounded amused, or perhaps it was exasperation she was hearing. She wasn't certain she cared.

"Won't know until I try, will I? I mean, eyes closed and everything?" Charlotte opened her eyes and focussed on him. "Ah. Nothing's gone blurry or fuzzy, so that's all right. Here, give me a hand up, will you? On the right side, please. The left's going to be a proper masterpiece."

"I saw it happen." Cordellet's voice, that theatre-trained product of years of exercise and vocal coaching, seemed suddenly uncontrolled. He moved to her right side, and helped her to her feet. "I saw your horse go up like a Roman candle—she just went completely mad, all out, and streaked off back the other way. I saw you fall. You frightened me half to death. Are you really all right?"

"I'm fine, thank you. Except for the bits that aren't."

"What happened?" He wasn't letting go of her, and she found herself disinclined to push him away. Cordellet was a nicely muscled bloke, she thought; he honestly looked too slender to be so strong. To her own surprise, Charlotte discovered that her legs were shaky.

She turned and stared at Lord Edward's Folly, pushing a tangled mass of red-gold hair out of her eyes.

That voice—that smell—they had come out of everywhere. Andrew, she thought grimly, that was Andrew Leight. And he might have been yelling from the ground or the sky or the stream, but damn it, Dagmar had got nervous and dancy when she first put her hooves on the stones of that bridge that led to where Susanna Leight-Arnold lay buried, and there was simply no way that was merely a coincidence. . . .

"Charlotte? Please. Can you tell me why your horse reacted the way she did?"

"There was a voice." It never occurred to her to sugarcoat her reply. "A voice and a smell. It smelled like something that hadn't been embalmed properly, a thousand rotting corpses, maybe a million. Horrible evil voice, from a filthy little man. It—" Her voice died away. "Sounds mad, I know."

"This has something to do with what's been going on at the house. Doesn't it?"

She turned and regarded him. "Of course it does. And of course, that nonsense this morning on the stairs, our good ghost, the one who never bothers or hurts anyone, poor Susanna. That woke you up, did it? You heard her, and the roaring?"

"Yes. But I already thought there was something going on." He saw her brows go up, and added, "Ringan Laine, opening night. Broomfield Hill opened the festival. I went up to congratulate him on a brilliant performance. You were there. Do you remember that? And do you remember how he suddenly changed?"

She thought back to that first night. "I was a bit tipsy, but I do remember it. Ringan—he went parky on you, didn't he? I could feel the chill. Couldn't imagine why, truly—I mean, you didn't put a move on Penny, did you? So what was all that about, then?"

"Damned if I know, but there was something." Cordellet shook himself. "He looked at me, and went icy. I mean, I could feel dislike coming off him, almost like a bad smell. There was something very animal about it, instinctive. And his eyes—narrow, cold—just different, somehow. I watched them change over, for a moment or two. They went upstairs, and next morning Penny had that cut on her mouth, and I could see a bit of plaster on one ear. And I'm wondering what happened, because although I don't know Ringan, I do know Penny, and she's not the type of woman any man could get away with knocking about. She'd have his guts for garters, Penny would."

"Well, Ringan isn't the type of bloke to do that, anyway. Yes, something happened. It goes back to something that happened to an actor here at a festival a few years back, something that likely had a hand in what killed her. There was a woman called Sinead Mc-

Creary—" She saw his face change, heard his breath catch, and spoke impulsively. "Oh, Julian, I'm so sorry. I forgot, you theatre types, you all seem to know each other."

"Sinead McCreary?" His voice was thin. "Donal McCreary's wife? Sinead was one of my closest friends. You're telling me that whatever it was that made your horse go berserk did something that hurt Sinead?"

"No. I think he—it—did something that killed her." She watched a muscle in his cheek jump. In a rare gesture, she stretched a hand out and touched him gently on the arm. "I'm sorry, Julian, honestly. Look, I think it's time I told you the whole thing, don't you? I mean, the bits that I know. Because I think maybe it will help, me, you, the whole mess, if you know what's what. All right?"

She gave him the story, omitting nothing. When she'd finished, she stood quietly, watching him absorb what she'd told him, watching as he pieced bits together.

"That voice." His brows were pulled into a straight, concentrated line. "That smell. You said your horse sensed it, that you felt something was off. And you'd just stepped onto that charming little bridge affair over there? And that leads to Lady Susanna's tomb?"

"Right." Her mismatched eyes fixed on his face. "So?"

"So," he said quietly, "are you quite certain Lady Susanna is the only occupant of the Folly?"

"Oh, my loaves and fishes." Her jaw had slackened. "I'm an idiot. No, of course I'm not certain—I've been inside maybe twice in my life and I always took it on trust, the same way I always took the truth of the family story on trust. But I've just now remembered the last bit of the song."

" 'A grave, a grave,' Lord Arnold cried, 'to put these lovers in.' " Cordellet tightened his hold on her. His mouth had thinned. " 'But bury my lady at the top . . .' "

" '. . . For she was of noble kin.' " Charlotte shook her head vigorously, sending her hair flying. "Julian, it doesn't make sense. Edward would never have buried Matty Groves in there with her.

Even if he'd gone half out of his mind after killing Susanna, he never would have done it. Matty—who was he, anyway? Just some bloke from Purbury. This was—she was his wife, the mother of his sons." She pointed with her left hand, wincing at the pain in her wrist. "Look at that thing. Marble, columns. It's a labour of love, a monument to her memory. He wouldn't have put Matty's corpse in there. He just wouldn't."

"But you weren't hearing Matty Groves, were you?" Cordellet asked quietly. "You were hearing Andrew Leight."

"Crikey! Yes, I was." Charlotte swung her head around, to stare at the graceful columns, the delicate curve of the dome, the beautifully carved oak door. "You think it wasn't Matty Groves that Edward surprised in bed with Susanna? You think he caught her with his foul cousin?"

"I don't know, Char. I've only just got this far, remember?" He wasn't looking at her. He, too, faced the Folly, dappled in sunlight, quiet, waiting. "But if you think all this black stuff is coming from Matty Groves, then what's the story with Andrew? No disrespect to the sanctity of the Leight-Arnold family history, but are you quite sure the song is accurate? Because I can't make sense of Matty Groves in there at all."

"My father." She turned her head back to regard him, aware that his arm still rested against her. Her mind was racing. "He found a mention this morning, in a journal from the month it happened, a personal entry. There was an unscheduled visit by some high-powered Bishop, just a bit before the murder. Da said he wanted to think about it, but it worried him, Julian. Something about that visit worried him. And now I'm wondering if you aren't exactly right, because—oh, damn." She shook her head, frustrated. "I can't seem to put it together. There's too many bits."

He said nothing. She pulled free of his hold at last.

"I'm going in to the Folly." She took a step towards the bridge, wincing at the ache in her hip. "I haven't been since before my mother died, and that's nearly thirty years. There's a brass plaque in there, on Susanna's tomb. I'm going to read it and see what it says.

I barely glanced at it when I was a kid—I was much more interested in all the big marble statuary. But that plaque, well, Edward commissioned it, so it's not likely to lie, is it?"

"No, most likely not. And I'm coming with you. You're not going in there alone. I'll go first."

They crossed the little stone bridge, Julian leading the way. There was no disturbance, no hateful taunting voice, nothing at all. It was just a stone bridge, no more than that. Below it ran the trout stream, small and quiet, a gentle burble of calm water. On the surface, bubbles broke where fish rose towards the early afternoon sun.

The heavy lock in the Folly's age-darkened door was as well maintained as everything else at Callowen. The key from Charlotte's pocket clicked the mechanism home with a soft whisper of brass teeth engaging oiled iron wards. There was no screech of rusty metal; the hinges were as functional as the lock and key.

Charlotte limped past Julian as he swung the door wide. For a moment, alone and silent, she regarded her ancestress's final resting place.

Lord Edward Leight-Arnold had commissioned a marble sarcophagus for his dead wife that would have rivalled any at Westminster. The polished stone gleamed dully in the soft light, a single brass plaque the only ornament along its sides. Aloft, however, three dancing angels rose towards Heaven, their wings looking lacy and almost fragile, their faces serene and beautiful. A second glance revealed that the two outside figures were there as support for the middle angel, and that figure had a startlingly familiar face . . .

"She looks like Janè Castle. My God, that's an amazing coffin!" Julian stepped inside, and stood dappled by streaks of dancing colour, punctuated by floating dust motes. "And lovely glasswork on these windows. I take it the lady about to be beheaded by the centurion-looking chap is Saint Susanna?"

Charlotte glanced up. "What—oh, the stained glass? Right. Susanna's name saint, most likely. What is it?"

"Name saint. Do you know, I'd forgotten," he said slowly. "I forgot that the Leight-Arnolds were Catholic."

"The Arnolds, you mean. Not very many of us, either. Catholic families who survived Cromwell and whanot. Not the Leight-Arnolds, they were Anglican. What on earth is wrong with you, Julian? You look as if you'd seen a—" She bit off the last word and fell silent.

"The Arnolds." He tilted his head. "Not the Leight-Arnolds?"

"Well, not the Leights, anyway." She was staring at him now. "They went thoroughly Anglican. Light speed, really. So we're a cross-church sort of family. What on earth . . . ?"

"I'm not sure—just trying to work something out here. Whatever it was, it's gone for the moment." He joined her at the marble monument. "What does that thing say?"

The brass plaque was so clean that it looked new. Charlotte, for the first time in her life, wondered just who was detailed to maintain all this. What invisible servant, equipped with a bit of rag and some precious, jealously guarded recipe for polish, crept into the Folly on Tuesdays and Fridays, to spend an hour lovingly rubbing the brass free of tarnish, sweeping the floors? And had that invisible servant ever felt the prickle of something wrong between his or her shoulder blades?

" 'Susanna Mary Gedlington Leight-Arnold,' " she read aloud, and the words echoed and circled upward towards the dome. " 'Wife most beloved, done to death most cruelly, her light lost in this life to the eyes of her lord and sons. In Heaven was she made, and in Heaven yet shall we meet again.' "

Charlotte faltered and stopped. Her throat was constricted, and the weight of unshed tears lay heavily behind her eyes.

"Hang on." Julian was clearly bewildered. "I don't understand. Wife most beloved? Done to death most cruelly? Was this thing put up by the man who supposedly killed her?"

Charlotte was silent. She was remembering a small warm moment on the stairs, a passage through her of something she somehow knew, was part of, understood on a level beyond rational thought. A ghost who had felt like a breath of sunlight. Her own outrage at the pursuer.

She straightened her back, feeling the jolt of pain in her bruised hip and wrist, and stepped away from the monument. The voice, the hate and rage—what had he said?

"Julian," she said abruptly, "listen. Before, when Dagmar got spooked and threw me—Andrew, that voice, he was talking to someone. Something about how whatever rights that person had here ought to have been Andrew's. He said—Julian!" Her eyes had gone wide. "I remember! He said, 'your house and your land and your lady gay, at least I've had the one and that's the one you'll be minding most . . .'"

"Edward?" Julian was glancing around the inside of the Folly, noting how bare, how devoid of anything other than its exquisite windows and ornate coffin, the small building was. "You think he was talking to Susanna's husband, Edward?"

"Of course! Who else? Julian, what are you doing?"

"Hunting. There's something to be found in here, I'm certain of it." He was circling the room, taking small steps, his eyes moving from wall to floor. "Your horse. She didn't want to cross the bridge, remember—and wasn't that even before you heard all that noise? If that voice was Andrew Leight's, and it came from in here—let's just say I doubt he's tucked in with Susanna, not after reading that plaque. 'A grave, a grave, to put these lovers in,' my arse. Help me look, will you? I'll take this half, you take the other. And don't ask me what we're hunting for. I've not the smallest clue. But I expect we'll know it when we see it. Give a yell if you see anything."

For several minutes, only the sound of even, steady breathing and slow footfalls disturbed the Folly. At a point in the curve of one wall, Charlotte suddenly stopped in place.

"Julian? Will you come look at this, please?"

The cross had been scratched into the precise centre of one of the large stones that formed the Folly's floor. It was so faint that only a concerted search in decent light would have revealed it. But it was no rough effort; someone had paid careful attention to detail. The edges were uniform, the cuts straight and sure.

"Well, now." Julian's voice held a quiet satisfaction. "There really was something here. Nice to be right. I wonder if that's what I think it must be?"

"A grave marker?" Charlotte felt suddenly cold. "No, I don't believe it. It couldn't be. The man who built this place and wrote the words on that plaque, he'd never have buried anyone else in here with her, certainly not Andrew Leight. It's ridiculous, Julian."

"Maybe. I completely agree that this little trip to the festival is making me think that one of my favourite songs in the world is a load of old bollocks. Let's get out of here, yes? Just lock the place up and get out into the sunlight."

They crossed the lawn in silence, Charlotte on the back of Cordellet's grey gelding. Her hip had begun a steady painful pulse, and her left wrist was swollen and discoloured. Halfway to the house, they saw a group of riders gallop out of the stables and swerve towards them. Dagmar, Charlotte reflected, must have not gone straight back to her stall. Otherwise they'd have had the search party out sooner.

"Ah. Here comes the cavalry. Took their bloody time about it." Julian glanced up at her. "Charlotte. How much do you actually know about your family's history? Really know, I mean?"

"Quite a bit. At least, I've always thought I did." The riders—all of them stable workers—were closing the distance. "Problem is, I'm beginning to wonder just how much of what I thought I knew is total pants. And however much I thought I knew, it obviously isn't enough."

Nine

"Oh, how do you like my feather-bed
And how do you like my sheets?
How do you like my lady gay
Who lies in your arms asleep?"

The rectory at St. Giles in the Green was a rambling square house, and Ringan's first thought was that it was probably comfortable and welcoming from cellars to attics. There was a sense of ease here, and of the slow passage of time. It reassured one that, whatever the problem might be, nothing was beyond an answer and some peace, especially in the study, with its books and ledgers, its faint tang of wood smoke and beeswax, the patina of age and care on the heavy furniture.

"What a nice house you've got." Ringan glanced around, taking in the gauzy curtains, the comfortable furniture, the angle of ceilings and bay windows, that seemed, somehow, to smile. He was visibly relaxing. "How old is it? Eighteenth century? It has those lines to it—very clean."

"Seventeen-nineties, so, yes. End of." Hibbert, who'd been speaking softly to an elderly housekeeper, sent her on her way and closed the door behind her. "It really is a pleasant house, the rectory, isn't it? Even if I hadn't wanted to come to this particular parish—and I did, very much—the offer of this house would have pulled me in."

"You wanted to come here? Specifically?" Jane's hands, with

their long musician's fingers, lay placid on the heavy wooden table, bathed in a pool of sunlight. "Why?"

"Oh, the history, of course. The Arnolds are basically the only great Catholic family in this part of the country, yet this church is comfortably Anglican. And of course . . ." His voice trailed off.

Ringan lifted an eyebrow. "The song, is it?"

"Yes. And to be quite truthful, that hint of the supernatural as well. I can't deny it fascinates me, the whole idea of the invisible world, but so far, my luck's been out—I've only been to the house a few times, and no sign of the Lady. I've seen the portrait, of course—oh, my." Hibbert swiveled his head, to stare at Jane. "I'm sorry, but—"

"I know." The tranquilly folded hands tightened for a moment, and then relaxed. There was a faint irony in her voice. "The resemblance has been noted, believe me. But there's no connection. It's pure coincidence, or six degrees from all other humans, or what have you. Let's get started. Can someone tell me what we're looking for? Or looking at?"

"Journals." Ringan, dropping into a chair, stretched a hand towards one of the bound volumes. "Journals kept by the resident priests at St. Giles, about six years' worth. Walter, did you say there had been one bloke for years and years, and that he got the boot, no explanation, around the time of the murders?"

"The Reverend Charles Lockereigh." Hibbert had a volume open, one forefinger lightly marking an entry. "Here's the first bit from the period Lord Callowen requested—February 1623."

"February? Bit late, isn't that?" Penny had her chin propped in one palm, her cloudy hair touched by bright slanting shafts of sun. "From what I remember of the registers at Wychsale House, the new year was a busy time for the blokes keeping the notes."

"He'd been ill, apparently." Hibbert cleared his throat, and read aloud. " 'Fourth February. This morning I have, for the first moment in many weeks, risen from my bed of sickness, and was able to go about some few regular duties without a great weight upon my chest. Tomorrow, an I feel so well as I do today, I will baptise the Anderley infant.' "

"Poor man. Winter colds are wretched things to have, especially when you happen to live in a time where there's no running hot water." Jane stretched her legs. "He sounds like a lamb, actually."

"Yes, he does. A very nice bloke." Penny's interest was clearly caught. "Walter, where's the first mention of Andrew Leight? Or of the Lady Susanna, for that matter?"

"It's Lady Susanna gets the first mention, as it happens, in May of 1623. It seems Andrew Leight, the cousin, was already here. And Lockereigh has something to—"

"He was here?" Ringan's head jerked. "Living at Callowen?"

"So it seems. 'Second May. Yesterday, at vespers, those who came to hear the gospel caught first sight of the maid who, an all reports be truth, bids fair to become the second mistress of Callowen.'" He stopped, seeing their expressions. "What's wrong?"

"Second mistress of Callowen?" Penny had gone very still. "There was a first wife in there somewhere?"

"Yes. If I may? It's all in here." Hibbert read on. "Where was I? Ah. 'She is very fair of face, and has all the rosy looks of youth. She is come with her mother to Purbury to succour an ailing aunt, Dame Mary Gedlington; I fear greatly that Dame Mary will not last out the summer, to see her niece wed and come to a great worldly position. Lord Edward has been most assiduous in his attention and indeed, to see the girl look up to him is a very pretty thing.'"

"There, see?" Jane's voice held a deep satisfaction. "She adored him. I'm telling you, she never had an affair with anyone. She just worshipped him—I could feel it."

"So could I." Penny was remembering the few lingering fragments of Susanna from the morning's episode. "She was more than grateful to him—he was most of her world. Is there more? Something about the first wife?"

"Oh, yes. 'Since the death of our Lady Joan in childbed, and the Callowen heir with her, so many years in the past now, we have despaired of our patron's House and estate coming from father to son. It is to be expected that young Andrew Leight will feel this marriage deeply, should it come to pass. I pray he may not prove a blight upon his cousin's coming happiness, and will accept God's will, that his circumstances change.' "

"Right." Ringan, suddenly restless, was up and pacing. "What have we got, then? Lord Edward, losing his great love and his only child in one go. But what did Andrew have to do with it? And why would he resent it or not resent it? Why would his opinion be worth anything?"

"So Edward was a childless widower. Not a bachelor." Penny was reasoning things out, hanging on to the flashes of Susanna, now faded almost to nothing. "No heir. Who? Oh, my God."

"Andrew!" Jane's bare arms had raised into gooseflesh, despite the warmth of the study. "What was that Lockereigh said, about not passing from father to son? A male cousin. Was Andrew the next in line?"

"If he was the heir—" Ringan bit off the words, sickened. It was an old, familiar story: greed, avarice, envy, lust. He went on, slowly. "If Andrew was the next in line, then yes, there's nothing more likely than Edward having him brought here. Learning the ropes, learning the business of the estate, the family history, the duties, the protocols. And would he resent the pretty young thing, bearing pretty children to knock him out of the running? Hell, yes." He caught himself, and shot an apologetic glance at Hibbert. "Sorry. But I'm not going to kid you—I hate Andrew Leight."

"Don't apologise. We're not in church." Hibbert smiled faintly. "Although hatred for one so long dead is rather extreme, surely? Still, you're quite right. It's no small thing, to be head of a great house. And if Lord Edward believed that he would never remarry? Bringing the heir to Callowen would have been his first order of business, to get on terms with the locals, at least. But how odd, and how unlucky, that there were no male cousins directly in the Arnold line. The Arnolds were keeping their faith hidden; but really, it's a fascinating question. I wonder if Andrew converted?"

There was a short silence. Penny broke it.

"What do you mean, converted?"

"To Catholicism." He saw the bewilderment on their faces, and raised a brow. "Surely you knew the Arnolds were Catholic?"

"We knew that." Something, a feeling, at the back of Penny's awareness, was struggling for clarification. "What I don't think any of us realised is that the Leight family *weren't* Catholic." She looked at Ringan. "This matters. I know this matters. If Andrew Leight was just some nobody from a socially useless end of the family, how could he inherit the title? Does it even work that way?"

"Oh, the Leights weren't nobodies." Hibbert shook his head vigorously. "The barony was impoverished, true, but they were a very old family, as old as the Arnolds."

Penny drummed her fingers in a light, insistent tattoo. "I'm still muddled. How would Andrew Leight—coming from an impoverished barony, and a minor one at that—possibly be the next in line for Callowen? I'm assuming the families intermarried, but when?"

"A good long way back, if I'm remembering properly, Edward the Second or thereabouts. Lord Stephen Arnold and a Leight daughter, I think her name was Margaret." Hibbert looked around, answering an unspoken comment. "I researched the family, of course, when I was first offered the living. The Leights were another Hampshire family, from a bit west of here; part of their ancestral demesne became Callowen land when that first marriage took place. I'd imagine the Leights jumped at the chance for an alliance with the Arnolds, wouldn't you? The Callowen title and fortune were established and important even then. Of course, there aren't any actual Leights left—the family died out and their land was reabsorbed by the Crown, around the time of George the Third."

"And in those days, when they got together," Jane pointed out, "everyone was Catholic. When did the change take place? When did the Leights go Protestant? Under Elizabeth?"

"That, I don't remember offhand. If it's important, we can find out easily enough." Hibbert cocked his head. "Is it important?"

"I don't know. Right now, we haven't got any way of knowing what might be important—that's part of the problem." Ringan had settled on the window sill, the sun leaving him a sharp dark line against a dazzle of refracted light. "Let's get on, all right? What's the next mention worth noting? And what did I say? You look awfully pleased."

"I thought you'd never ask. The next bit is Lockereigh, after the wedding. Christmas of that year, 1623. It's, well . . ." Hibbert hesitated. "I find it interesting. I'm not sure what it's really about, and this is only a note, but still. Listen. 'I find myself most perturbed in spirit. The House of Callowen having been enriched by the youth and most virtuous beauty of Lady Susanna, on this the day of birth of Our Saviour, all those concerned should on this day be taken with great rejoicing. Yet I fear 'tis not so, for having read the sacrament and joined this new-made lady to her lord, I did espy upon the face of Andrew Leight as he gazed upon his cousin a look of such blackness that my own head did for some short time turn light, and my heart felt the sudden weight of dread within it. Truly, in such a guise did he seem as to be one of those darker Spirits, the like of which we are told are doomed to eternally disport themselves in damnation.' "

"He was looking at Edward." Jane's face was parchment-pale, her resemblance to the Mytens painting at its most marked. "Hating Edward. Not Susanna—he didn't give a damn about Susanna. She was unimportant to him. Susanna was just his weapon, his way to get at Edward. It wouldn't matter to him that Edward didn't know, would it?" She wrapped her arms around herself. "It was enough that he was hurting something Edward loved."

"Andrew the man, becoming Andrew the incubus. And he wasn't even dead yet." Ringan spoke grimly. "Penny, lamb, remember what you said to me? That maybe an incubus was really just a sort of thoroughly rotted-out person who kept getting worse and worse, even after they were dead? I think you were right."

"You know, I don't want to seem inquisitive." Walter Hibbert's voice was diffident. "But would it be allowable for me to know what you're all talking about?"

His three guests stared at him. He added, mildly, "Because you know, I'd probably be able to find you what you need rather faster if I knew just what to look for. But, of course, it's entirely up to you."

"Oh, crikey." Ringan grinned suddenly. "That's right, you haven't been up to the house since the festival started, have you? You don't know what's been going on. You must think we're a collection of raving nutters."

Taking Hibbert's murmured disclaimer as encouragement, Ringan promptly gave the entire chronology of Andrew Leight and his burgeoning presence at Callowen, from their first night at the festival. Jane added the details of her exhausting dreams of that first night, and her other encounters of hearing the voices of Lord Edward Leight-Arnold and Matty Groves at Annie Whitlaw's. Penny added the details Roger Searle had found concerning Susanna's diary. She told Hibbert about Sinead McCreary's death, of how they had come to believe that the twisted evil thing her husband Donal had seen move through his sleeping wife at Callowen was the deformed shade of Andrew Leight. She said nothing about her own sensitivity to the unseen world; that much, at least, Hibbert had already guessed.

"So Andrew Leight, a Protestant poor relation, was brought to Callowen House by his cousin." Hibbert's interest, and his grasp of the tangled story, were clear, and the others nodded. "His cousin's first wife had died in childbed; there was no one to supplant him. Then Edward goes and falls madly in love with this radiant young thing, not nobly born, and Andrew sees his hopes of inheriting slipping away. I wonder how long Andrew had been there? How long he'd been telling himself that the lands, the title, the wealth, the power, were destined to be his? Meant to be his? Should have been his?"

Hibbert was interrupted by a sharp rap at the study door. It swung open, and, without awaiting an invitation, Miles Leight-Arnold stalked into the sunny room. He came to the end of the long table and glared generally around.

"You need to come back to Callowen," he told them. It occurred to Penny that she'd never seen anyone holding back so hard on anger. "My daughter's in bed with a fractured wrist and a bone bruise on one hip, the entire place is in an uproar, and it needs to stop. This whole nonsense—Andrew Leight—it all began when you people showed up. I don't know why the bugger's woken up so fast and furious, and I don't give a tinker's damn. He's ruining my festival and scaring people all over the place, and now he's injured Charlotte. I won't have it. You woke him up. You can bloody well drive him off."

They gaped at him. He slapped the table with an open palm, sending a resounding echo through the room. "Don't sit there with your mouths open like a bunch of flounder, damn it! Something you did brought Andrew up to this pitch, and now you've got to get rid of him. And get this straight: you're not to touch the Lady Susanna. She's our house ghost and I won't have her meddled with. If she goes as well, you'll regret it."

That evening, as Julian Cordellet took the stage for his scheduled one-man show in Callowen's ballroom-cum-theatre, a significant portion of his audience's attention was regrettably elsewhere.

A tight-jawed Miles Leight-Arnold, at a first-row table, had his daughter at his side. Charlotte, in loose-fitting clothing that allowed for easy movement, was paler than usual; her left wrist now sported a moulded cast, and the entire arm rested in a shoulder sling, both provided by the family doctor after a hasty visit. It was, perhaps, the curtailed use of both hands that had led her to leave her hair alone. It hung free to her waist in a rosy shower, and drew nearly as many looks as the sling did.

The official word, passed rather too casually among the guests, was that she'd been thrown from her horse. The explanation, as Ringan dryly remarked, had at least the merit of being true, albeit incomplete. At Charlotte's other side sat Albert Wychsale, looking rather shaken; several times he twisted around, scanning the tables. When the Broomfield Hill contingent took their seats, he seemed to relax.

The band, in a group, had chosen tables at the rear. They had the rear row to themselves. After Lady Susanna's appearance that morning, nearly a quarter of the guests had made their excuses, packed up, and fled Callowen as if the ghostly wailing had been a harbinger of the Black Death. Jane was in the centre, surrounded by a protective phalanx of her fellow musicians. Liam sat at her right shoulder, with Matt and Molly Curran beside him; Ringan sat at her left, with Penny on the aisle. The impression, that Jane was somehow being guarded from some nebulous threat, was impossible to miss.

If the remainder of the handpicked audience knew something was up, they quickly forgot about it. Julian had the kind of stage persona that was as electrifying as it was rare. Minutes after Jack Halley brought the house lights down, Julian was deep into his monologue and almost everyone was enraptured to the exclusion of all else. Charlotte, whose traditional habit of skipping any of the festival performances that weren't music was legendary, watched with her lips slightly parted and her head tilted. She looked surprised. At her side, her father's jaw slowly relaxed.

"He's damned good." Ringan leaned over and breathed into Penny's ear. His voice was the barest tickle of sound, impossible to hear more than an inch or two away. Ringan, who often found himself wanting to throttle people who spoke during performances, felt safe in his whispering. "I had no idea."

"Isn't he?" Penny, mindful of her own dislike of chattering audience members, breathed back into his ear. "He's brilliant onstage. You should see him when he really lets it rip. He'd make Errol Flynn look drab."

She leaned forward and peered around Ringan at Jane. It was hard to be certain in the dimness, but her friend's profile seemed calm; she looked to be feeling nothing more than appreciation for Julian's performance. Penny, exhaling softly, sank back in her seat. With a mental apology to Julian for abandoning his performance, she turned her attention inward, to the problem Miles Leight-Arnold had dropped into their collective laps.

As accustomed as they'd already become to Callowen's peremptory way of dealing with his fellows, today had been something new. Charlotte's injury seemed to have pushed a button in him; his eruption into Walter Hibbert's quiet study had been the act of a man who'd gone beyond the niceties of *politesse*. The command had been plain enough: get rid of Andrew Leight, but leave Susanna where she was.

So, too, had been the attendant threat. And while the dumping of all responsibility for the exorcism into their laps was infuriating, Penny couldn't make herself feel it was entirely unfair. Although Andrew Leight had certainly done damage in the past, his new power and strength did, in fact, coincide with Broomfield Hill's arrival.

The terrifying thing was, Miles Leight-Arnold had the money, the power, the prestige, to make them all sorry they'd ever opened that invitation to Callowen House. A wry smile, unseen in the darkened ballroom, touched the corner of Penny's mouth. She was already sorry. Once this was done with, she thought, she was certainly never coming within ten miles of the place again.

Without realising it, she reached up and rubbed her temples. Her mind circled around the problem. She and Ringan were no strangers to exorcism. They'd done two of them, both musical, and in both cases, the exorcism had worked. This situation was something different; there was no way she could see that a simple musical exorcism, merely playing the song that chronicled the story, was going to work. For one thing, they didn't know whether Andrew Leight would respond to the song in question. Why would he, after all? He wasn't even mentioned in it. . . .

Or was he? She ran the words through her head, breaking them down, concentrating. Julian Cordellet's beautiful voice washed over her. She didn't hear him.

What, precisely, was the story the song told? It was an old story: a saucy young wife with a roving eye, getting caught and killed for her pains.

But that was wrong, wasn't it? Jane had seen and felt and understood Susanna, and she'd stated flatly that Susanna had been no wanton. Not that Jane's opinion on this one was needed, not since Penny herself had shared those few intense minutes of memories, sensations, impressions. Right from the start, Penny thought, the lyric had got it wrong.

Then there was a bit about how Susanna had seen Matty Groves, and invited him into her bed, and how Matty had recognised her and at first refused her. But that was rubbish as well. From what Jane had told them earlier, Matty had been Susanna's page, or groom, or something—some sort of personal servant. So how would he not have known who she was? It wasn't feasible; hell, Penny thought grimly, it wasn't even possible.

She rubbed her temples, fingertips moving in slow circles. The threatening headache was getting more intense. Penny forced her concentration back to the song.

The first verses, then, were straight-out lies. She strained her memory, reaching back for the versions she'd heard and hummed atonally along with in the past. Right, she had it now: Susanna convinced Matty that Lord Edward was out on estate business, far away from Callowen. Taken with her youth and beauty, he'd consented, and they'd gone off for a bit of slap and tickle.

The servant who was standing by
And hearing what was said
He swore Lord Arnold he would know
Before the sun was set . . .

The four lines came into her mind complete and whole. She blinked in the darkness, turning them over.

It didn't make sense, not any of it. Matty Groves, that invisible boy, had been Susanna's own servant. And if he hadn't been indulging himself in his mistress's bed, he certainly hadn't been telling Edward anything; what Jane had heard, in the pleasant chintzy room upstairs at Annie Whitlaw's, put that much past argument. Penny suddenly remembered Miles telling them that, according to family legend, Andrew had been the "servant" mentioned.

But that made no sense, either. Even if Susanna had been having it off with a third party, as yet unknown to any of them, Andrew would have been the last person on earth to tell Edward about it. If anything had come clear about the man who had been Andrew in life, it was his penchant for keeping secrets, as a form of power.

So who was the servant? Who had run off to Lord Arnold, carrying tales, bringing down the wrath of her husband, bringing death at the end of the swordpoint? And if Susanna had been innocent, if there had been no adultery to interrupt, how had they died? What had actually happened?

The headache was throbbing now, a steady starburst of pain pulsing behind her right eye. She tapped Ringan on the wrist. He brought his head close.

"I've got a foul headache." Speech was unexpectedly difficult; her lungs were contracted with discomfort. "I need air."

He nodded, looked at Penny questioningly; interpreting that look, she shook her head, no, and got unsteadily to her feet. The starburst of pain had become more of a Roman candle. She found herself fervently hoping that this wasn't a migraine—she hadn't had one for twenty years and she didn't fancy one now. She moved quietly towards the open doors, thankful that they'd had sense enough to choose seats at the rear.

Ten feet from the doors, she stopped. So did Julian's beautiful voice. A hush, as nauseating as it was unnatural, settled on the charming room like the devil's rain.

There was darkness here.

Penny, suddenly and too late understanding her own physical discomfort, her inability to breathe properly, swung around towards Jane. Every nerve in her body was suddenly jangling, screaming a warning: *go get out move hurry go.*

With a thunderous echo, the ballroom doors slammed shut. It happened fast, a speed too quick for the human eye. They all heard the sickening screech of metal gouging wood as the heavy bolts at the bottom of each door were forcibly dragged across the parquet floors of the hall.

The moment of total quiet that followed was broken by Charlotte's voice. It rang out, clear and imperative.

"Ringan! Get Penny out of here—*hurry!*"

Penny wrenched her head around. Charlotte was on her feet, backlit by the stage lights; her hair was wild and electric. She looked uncanny, and imposing, and very beautiful. As Penny struggled to focus, she saw Julian jump from the stage and stop at Charlotte's side.

A voice, an echo of the charnelhouse, filled the room.

You filthy Catholic scum . . . you with your fine silks and your hawks and your hounds, you with all your privilege, you should have burned, all of you, this is mine, it should have been for me, 'twas meant for me

"Out." Ringan had reached Penny's side. He was struggling, his chest heaving, as if trying to walk through water. "Now."

The words were forced out, small and harsh and barely registering under the weight and malevolence of the cold rasping horror that seemed to be pouring out of the walls. The ballroom was in pandemonium, women screaming, men overturning their chairs. Penny heard none of it; something seemed to be swathing everything except Andrew Leight's voice in a dull, heavy muffler of silence.

Ringan, his teeth chattering and his hands shaking, managed to get Penny by the arm. He turned back long enough to see that Liam, seemingly barely affected, was forcibly dragging Jane along with him. He was pulling her, not towards the main doors but the French doors, those tall, elegant windows, opening out onto the lawns. The Currans, husband and wife, were right behind, at Jane's back—Molly was actually pushing. If anything wanted to get at Jane, it would have to go through them first.

"Windows," Ringan told Penny, a tiny dart of a voice that just reached her, nearly obscured in the verbal hellish wind rocketing through the room. "Lawn. Go."

We won't make it, Penny thought madly, he won't let us, the windows will slam and we'll be trapped and he'll kill us all, he's all about death and revenge, oh God my head it hurts . . .

Your fine lady, your fine sons, all of it, mine

The voice was loud now, too loud. It was everywhere.

"Go," Ringan managed, and gave Penny a hard shove between the shoulder blades. She fell forward through the nearest French door, and went sprawling in the grass, just as the glass blew out behind her.

It shattered all at once, two dozen doors, each with a dozen panes of glass, exploding in a cacophany of sound and prismatic light, as thousands of shards rained outward onto the grass, reflecting and refracting the moonlight. Somewhere above the impossible violent storm of noise were the screams of the falcons in the mews, the furious barking of the Callowen hounds, the terrified slamming of hooves against stall doors in the stables.

Penny, on her knees in the cropped grass, covered her head with her arms, protecting her face. The ground shook around her as the remainder of the audience stampeded through the empty doorframes, streaming in lines, in an instinctive search for safety and light.

All this time, having to mind myself, saying aye, surely Edward, and nay Edward, all this time and you knew nothing you sorry fool of a heretic, you can't do no harm to me, you'll not touch me for it, mine, your lady, your sons, your land . . .

"Shut up! Shut up shut up shut up!"

Penny, with fragments of glass in her hair and her head about to implode in upon itself, sucked down the sweet warm air. The voice was Charlotte's. It rang out through the ballroom, across the gardens, coursing across the sky. It was strident with rage.

"You shut up, you foul little tick! Get out of our house! We don't want you here—we don't acknowledge you. You're not an Arnold, you aren't our ancestor, you aren't anybody or anything. You're bloody worthless, is what you are! *Get out!*"

"Oh, my God." Jane was on her knees, her hands feebly clutching at the damp grass. Her voice was threadbare. "Sick, I feel so—"

"Get *out!*"

Into the silence that followed came weeping. Light, vagrant, the same voice that had woken the denizens of Callowen House that morning, it rustled down stairways and curled into corners: the Lady Susanna, weeping for her loss.

Something that was not a cloud moved in the ballroom, shaking down from the gilded ceiling like black dust. It bent back in upon itself for a moment as it crested Charlotte, as if unwilling to touch her. It moved through wall and window frame, visible, deformed, off into the moon-touched darkness, and faded out: Andrew Leight, going to roost for the night.

Penny dragged herself upright. She looked across at Jane, and then at Ringan, supporting her with an arm around her waist.

"Miles was right," she told them. "This has to stop."

The next morning, at the long table at St. Giles in the Green's comfortable rectory, Walter Hibbert passed around bacon and toast prepared by his imperturbable housekeeper, and regarded the small horde of people who had shown up at his door at nearly midnight, asking for sanctuary.

His curiosity, which he'd resolved to keep firmly in check until everyone had eaten, was nevertheless at boiling point. He'd gone to bed for the night, only to be roused by the sound of automobiles screeching to a halt beneath his windows, of car doors slamming, of voices, of an imperious pounding at the front door. He'd hurried down and found himself ushering in Ringan, Penny, Jane, Charlotte, a startlingly handsome and familiar-looking actor, and Lord Callowen himself.

Miles had been tight-lipped, visibly shaken, and even more peremptory than usual. His demand was simple: this was a church, an Anglican church but under the Arnold family's patronage, and he was demanding sanctuary for his guests and for his daughter, as well. Of course, he hadn't actually used the word "sanctuary"; he'd merely announced that beds were needed for everyone there but himself, and would Hibbert see about sending people off to their rooms now, thank you very much. But that sanctuary was wanted was quite clear.

Hibbert, rising to the occasion, had put Jane and Charlotte in one guest room, Penny and Ringan in another, and settled Julian Cordellet on a comfortable divan in the rectory's enormous front room. He'd found himself oddly thrilled. Not only was the lord of the manor asking for his help, he was asking the kind of help that likely hadn't been asked of a priest in England in a good long time. Hibbert noted Penny's drawn, exhausted look, Jane's withdrawn silence, the cast on Charlotte's wrist, the furious jut of Ringan's beard. He noted, too, the way Cordellet's eyes followed Charlotte until she was safe behind her borrowed bedroom door, and wondered how she'd come by that injured wrist.

Hibbert then turned his attention back to Miles Leight-Arnold, swallowed his curiosity about what had brought them here at midnight, and reassured his noble patron that his guests and his daughter would be safe and comfortable for as long as was needed, and was there anything else he could do for Lord Callowen? Miles had shaken his head, offered a curt thanks for the help, and driven off into the night, presumably back towards Callowen House itself. Hibbert, hearing nothing at all from behind the guest room doors, had gone back to his own bed. There he lay awake for a while, puzzled, his mind busy.

Now, after an uneventful night, Hibbert let his guests finish their breakfast before he spoke up.

"Well." He waited until he was sure he had their full attention. "I was too busy getting everyone settled last night to ask just what was going on. First of all, Lady Charlotte, I see you've hurt yourself. I'm awfully sorry."

"Ta." She regarded her broken wrist for a moment. "Bloody Andrew Leight frightened my horse. He's such a *git*. I really truly abominate that wretched ghost." She glanced up, as if expecting disagreement, and added defiantly, "Well, I *do*."

"Don't we all!" Ringan's agreement was heartfelt. "Do you know, this is one ghost I'm looking forward to exorcising? Especially since if there's actually a Hell, that's where he's headed. Burning Andrew. Dear toasty little rapist." He grinned sourly. "I can hardly wait."

Hibbert abandoned any idea of subtlety. "Something happened last night, I presume. May I ask what it was?"

Surprisingly, it was Julian who spoke up. His recap of the performance, and the intrusion of Andrew Leight into the ballroom, was clear, terse, and completely terrifying. Jane, pushing a cooling mouthful of poached egg around on her plate, began to shake; Penny reached out and put an arm around her shoulders, and whispered into her ear. When Julian had finished, Ringan spoke up.

"So here's the thing. We've been told by Char's dad that it's our fault his nasty little tick of an ancestor is kicking up such a fuss. He may be right—Penny's a sensitive, you've seen that, and Jane looks too much like Lady Susanna for anyone's peace of mind. Maybe we did wake him up. But I'm damned if I'm going to let Callowen saddle us with the responsibility for it. Sorry, Char, but I nearly dotted him one yesterday. This power-and-privilege rubbish is beginning to get up my nose."

"Besides which, it's a load of rubbish." Penny was fierce in her agreement. "Maybe Miles should try some of that high-and-mighty act on Donal McCreary, and see how far it gets him. Andrew was here and he was active before we got here. And Miles damned well knows it."

"Oh, I think so, too." Charlotte nodded vigorously, sending her hair into her plate. "But you don't, not really. You still feel guilty, don't you? I mean, otherwise, you'd have told Da to go to hell, wouldn't you? And, well, you didn't."

Her honesty was devastating, and reduced both Penny and Ringan to silence. Impossible, Penny thought, impossible Char, with her clear uninhibited way of looking at everything, her inability to hang convention as a cloak to mask the truth. And impossible to argue with the truth behind Char's statement, either. The guilt, the sense of personal responsibility for the awakening of Andrew Leight, was present in at least three of them. Looking at Ringan, she saw the same thoughts reflected in his face, and let out a sigh.

"I do feel guilty," she said simply. "I do feel as if I woke him up.

I keep remembering Lumbe's, and Agnès de Belleville at the theatre, and feeling that somehow, just being who I am made them more, I don't know, more *there*. More dangerous—more potent. That's why I didn't tear a strip off Miles yesterday. Damned Protestant ethic of mine, there's no shaking it."

"Well, I don't feel guilty. And even though last night wasn't the time for it, Char's daddy and I will have words, you may be sure. I'm through being pushed about." Ringan sounded grim. "Look, let's get down to it, all right? We're going to need all the information we can get—we want some weapons. First, though, Charlotte, why did you tell me to get Penny out of the ballroom last night? Why not Jane? After all, we've been assuming it was Jane he was after—her looking so much like Susanna."

Charlotte opened her mouth, then closed it again. For a moment, she looked puzzled. Her face cleared.

"Of course! I couldn't remember for a sec, except for just the feeling, it was simply enormous, that Penny ought to be got clear. But there was something, and I've only just remembered. I could see him, sort of. He was all shadowy, and twisted up, and the feeling hit first, that was how I knew I really must turn round, so I did, and there he was, hovering, all winged and twisty and really totally filthy to look at. Deformed—I can't describe how. He was—I don't know, like something out of old books about devils, demons . . ."

Her voice trailed off, and she swallowed hard. The rest of the group was silent. "Ugly," she said finally. Julian reached out and touched her shoulder gently, but said nothing.

"Right." Ringan was watching her intently. "I understand that you felt it. But why Penny? Why did you feel she was at risk, and not Jane?"

"Really, Ringan, you're awfully dim this morning," she told him, with some asperity. "I told you, I felt him first, or maybe it was hearing. I knew he was there, anyway. And I felt he was behind me, so I swung about in my chair and I saw him. He—it—Andrew, just sort of detached himself from the ceiling, and he was right above Penny's head. He wanted Penny."

"Over my head?" Penny sat very still. She was aware of something new to her: fear, the genuine article, verging on panic. She licked her dry lips. "It—he was above my head? Mine? Coming after me?"

"Descending," Charlotte said, and the single word was chilling. "Slow, a deformed twisty cloud-thing. He had—right, this sounds completely loopy, but it looked almost like wings, big wings, made of the dark, or maybe the shadows. And I saw where he was going—he was coming straight down at you. So I shouted for Ringan to get you the hell out of it."

"Excuse me." Hibbert looked around at the frozen faces. "But Ringan's right; you're going to have to find a way to get rid of this creature. All we have now are a few scattered bits of knowledge, and more is certainly needed. I ought to be able to help. Unless you've learned a lot since yesterday, research is indicated. I take it we're all agreed that the song is inaccurate?"

"We're quite certain it is—" Penny broke off as Julian suddenly exclaimed. "What is it?"

"The Folly! My God, with all the brouhaha last night, we completely forgot!" He saw eagerness in Charlotte's face, and spoke to the rest. "Yesterday, in Lady Susanna's tomb, after Charlotte was thrown. Two things, and they're important—they must be. First off, her tomb itself? If an angry cuckold commissioned that thing and wrote the inscription, I'll personally eat all three marble angels, with vinegar and salt. Char, you agree, don't you?"

"Of course I do! 'Wife most beloved, done to death most cruelly, her light lost in this life to the eyes of her lord and sons'? That little lot was put together by a man in mourning for his wife, not one who'd killed her. It's rot, that song, total pants." Charlotte suddenly caught her breath. "Oh, Julian—the cross! We forgot about it."

"Yes, that's the other thing." Julian explained about the faint yet expertly rendered cross on the Folly's floor. "We couldn't think of any reason for it to be there, unless it was a marker of some kind."

"Someone else, buried in the Folly." Hibbert was nodding furiously, bright spots of excited colour on his cheeks. "That would have been logical, you know; mark the site with a cross. Whoever it is, they couldn't have been loved too much, could they? No name, nothing but that one thing. Matty Groves, do you suppose?"

"Or Andrew Leight." Jane spoke up, finally. "This is why I came down to St. Giles yesterday. I wanted to find either or both of their graves. Walter, is there anywhere we could check to find those two burial places? Surely, there would be something in the church records?"

"Yes, but those aren't kept here. They're the property of the diocese." He saw her dismay and added, "But don't worry, we can always have a nice wander round the churchyard. And we really only scratched the surface of our incumbents' journals, before Lord Callowen, er, dropped by yesterday afternoon. They'd be a good place to begin. Can someone please clarify what we're actually looking for?"

"Details," Ringan replied. "Anything to clear all this muddy water. Lots of things—where is Lady Susanna's journal? If we can find that, it may get us a lot farther along. How did Andrew Leight die, and where is he buried? If the song is wrong, then how did Matty Groves die, and where is he buried? Hell, what did Matty Groves have to do with anything, for that matter? Is there someone beside Susanna buried in the Folly, and if so, who? That might call for a trip to the diocese, and we haven't got a lot of time. Why was the Reverend Lockereigh dismissed and replaced right around the time of the murder?"

He paused for breath, and Jane broke in. "I have my own question. How was it possible for me to hear those voices, Matty's voice, Lord Edward's voice, miles away from Callowen, at Annie Whitlaw's bed and breakfast? It isn't happening here, but it did there. Does the bed and breakfast have some connection?"

Ringan looked suddenly dispirited. "My God, that's a lot of individual bits and pieces to worry about."

"If we're talking about big questions, let's not forget the biggest of all." Julian spoke quietly. "We have a song that's wrong in its details, but we also have the bare fact: there was a violent death, maybe more than one. What exactly happened that day? Who died? And who did the killing?"

"It is a pile, isn't it?" Penny got to her feet. "But honestly, I'm glad to be doing something. Because guilty twinges aside, I really think Andrew Leight needs to disappear. So let's get started."

Ten

"Oh, well I like your feather-bed
And well I like your sheets
But better I like your lady gay
Who lies in my arms asleep"

As the long night hours marched closer towards sunrise, Miles Leight-Arnold lay in his bed, staring into the darkness of Callowen's sumptuous master bedroom suite. He was wide awake, and had been since dropping the others at the St. Giles Rectory.

The truth was, he was seriously rattled, and for a man unaccustomed to introspection, the experience was one for which he had no reference point. He shifted from his side to his stomach, fetching up eventually on his back, staring at the dim outlines of the canopied bed, the room, the ceiling, which, tonight, seemed uncomfortably high: a refuge for impossibilities.

His mind was busy, too busy. It cycled infuriatingly from his daughter, to the festival which had been his particular joy and which had now spun completely beyond any pretense of control, to the sobbing that had wrenched him from sleep that morning, to the now almost-faded memory of a charming woman called Sinead McCreary, a woman who had come to Callowen to entertain, and who had left damaged beyond repair.

Beyond control, he thought, and realised how exhausted he was. He was so tired, he could barely parse his own resentment.

The last scion of the ancient and powerful Arnold line was accustomed to control. It was his, not only by the birthright that had given him power and position and wealth, but by virtue of his own personality. He was a man of enormous will.

Off in the distance, in the safety of the Callowen mews, one of the hawks screamed and then was quiet. Miles rubbed one pyjama sleeve across his gritty eyes, and wondered what he was going to do about the festival, and whether Charlotte's wrist would heal properly.

He had a moment of resentment, darker than the pre-dawn hour surrounding him. Damn Andrew Leight, he thought, and felt his own anger at the evil infesting his home as a bitter sting at the forefront of his psyche. Damn him for being here, for ever being here, alive or dead. Damn him, for hurting my daughter . . .

Another scream, the high-pitched *scree!* from one of the younger shortwings. Miles, ignoring it, suddenly gave in to the anger that he had clamped down on so hard until this point.

Andrew Leight had damaged Charlotte. He had dared—*dared*—to damage the daughter of Callowen House. Had he been trying to do that? Worse, considering what had happened to Sinead Mc-Creary, had he been trying to kill Charlotte?

A small voice in his mind provided the answer, stark and comfortless: *of course he had.* Miles thought of the damage Ringan had apparently done to Penny, of Jane's memory of a brutal rape that had happened to someone else, but was now as deep a part of Jane as if she herself had been attacked. He wondered how long he, himself, had been oblivious to this canker in his house. Certain things, excuses made by the locals and by previous visitors to Callowen at festival time, would make all too much sense if viewed under the harsh light of that possibility.

He found himself wanting to writhe. He rarely felt humbled by anything, especially an awareness that he had been obtuse. The sensation was not enjoyable.

The walls of his room were more visible now, streaked with the first grey of dawn on the eastern horizon. Miles forced his mind back to Andrew Leight, as he had been in life. Had he always been twisted, ugly, somehow subhuman? What would he have been had he been alive today? Probably a serial killer, Miles thought grimly, one of those men one saw on the evening news, being led off in handcuffs between two sturdy policemen, an appalled yet suitably professional newsperson speaking in hushed tones about the bodies dug up in said serial killer's garden or retrieved from a cellar under the killer's house. There would be footage, and a trial, and endless speculation on the parts of paid professionals and dedicated amateurs alike, wondering how he'd got that way. Bad genetics? Original sin? Abusive family, perhaps? Everyone had seen something like it on the television, the news that Killer X had been a quiet child, or a misogynist from birth, or had started down the path that led to dismembered transients or strangled lovers by pulling the wings off insects, or torturing small animals, or . . .

A scream, deep and angry, breaking off abruptly. It was the voice of Gaheris, down in the mews. Another scream, a horse this time, a high call of fear.

And suddenly, without conscious thought or deliberate decision, Miles Leight-Arnold was out of bed, barefoot, grabbing the powerful torch from his bedside table, holding it like a weapon as he ran from his room, down the empty corridors of Callowen's family wing, past Lady Susanna's painted smile without so much as a glance, down the staircase, out across the damp grass towards the mews.

The low-slung building, with its six discrete stalls, had housed the Leight-Arnold hawks for centuries. Beyond the mews, the stables were a much larger blocky shape in the burgeoning dawn. As he ran, Miles became aware of the noise levels that he had somehow, to this point, missed hearing. It was astonishing. The horses, all eight of them, were screaming, sounds of fear and anger; one whinny cut across the rest for a moment, the distinctive voice of Charlotte's mare, Dagmar. The slamming of furious hooves beating futilely against wooden stalls rose to a clamour and was lost as individual noise, as it blended with the cacophony of rage and terror coming from the birds.

Miles stopped, disoriented, his head swinging from stables to mews. Who to calm first? The horses, he thought; they were able to do more damage, to themselves and to their surroundings; the birds were jessed. He glanced over at the door to the mews, noted that it was firmly shut as it always was, and ran for the stables.

By the time he'd pulled away the heavy crossbar and pushed the wooden doors completely open, the horses had already begun to quiet down. That something had spooked them badly was obvious in the rolling eyes where too much white showed, the twitchiness and unwillingness to let him approach without soothing and blandishment, the way even the generally placid Dagmar skittered away from him, jerking her neck, tossing her head wildly from side to side, voicing her unease. He saved his own Lothian for last, stroking the silver neck, offering comfort. There were flecks of foam at the corners of Lothian's mouth, as if he'd been running hard, visible now as the sky outside began to lighten into day.

Perhaps the final approach of morning had lulled him, or perhaps the impending morning made danger seem impossible. Whatever the cause, the scream from the mews took him totally by surprise. It was the voice of the peregrine Gaheris, in an extremity of rage, shocking in its power.

Miles ran. Behind him, the horses moved uneasily, but were quiet. As he reached the lawn, the first sunlight of the day touching the grey horizon with brilliant colour, he stopped in his tracks.

The mews door, firmly shut not ten minutes earlier, was open and swinging. The steady *clack!* of the moving door against the side of the ancient building was horrifying, impossible. The morning was dead calm. There was no wind, not even a breeze. The door swung, and hit, its iron fittings slapping against the outer wall. The sun was higher now, the grass showing lines of rose and gold.

Miles moved forward, towards the mews. There was nothing in the world he wanted to do less; the sense of threat, looming, waiting, was palpable in the clear summer air. His heart was erratic, rocketing with an accelerated, uneven rhythm against his ribs. There was darkness, something alive, something dead, something with evil murderous intent . . .

Gaheris called, sharp and high.

Pulling the wings off insects. Torturing small animals . . .

Miles Leight-Arnold steadied his breathing, took hold of himself, and walked into the mews.

The group in the rectory study bore a strong resemblance to a ragtag lot of university students, swotting for a major exam. Each had an ancient leather or buckram-bound register, detailing in fine calligraphy the day-to-day minutiae of centuries past; each had a small spiral-bound notebook, purchased from the stationers' shop in Purbury during a hurried trip by Ringan.

"I think I've found something."

Hibbert, who had been reading at a faster pace than the others, put his pencil down and rubbed his eyes. Everyone else, glad for the break, looked up at him.

"I've been reading all Charles Lockereigh's personal notes, the ones he made after Edward and Susanna's marriage. There's a lovely piece in here, from April 1624, about Edward getting a 'distinguished and most estimable painter from the Lowlands, to take the Lady's likeness.' " Hibbert looked sad. "I've seen the Mytens painting, of course; she looks incredibly happy, very young and vivid and bright, with her whole future stretched out in front of her. And that's interesting, isn't it? Significant?"

"You mean because, from the look of it, Andrew's campaign of terrorising her hadn't begun yet?" Penny's mouth was a thin line. "Yes, it's significant, for the timing at least. So the painting was done before her first child was born?"

"Richard was born in 1625. It was a very warm day, early spring—she was a few days before her time. There'd been storming for days before, and trees were down all over the estate. Edward had to ride out that day, to see what damage had been done." Jane spoke with certainty. "The baby had curly brown hair. A very pretty little boy. Charles was just a wee thing when his mother died, a year old or so."

They stared at her, chilled, knowing she was giving them facts, not wanting to think about how she knew those facts. She managed a faint smile.

"No, it's all right. Those voices I heard, back at Annie Whitlaw's place—Matty's, Edward's. I knew about the children. I could see them, feel them, the way Susanna did. Don't look so horrified. Really, I'm all right. Walter, what was it you've found? I take it there's more than the Mytens sittings."

"Oh, yes, much more. Listen to this." Hibbert read slowly, inflecting his voice; unconsciously, he was articulating the man behind the words. Penny and Julian, the trained actors, shared a quick appreciative glance.

" '23 September 1624. Today at morning mass it was given to me to offer thanks to Our Lord and Heavenly Father for tidings of great joy. The Lady Susanna goes with child, and, should God grant us this blessing, will be brought to bed in March of the new year. The Lady's contentment shines from her for all to see, and Lord Edward can see nothing and no one, so deep is his happiness at this, and his care of his Lady.' "

"So, they announced her pregnancy—Richard, I suppose, the elder child—to the entire village, at essentially the end of her first trimester. It seems a bit early to have said anything, what with infant mortality rates being high in those days—there was a huge plague outbreak in 1625. It seems they were tempting fate, but still, how lovely. It must have been delicious for Susanna, such a happy thing." Charlotte, absorbing this history of her own ancestors, was visibly moved. "Is that what you wanted us to hear, Walter?"

"No. There's more, part of the same entry. Where was I? Ah, right. '. . . his care of his Lady. No sooner had I given out the news from the pulpit, than my gaze did come to rest upon Andrew Leight. So terrible was his visage, so twisted and full of hate his features, that I was like to swoon, and did for a moment fear that he might burst into consuming flames, as would a minion of Lucifer in such surroundings. No doubt remains in me, that he means grievous harm. I fear greatly for the safety of the child and the

Lady alike. Yet how to best express this to Lord Edward I know not, for he will hear nothing, no word, spoken against his own kin. In such a fashion can an honest man's loyalty be used against him, against all the best meanings of man in the service of God, and after the pursuance of His Word.' "

"Well, that paints it in a bit, doesn't it? Andrew's resentment was right there for everyone to see, except, apparently, the one person who could have nipped it in the bud." Ringan shook his head. "Damn. Well. From Lockereigh's earlier entries, at least the bit we've found, we already get the picture of Andrew Leight there, young, learning the estate, being trained—being reinforced in his belief that someday, Callowen was his. And then, bang! Here comes this gorgeous young dolly-bird, not even particularly well-born from where he's sitting, and his cousin, the confirmed widower, falls madly in love, marries the girl, and she turns out to be as fertile as a bucket of potting soil. And there go all his hopes and dreams. I wonder what he had in mind, that 'grievous harm' Lockereigh talked about?"

"Murder, possibly."

There was a momentary stillness. The words had been spoken with all the weight Julian could give them.

"I've got something here, as well—first mention of Matty Groves." He looked up from his own densely written page. "This is a later register, and Reverend Lockereigh has no illusions at all about just how dangerous Andrew Leight is. Listen."

Julian cleared his throat. His beautiful voice brought Charles Lockereigh into the sunny room.

" '24 July 1627. I am in much worry and indecision. This morning, I was summoned to the House, to administer last rites for John Bolling, the head groom, who in the course of breaking a young horse was thrown hard, and struck his head. He will be sore missed, and deeply mourned, for he was much loved.' "

Julian paused. " 'As I passed through the western grounds on my return to St. Giles, I espied, in a charming garden where roses bloom rampant, the Lady Susanna, in company with Andrew

Leight, in what appeared to be no light conversation. It seemed to me that Andrew spoke to her in such a way as caused her grave distress, so that she shrank back from him. As I watched, he took hold of her, closing his hand with some force around her forearm, hard enough indeed that she did cry out. As she did so, I saw him raise his free hand, as if he would strike her, and I called out to them. He at once released the Lady, and strode away from us, hurrying, so that I might not catch him up.'"

"Miserable evil hateful man." Penny's hands were clenched hard. "Go on, Julian. There's more, right?"

"Oh, yes. 'She came to meet me, and through her distress spoke kindly and sweetly to me, but there was no hiding the mark of Andrew Leight's anger on the flesh of her arm. As she spied my gaze returning to that bruise, I made as if to say something to her of it, but was forestalled as the Lady's page, young Matthew Groves from the village, caught us up with a summons from the House for his mistress, that Lord Callowen, having come home too late for his servant's passing, did desire that his Lady might bear him company in his grief. I was, therefore, compelled to depart with my purpose of speaking frankly to the Lady unfulfilled. Yet I fear that this cruelty is no less than a common occurrence. I must pray for courage to speak with Lord Edward, that he might remove his cousin from his Lady's company.'"

"Matty was Susanna's *page*?" Char was outraged. "But he must have been a child! She wouldn't have had a lusty teenager as her page—it simply wasn't done. And, well, that just puts the lid on it. The song is a load of old bollocks, and all this time, people have been going around singing this as if it was true, and it wasn't. It's all a big lie, like Richard the Third, and she wasn't guilty of anything! And I'm damned well going to clear her name!"

She paused for breath, her cheeks flying banners of furious scarlet. Julian, faintly smiling, touched her hand.

"We will, Char. But we need to know what did happen, now that we're clear on at least one thing that didn't. And that means more work. I say we get down to it. There's no performance tonight, obviously, so unless someone here has a pressing engagement elsewhere . . . ?"

For the next hour, the only interruption to the sound of even breathing and the careful rustle of pages was the soft spatter of a passing shower, beating lightly against the rectory's outer walls. At the end of the hour, Jane set her pen down.

"There's something else here. I can't help thinking it's important, somehow, but I'm damned if I know how it fits, or why. It has nothing to do with Susanna, or Matty Groves—it's about a visit that a bishop made to Charles Lockereigh."

Everyone was silent. She peered at the page.

"'1 September. I am in great distress, and uneasiness of mind and spirit. Bishop Wolvesley having come to Purbury expressly to speak with Lord Edward, as I thought, I had no notion of the prelate stopping first here at St. Giles. It is clear to me that Lord Callowen had no prior notice of this event. More unsettling, however, was the news he shared with me, and will tomorrow bring to Callowen, of the arrest of Sir Hervey Leight.'"

"Sir Hervey Leight?" Penny said, bewildered. "Who was Hervey Leight? A relative, obviously, but—"

"Andrew's father. It gets worse. Listen." Jane read on, her face looking pinched and tired. "'I enquired of the Bishop with what crime Sir Hervey was charged, and was much taken aback to hear that he was taken for the murder of his own wife, the Lady Margaret, whom, it is said, he did kill in rage and uncontrollable passion.'"

Ringan made a strangled noise in his throat. Jane kept her eye on the ledger.

"'I found myself wondering how such news would be received by Andrew Leight, who looks to lose mother and father all together, this being a high crime and most mortal of sins. Yet I could not but reflect that the capability for such a heinous act by the father might cause no surprise, for I have with my own eyes seen this same cruelty and violence in the son. I grieve for Lord Edward, the more so that the Bishop did hint at issues concerning the arrest that spoke more to his thought of the schism between churches, and that same schism between King and Parliament, than of the sin of Cain itself.' "

"Between King and Parliament." Char shifted her cast, her vivid face clouded. "And between churches—oh, heavens, I wonder if Sir Whatsis, Andrew's dad, was a King's Man in Parliament. One of the people who spoke for the King's Party."

"A what?" Ringan blinked at her. "Char, look, I know it's been a very long few days, but it would help if you remembered that we didn't all get firsts in history. Well, I didn't, anyway. Could you clarify, please? What are you talking about?"

"Committees," she said briefly. "It was an old Tudor trick: the most powerful parties stocked Parliament with committees, each one headed up by a handpicked spokesman. I wonder if Hervey Leight was one of them? That entry—Lockereigh said issues between King and Parliament. It would fit."

"If he was—" Ringan shook his head, frustrated. "No, I'm not following it. It's awfully muddy. Wasn't the King at the time Catholic? Isn't that what led to the whole Civil War—Cromwell, Roundheads, Cavaliers, all that? Why would a Catholic king have had a Protestant running one of his shows for him?"

"Where in the world did you get that idea? Charles wasn't a Catholic, he was an Anglican." Charlotte's usual style of speech had been replaced by a tremendous authority; this was a woman in her element, speaking not only about her family history but about her speciality. "We're talking about the years leading up to Cromwell and the Puritans, you're right about that. The Stuart kings—James had a tutor, I've forgotten his name, but the bloke was a stick-straight Calvinist. The Catholics couldn't stand James. Remember the whole Guy Fawkes bit, Gunpowder Plot, all that? Charles was rather more sympathetic, mostly thanks to his wife—she was French, and Catholic. So he slipped favours to the Catholics behind the scullery door. Mostly, the Catholics were heartily loathed, all sorts of sanctions and whatnots. And since Parliament was essentially completely Anglican, with the schism coming between the Anglicans and the Puritans—"

"—that meant having an Anglican with strong ties to one of England's great Catholic houses would have covered all sorts of ground for King Charles." Walter had caught up with Charlotte. "This is very plausible, I must say. If Andrew's papa was a King's Man in Parliament, what would his arrest have meant for Andrew? And how do we find out for certain?"

"Parliamentary records." Charlotte was on her feet, scrabbling with her usable hand in her purse. "That part's simple. Da's a peer of the realm, remember? He's a member of the House of Lords, the silly half of Parliament, but still, it's Parliament. I'll make him ring down to the archivist in London and find out. Oh, damn it all, where's my phone?"

The call was short and to the point. Charlotte demanded her father, got Roger Searle instead, and was told that her father was feeling unwell, and was resting. With a succinctness and brevity that astonished her companions, Charlotte relayed the information she wanted to Searle, told him to call London and use all the influence the Callowen name could command to cut through any official red tape and get the answers quickly, told him she'd explain what was going on when she got home, and rang off.

"Did you say your father's sick?" Hibbert, mindful of his duties as host and suspecting they were in for a long wait, called for his housekeeper and offered his guests a light meal. "What's wrong? I hope Lord Callowen's all right."

"I didn't ask." Charlotte looked guilty. "My mind's gone all focussed on this. If it was serious, I'm sure Roger would have said." She glared at her phone. "I know, I know, watch it and it won't ring. But still . . ."

The call from Callowen House came less than an hour later. Armed both with a precise date and the Callowen name behind the request, the unknown archivist in London had performed with spectacular efficiency. Charlotte listened, her phone propped precariously to one ear as she scribbled down notes. When she rang off, she took a deep breath and faced the others.

"He wasn't a committee head," she announced. "He was the

Speaker of the House of Commons, for that session of Parliament."

Everyone was silent, staring at her. She licked her lips. "And on 28 August 1629, Sir Hervey Leight was dragged out of Commons and taken into custody under the King's pleasure, for the crime of murdering his wife. The archivist told Da there was a footnote— King Charles actually sent along the name of his chosen temporary replacement for the empty seat, on the very next day. And I'll give you one guess what that name was."

"He wanted Andrew Leight?" Ringan's nerves were jumping, touched by the spur of solid information, a trail to follow, the promise of action close at hand. "To replace his father?"

Charlotte nodded. Her voice was tight. "The date. Did you notice? 28 August?"

"Susanna's murder," Ringan said grimly. "What was the date of that?"

"September 2." Penny was trembling a bit. "Just enough time for the order to come down to the Bishop from London, and send him screaming off towards Callowen, with no time for advance notice that he was coming. He must have stopped here, at the rectory, the night before Susanna died."

"I wonder if he had a premonition?" Jane spoke softly. "Perhaps bad dreams? Bad dreams—they do seem to follow Andrew Leight about, don't they?"

"Personally," Ringan said thoughtfully, "I'm wondering if the news is what pushed Andrew Leight over the edge in the first place, from secretive sadist to barking mad murderer."

The first thing Miles Leight-Arnold heard, as he forced his feet to carry him over the threshold and into the dark building that housed his birds, was a deep, ragged breathing.

The windows in the mews were useless for light; they were mere slits, cut high up in the walls, there for ventilation and nothing else. The room was a long rectangle with a line of six stalls, each with a perch holding a hawk. It had never been wired for electricity.

Miles realised suddenly that he had set his heavy torch down in the stables as he'd tried to soothe Lothian, and left it behind.

"Damn," he said, but the word stayed deep in his chest. Whatever, whoever, was the source of that edgy breathing in the shadows seemed to be using all the available air. He himself could barely get enough oxygen into his own lungs to stay conscious and alert, much less to waste anything on speech.

He forced his head to turn to the right; his neck, perhaps responding to the instinct that told him of danger directly ahead, seemed made of granite, unbending, immovable. The shortwing in the first stall, deep in the moult, was twitching and uneasy. Miles moved past her, and past the next three birds; the hawks were quiet now, too quiet. These were unhooded, their eyes fierce and staring in the dimness. He understood, suddenly, that they were not relaxed, but rather hunched against something. These were birds wanting to strike, to attack, to kill.

The ragged breathing was louder now. It seemed to intensify as Miles approached his favourite bird, jessed to his perch at the end of the row. The noise was stealthy, uneven. It somehow conveyed the impression of a bestial excitement and arousal.

Gaheris screamed. And, quite suddenly, Miles stopped being frightened.

He strode past the fifth stall without a glance at the occupant, walked straight into the final stall, and kicked aside feathers. There was a small drift of them, perhaps eight or ten, under the stall. Gaheris, enraged and insane, held his beak open and ready to strike. His flat glare moving to Miles, he bated, pulling in vain against the short jesses, trying to free his best weapon, the murderous talons, for use against the invisible enemy that tormented him.

Your hawks, your horses, your pretty hounds, this should have been mine, all mine

Miles shook his head, like a swimmer trying to come clear of heavy water. His ears were roaring, the scratchy breathing mixed with the scrabbling of the birds and the impossible words cutting into his awareness.

As he watched, Gaheris jerked his left wing, and screamed. A feather came free, fluttering down to join the small heap on the mews floor.

"Get the hell away from my birds." Miles didn't know if he'd shouted it, or whispered it, or if he only spoke in his own mind. Heedless of anything else, of the danger to flesh and bone, he pulled down the pyjama sleeve on his left arm, as far as it would go. Murmuring words of comfort, he undid the jesses, and, lifting Gaheris from his perch, shifted the peregrine to his sleeve.

From around him, behind him, from everywhere and nowhere, came a deep, horrifying chuckle.

He felt Gaheris close hard around his forearm, saw the small patch of red staining his sleeve as Gaheris, frightened and furious, closed his talons and pierced flesh. Miles was aware of searing pain, and felt a hunger in the air around him, deep, furious, something smelling his blood with avidity and pleasure, someone, something, perhaps it was the birds themselves, catching that scent of the kill on the air . . .

"No." This time, he spoke aloud. The icy rage, the cold power, in his own voice startled him. "You don't get my birds. You don't get my horses. You don't get my daughter, either. You get nothing, do you hear me?"

The breathing stopped, as if in surprise. Miles, blood dripping from his left arm and staining the hawk's feet, backed out of the mews, into the daylight, into morning sunlight and dew on the grass and clean air and sanity.

"My Lord!"

He heard the call, his stable chief running towards him across the grass, as the Purbury clock struck six off in the distance. The servant came to a halt a few feet away, staring at the bird, at the lord of Callowen, at the blood dripping on the grass.

"Go find me a heavy towel, or a chamois cloth." Miles, his arm in flames, spoke tersely. "No! Don't go into the mews—find something in the stables. I need to put Gaheris away. And then, for Christ's sake, go back to the house and ring up the doctor. Tell him I'll need a tetanus shot, and probably some stitches."

Eleven

"Get up, get up," Lord Arnold cried
"Get up as quick as you can
It'll ne'er be said in fair England
I slew a naked man!"

After a heated discussion, Penny and Jane accepted an invitation from Walter Hibbert to remain under the rectory's roof for as long as they felt it was necessary.

There had been some argument about it, with Penny surprising them all by insisting that she ought to be at Callowen. Ringan, listening to this, had told her she was out of her mind, and threatened to tie her up, toss her in the boot of the Alfa, and drive her back to London if she looked to go anywhere near Andrew Leight. As the back-and-forth got progressively more high-pitched, Charlotte stepped in.

"You're both wrong," she announced. "And both right, as well. Ringan, you're right, of course you are. But being right isn't enough, not right now. Penny's going to be wanted, when we figure out how to get rid of Andrew. It's just that, for right now, until we can sort out the mess—"

"Like hell she's going to be wanted!" Ringan was breathing heavily. "Wanted by who? I'm not having her near the place. You said it yourself, Char—he was after Penny. Why you think she'd be safe within a country mile of Callowen is beyond me. I won't have it. She'll go back within striking distance of Andrew Leight over my dead body."

"I didn't say she'd be safe, did I?" Char's reasonable tone, combined with the terrifying sense of what she was saying, lent her speech an air of surreality. "I said she'd be wanted. And she will. Because Penny's the source of this, isn't she?"

"What in hell is that supposed to mean?" Ringan's jaw was locked hard. He spoke through his teeth. "Your bad boy incubus was scooting merrily through the walls of Callowen's guest bedrooms before we got here—Sinead McCreary, remember? He's been there all along. I'll be damned if you're saddling Penny with the responsibility for this, Charlotte, and anyway, what about Jane? It was Jane he went for, before he ever—"

"Ringan." Jane's voice stopped him in mid-sentence. "Wait a bit. I think I know what Char means." She swallowed hard. "And if she means what I think she does, I think she's right."

"It's both of us. Isn't it?" There was a note of resignation in Penny's voice, an acceptance of the situation, that shook Ringan to the core. "Jane, looking so much like Susanna. Me, being some kind of, I don't know, power station? Battery? That's what you mean, isn't it, Char? He was floating around but his power was really just dormant, or something. He woke up to this level because of me, and because of Jane. We were a sort of one-two punch—we acted as, well, as Pygmalion. That's what you're saying. Right?"

"I'm sorry, Penny. Yes, that's just what I meant." Char looked sympathetic. "And that's what I think. No, Ringan, don't. Just stop and think a moment. What's the use of getting cross with me? I'm not what you ought to be mad at; I'm just saying what I believe the situation is, truly. I understand about Sinead McCreary, but from what you told us about it, it was nothing like the sort of firepower Andrew's been showing since the start of the festival, was it? Really, what happened to your friend's wife sounds almost accidental, as if Andrew went for a bit of a reccy and she happened to be in his way, and was sensitive to him, or vulnerable, or something."

Ringan was silent. His lips, and the flesh above his beard, looked bleached. Penny tried again.

"Ringan, think. Last summer, with the weaver in your tithe

barn. Then at Christmas, Agnès de Belleville at my theatre. I seem to have something that switches them on, or wakes them up." Her eyes were suddenly wet. She laid a hand on Ringan's arm. "I don't know how and I don't know why, I just know that's the way it is. Oh, and I hate it. Mustn't forget that much. I hate it and wish it would stop. But it does mean I can't just walk away. Miles was right, damn him. I woke Andrew up, just by walking in the front door. I'm responsible."

"So am I," Jane added. "If he sparked up because Penny was there, I gave him something to spark up for. And then I went and made it worse, didn't I, by going and dreaming for Susanna, and letting him relive his nasty little triumphs all over again? No wonder he's got so strong; I might as well have been spoonfeeding him. I'm responsible, too."

"Oh, hell." Ringan's shoulders slumped suddenly. "Right. Fine. Brilliant. I can't even dot Char's infuriating daddy one in the jaw, because he's right. So, what do we do next?"

"If you're seriously asking? I'd say we proceed as we began." Julian, who had stayed out of the argument, spoke up. "If knowledge is power, we need more of it. Jane, you said you'd come down to the church to hunt for graves. We still don't know how Andrew or Matty actually died, or where they're buried. Why not go ahead with that?"

"I will." Jane smiled, albeit faintly. "Very sensible."

"I'm only getting started, with the commonsense. You just wait." He grinned at her, the heart-shaking matinée idol's smile as effective as it was attractive. "Right, here's me being bossy. Char, you're the historian. We need to know more about what happened on the political end of things. Where's all that info likely to be stored? Back up in London?"

"What a weird question, Julian. There's going to be bits all over. We need a starting point." She considered for a moment. "I think the bulk of it's likely to be at the British Library, you know, the big one at St. Pancras. They've probably got some awfully tasty stuff stashed away in the King's Collection—" Char broke off as

Ringan and Penny both made a noise. "What? Did I say something useful?"

"Stroke of luck, that's all," Ringan said. "We have a very good friend there—the curator, Madeleine Holt, Lady Madeleine Holt. She helped us out with research at Christmas last year, when Penny was having trouble with a ghost in her theatre. Maddy's a life-saver. And there's also this: she knows about ghosts, and believes in them. We won't have to convince her we're not out of our minds, or anything. She's seen for herself, firsthand. She'll get it, straight off."

"I'll call her." Penny was aware of something stirring, deep down where her intuition seemed to be buried. *First lucky break,* she thought, and felt an odd tingle of excitement. Andrew Leight had had all the luck so far; could this be the first turn of the tide their way? "I'll call her right now. She'll jump at it, I know she will. Here's hoping she's not off digging through some medieval pornography in Périgord, or something."

"That leaves the pair of us." Ringan cocked an eyebrow at Julian. "Why do I think you're going to suggest something that requires the flexing of manly muscle? Or is that just wishful thinking? I'm tired of sitting on my bottom, reading."

"Sharp eye you've got." Julian was grinning. "I was thinking, there are two things we could be doing. First off, there was the mention of Lady Susanna keeping a diary, wasn't there? And of the Callowen steward handing it over to Susanna's bereaved mum?"

"Dame Gedlington." Hibbert broke in eagerly. "Are you talking about trying to track down where that pile eventually fetched up? Because the Gedlingtons died out long ago."

"Genealogy research," Ringan said glumly. "Damn. Sorry, Julian, of course you're right and it needs to be done, but I've gone all itchy from doing nothing. I want to get my hands on something solid. I'm tired of mucking about with books."

"Actually, I was going to suggest that Walter look into it, that is, if you're willing, Walter?" Julian tilted his head at Ringan. "You called it, mate. Muscle for us. All our muscles."

"What—" Ringan, bewildered, suddenly understood. "Oh, my. That cross on the Folly floor. Is that it?"

"That's it," Julian agreed. "Time to dig in the ground, and not in the records. We'll need permission from Lord Callowen, of course. And it might not be easy to get."

"You'll get it," Char said flatly. "I'll go back there now and wave my injured wrist at him, and tell him that if he's going to storm around coming the lord over everyone, issuing imperial fiats about exorcisms and whose fault things are, he'd damned well better be front and centre with some cooperation. If he wants to sit outside the Folly with Gaheris on his wrist, that's fine with me, but we need to track down the facts, and I'm feeling a bit shamed that it's all been Penny and Ringan and Jane. Susanna's our ghost, damn it, and Andrew's our problem."

She sounded quite fierce. Ringan grinned at her. "Good on you, Char. Me and Julian, we'll just stand outside until you've scared your father into submission."

"Right." Char took this suggestion at face value. "In fact, if Penny wants to call Lady Whatsername at the British Library from right here, she can stay here while we three go back up and tell Da what's what."

"I wonder if Albert would want to help?" Penny, who had been poised to take her phone into the garden for the call to the King's Collection, spoke impulsively. "Sorry, but what Char said about Miles playing the lord—it reminded me. Albert was right there when Broomfield Hill played the ghosts out of Ringan's barn; in fact, he was the one who got us an item we needed for the exorcism, by going in and being all peerish at the people who had it. Coming the lord, in fact—sometimes it's damned useful. And really, Albert's a useful bloke. Besides, he probably feels responsible as well, since he was the one who wangled Broomfield Hill their invitation to Callowen. Albert has rather a lot of conscience, and I think it might be giving him some problems right about now. Ringan, do you think—"

"Yes, I do. We'll gather him in on the way to the Folly, and see if he wants to help. So, if everyone's ready?"

Ringan got to his feet. He was aware of a surge of energy in himself, the release that comes when one has been kept immobile too long. He felt it as something tangible; the frustration imposed by his own inaction, all the pent-up irritation of a man forced into the position of watching helplessly while things happened around him, was transmuting into reaction. He was being given the opportunity to act at last, and he could hardly wait. "Jane, finding as many final resting places as possible. Penny, calling Maddy Holt in London and seeing what we can use. Walter, tracking down what happened to Susanna's diary. The rest of us will trot off to tackle Charlotte's infuriating papa. Let's get a move on."

The next morning, Ringan, with Julian and Albert on either side of him and the Leight-Arnold contingent leading the way, stood at the foot of the bridge that led to Lady Susanna's tomb, and made a dismaying discovery.

He really did not want to set foot in the place. Nor was he alone in that reluctance.

"Damn it." Julian, at Ringan's left, kept his voice pitched low. "*Damn it.* Is it my imagination, or does that dignified little monument seem extraordinarily ominous to anyone else?"

"Not your imagination." Albert Wychsale sounded unhappy. Despite the warmth of the summer day, he shivered suddenly. "I'm glad we agreed to do this in full morning sun. If we have to do it at all, that is."

"Well, you said you wanted to help," Ringan pointed out, reasonably. He sounded unsympathetic. "Really, it's best to get it over with."

In truth, he himself was a bit dazed by how quickly this expedition had been organised. Penny, having set up a meeting with Maddy Holt at the British Library for the following day, had taken the keys to Ringan's car and headed back towards London. That taken care of, Charlotte got up a full head of steam, and led the charge for her father's permission to attack the Folly's floor.

Lord Callowen had been tracked down just before dinner. Rather to everyone's surprise, he'd been located in the muniments room, frowning over one of the family journals from the period on everyone's mind. His left forearm was heavily bandaged, but he seemed disinclined to talk about the injury.

The festival, for this season, was in ruins, its reputation perhaps beyond repair; the glaziers were replacing the panes of the ballroom's French doors. Guests had been sent on their way with their host's regrets. The performers had been paid and dismissed. This had led to a lively argument between the uninvolved members of Broomfield Hill and those who remained, with Liam flatly refusing to budge and both the Currans backing him up. Jane had prevailed, in the end, but it had taken some heavy promises and reasoning.

Miles listened to his daughter's impassioned arguments in silence, waiting only until she paused for breath.

"Y'know, Char," he told her irritably, "for someone who claims to disdain professional theatre, you're a damned drama queen. Don't stand there waving your poor wee damaged wrist at me; this isn't the Globe Theatre and I'm not buying it. Besides, it's not needed. I agree with you. We'll do it in the morning. As early in the day as we can, in fact."

His daughter gawked at him. Someone in the small crowd of males at her back swallowed a choke of what might have been laughter.

"I didn't know about that cross on the Folly floor—you'll show me, tomorrow." Miles nodded at the group over her shoulder. "Were you all thinking I'd say no? Bunch of idiots. I was there, in the ballroom, remember? Besides—no, never mind. I'll just say that I've been upset with the wrong people, and I'm sorry for that. But Char? Just because I don't want to play some sort of Irate Papa from a Victorian pantomime, that doesn't mean I'm not upset about you getting hurt. I *am* upset. I've got reason to be upset. I've been reading up a bit—trying to expand what I thought I knew about my family history." His voice changed, becoming somehow less distinct, less imposing. "From the looks of it, I'd say I didn't know much. But it's hard to tell. There's not a lot in here."

"Miles, have you found something?" That shift in tone had not been lost on Albert Wychsale.

"No. Just the reverse, in fact. Looks to be a section that's gone missing entirely. Remember Lord Edward's steward, the one who gave Dame Gedlington her dead daughter's effects?" Miles smoothed out the pages of the register, and ran the tip of his index finger down the central crease. "Looks as if someone's taken out a page or three. There's a gap in the dates, and you can feel where the pages have been cut—it's very skillfully done, down as far as it could go without being too obvious."

"You mentioned Lord Edward's steward." Julian was concentrating, his eyes narrowed. "Why?"

"Because everything leading up to the missing section looks to be written by him, and the bit afterwards. He must have been Callowen's official diarist, the secular one, that is. We heard that section, about him giving Susanna's mother her bits and pieces—Penny read it. So I'm thinking someone cut out a few days' worth of entries. I checked the dates. The last entry in here happens to end at the very bottom of a page. The date of that is 31 August, and then"—he glanced down at the cramped script—"14 September. That's two weeks gone walkabout. And of course it's the two weeks we wanted, presumably including whatever really happened on 2 September. This wasn't a clean simple killing. Someone took the time and trouble to remove those pages. There was more than that going on."

Everyone was silent. Miles closed the register. Pushing his chair back, he stood up.

"You say Penny's gone off to London? Good. Any luck, she'll sort things out at the Library. It's a damned good library; we have some papers there ourselves, family stuff on permanent loan. Besides, she's better away from Callowen, and I'm thinking Callowen's better with her off and away. I have the feeling things will be a bit more quiet with her not here. So, tomorrow morning, first thing after breakfast? We'll take some tools down to the Folly and go have a look at who's been keeping Susanna company in there, all these years. Just us, mind you. I'm not risking having any of the staff near this mess. That means everyone's here for the night, and no arguments. You can always run screaming if anything happens."

"Your arm—" Julian began, and was cut off at once.

"My arm's fine. Just a bit sore. I had to shift the hawks this morning and I got sloppy. It's nothing. Now for heaven's sake, go away, all of you. I'll see you in the morning."

The night had passed without incident. Ringan, alone in the ornate bedroom, had found himself alternately missing Penny's presence in the big bed and being oddly comforted by picturing her in the safety of her Muswell Hill flat. He only hoped she was missing him as well.

The following morning, Miles led the way to Callowen's South Lawn, where they found a small two-seater ATV loaded with an assortment of tools—pickaxes, shovels, sledgehammers, crowbars. The plan, Miles announced, was that he and Char would drive the equipment to the Folly, and await the others. "Give you a chance to digest your breakfasts properly," he'd grunted.

"Da didn't get his ride this morning," Charlotte confided to Julian, standing beside her. "He always gets cross when he doesn't get his ride. He says it keeps him regular. And I think his arm's being uncooperative. Actually, I think he wants us to go in two groups, so no one will notice and wonder. Isn't that right?" She caught her father's glare, and abandoned the subject. "Anyway, we'll wait for you there."

Now, clustered in a small, oddly primitive knot at the spot where Charlotte had been thrown from her horse, none of Lord Callowen's guests felt anything other than deep reluctance at the thought of walking across that bridge and into the building.

Charlotte, however, was made of sterner stuff. Without a moment's hesitation, she stalked across the bridge, her father at her heels. She then set the enormous key in the lock, twisted hard with her uninjured hand, and pushed the Folly door open.

"Come along," she called back over her shoulder. "And bring some of those tools, please."

Inside, the Folly looked no different than it had for close to four centuries. The three marble angels strained towards an apparently unreachable Heaven, the brass plaque gleamed, dust motes danced in the warm still air, filtered through the stained-glass robes of Susanna's patron saint as she knelt before a Roman with a sword and serenely awaited her own beheading in the service of God. The room was airy, spacious, quiet; there was light here, and a sense of peace. The ominous sense of threat, whatever its source, had not followed them indoors. The room was just a room, no more.

"I hate this." Ringan, not realising he'd spoken aloud, saw four heads swing in his direction, and flushed. "Sorry. It's just that I feel like a tomb robber, a resurrectionist, or something—Burke and Hare. Let's get it done, all right?"

Charlotte found the spot immediately. For a few moments, she and her father stared down at it. Miles stooped, and traced the rough-hewn cross with one finger.

"These stones?" he said. "They don't look to be sealed, just set in place. Beautiful work of fitting them together—those period stonemasons knew their job. We may not need to break this, after all. Damned good thing, too. Rather not destroy a bit of family history if I don't need to. How many crowbars have we got? Maybe a chisel? Let's try prising it up."

In the end, the operation was simple enough. Albert and Miles held the chisels on opposite sides of the stone, while Ringan and Julian, sweating and careful, slipped bars on the remaining sides of the square. The stone rocked, inching upwards in small increments. Charlotte stood apart, her good hand on Susanna's marble coffin, her injured wrist immobile in its sling; her lips were slightly parted, her eyes curiously blank.

After a quarter hour of work, the slab had come free enough of its fellows to allow Julian to get the hook end of his crowbar beneath it. Albert and Ringan got their hands on the far edge. Between them, their chests heaving, they rocked the stone completely free, and moved it clear.

Whoever had buried the small coffin had set it shallow. Ringan, staring down into the hole at the lid of plain wood, wondered whether it had been laziness, or whether the need for secrecy and speed had driven them.

"God," Miles grunted. His hawk's face was streaked with sweat and grave dust; the white bandage on his left arm was torn, two tiny dots of blood showing where a stitch had come undone. "You know, I'm not sure I believed we'd find anything. Let's get another stone out. Sorry I can't be a bit more help, but I'm supposed to keep this arm from too much use, and I've already bunged it up."

It took the removal of three slabs to fully reveal the coffin. It was plank wood, rough, unfinished. Yet someone had cared enough for whoever was to rest here to have cut another cross into the lid. Like the cross that had marked its placement, it was simple, the merest outline of the symbol.

The group stood in a silent line, looking down. Only Charlotte stayed where she was, her face smooth and blank, as if listening to voices the others couldn't hear.

Albert spoke first. He sounded bewildered.

"I don't understand," he said. "That's a child's coffin."

"He was a child." Charlotte spoke softly, so softly that no one heard her.

" '*A grave, a grave,*' Lord Arnold cried, '*to put these lovers in But bury my Lady at the top For she was of noble kin.*' " Ringan turned to Miles, his face set and hard. "More nonsense. Susanna wasn't noble, she was a commoner. Susanna didn't put cuckold's horns on Edward, she was brutalised by Edward's cousin. And Matty Groves? He was her page. Charlotte told us he'd have been no more than ten or eleven years old—a child. Lovers? I don't think so. But I think we've found Matty Groves."

"A poor wee thing, God rest him. At least he can rest, sleep soft in consecrated ground."

They all heard her this time. Julian swung around first and took a step towards her, only to stop, staring.

"Slain in defense of his mistress," Charlotte told them, and her voice was musical, distant, close to song. "Slain, and hid deep, and none to do him justice or let the truth out. None to stop the calumny against him, and against her. Poor bonny boy. He tried to stop it—no blame or shame to him, that he failed."

"Char?" Miles was white-knuckled. "Char, stop it. Whatever it is you're doing, stop it now." He bit down on the rest of his words, wincing back as Albert's hand closed down hard on his injured forearm.

"Susanna," Albert breathed. "I think—"

"It's a wonder he can rest at all." Charlotte swayed a bit, her hip planted against Susanna's tomb. "It's a wonder there's any rest for any of us, when all's said. And you left her alone, time after time, left her to Andrew's use. Small wonder she walks. And Andrew?" She smiled suddenly, a heart-freezing twist of a mouth that seemed completely unfamiliar. Her eyes were filmed. "Small wonder he flies, as devils do."

Julian moved so quickly that he had reached Charlotte before anyone could be certain of his intent. He got one arm around her back, and wrenched her free and away, breaking her physical contact with the marble. She blinked, staggered, and slumped suddenly against the curl of his arm. After a moment, her eyes cleared. She licked dry lips, and swallowed hard.

"It's all right," she told them. "There's no need to worry about poor Matty; he's been sleeping easy. But Andrew's not in here. He never was."

Any doubts Penny might have harboured concerning Madeleine Holt's willingness to help were dispelled the moment she walked into the small, airy office at the British Library. Maddy greeted her guest with coffee, pastries, and unfeigned enthusiasm.

"Penny! I haven't seen you in ages—how are you? You look sensational. Here, come in, sit. I'm just pouring espresso—you take it black, no sugar, right? God, it's good to see you! How are you, and how's Ringan?"

Dr. Madeleine Holt, curator of medieval documents at the British Library, history scholar, and former punk rocker, pushed a chair towards Penny. Penny settled in with an almost inaudible sigh of relief. No matter what the circumstances, there was something intensely comforting about being here, in Maddy's office, once more.

"Here, have a coffee. You look as though you need it." Maddy had heard that tiny sigh. "Penny, what's up? Something's wrong, isn't it? I'm getting the feeling there's more happening than just you wanting some gen about the Leight-Arnold family."

"Perceptive, you are." A rueful smile touched Penny's lips. "But actually, I was just remembering the last time I was in here. Wasn't I asking for your help in getting rid of a ghost then, as well? It's just—oh, hell, might as well admit it. It's guilt. I feel as though every time I come see you, it's because I'm screaming for help. I'm a rotten friend."

Maddy grinned at her. "Considering I was in America for six weeks, I was about to apologise for not being around enough to ring you up. But if you want to carry the weight? Perfectly all right with me." She watched Penny's face relax. "Besides, weren't the Tamburlaines on tour? Really, don't be silly. Just drink that nice cup of liquid energy and tell me what's going on. You were very mysterious on the phone yesterday. What's all this about the Leight-Arnold family, and how did you get involved with them? Were you invited to do the festival? I know about Callowen being haunted, of course, and about the famous song. Is it that?"

"I wasn't invited to Callowen. At least, not to perform—Ringan was, with the band. As to the ghost? Well. That bit's complicated." The coffee, strong and undiluted, was kicking Penny back to some semblance of physical energy. She explained about Albert Wychsale's wangling of an invitation for Broomfield Hill to participate at the Callowen Festival. Maddy, perched atop her desk with her legs swinging gently, listened.

"So Broomfield Hill got the nod? What a bit of luck for Ringan! But—wasn't there something about it, something you were involved in before, at Callowen House?"

"Not me, Maddy. Donal McCreary—you met him, at the Bellefield. His wife Sinead died because of something that happened to her, at Callowen. Something—someone—some sort of ghost or something evil, moved through her while she was asleep. She died a few months later."

"That's right. You told me about it, I remember now. But I'd forgotten her name." The swinging legs stilled; there was something disturbing about Penny's choice of words. "I take it you think this ghost is back. But Penny, what do you mean, some sort of ghost? How many sorts are there? I mean, dead people who can't rest are just that, surely? Just ghosts."

"That's what we thought." Penny lifted her face to Maddy. Her lips trembled slightly, and for the first time, Maddy noticed the faint line of the nearly healed cut there. "Turns out we were probably wrong about that. Because what do you call a ghost that uses the living to attack and hurt each other, so that it can act out on what it did while it was alive?"

"I don't know." Maddy was staring. "I'm not sure there's a word for anything that horrible. Sounds devilish to me. Are you saying— right, I'm just going to belt up and let you talk. Look, if you don't mind my asking, what happened to your mouth? What's been going on?"

Penny, her voice under as iron a control as she could impose, told Maddy the entire story. As Maddy listened, her memory returned to the last time Penny had come to see her, and she became aware of an unease that had not been there before, even in the presence of the long-dead madwoman who had taken over Penny's theatre. There was something about the story of this man, this Andrew Leight, that brought up a kind of outrage in Maddy. She was unfamiliar with it, and unprepared as well. She had no way to deal with it, no tools to combat it. That the outrage was tinted with fear for her friends only added to her unease.

When Penny finished, she blurted out the first words that came into her head.

"Oh, Jesus, Penny, this is insane. It's insane and it's horrid. You should have called me sooner. Why in hell did you wait so long?" She heard her own words, and felt their complete inadequacy. "I'm sorry. That sounds—I know it sounds—it's just that the idea of Ringan . . ." She bit back the words.

"It wasn't Ringan, Maddy. Not really. Believe me, there's nothing you could suggest for Andrew Leight in the way of eternal damnation or whatever that hasn't already gone through Ringan's mind, with add-ons." Penny emptied her cup, and took a small bite of pastry. "As for calling you sooner, this whole mess only boiled up a few days ago. I called you as soon as Charlotte Leight-Arnold said there would likely be information in the King's Collection. And by the way, I'm hoping she was right, because if she was wrong . . ."

"Not to worry, she was right. There is, are, not only court archives and notes but a few documents from the Callowen personal archives as well. They were donated by the present Lord Callowen's esteemed papa, donkey's years ago." Maddy circled round to her chair, and moved the computer mouse. The screen flickered to life. "Here, let's have a look at the archived data first."

"Archived data?" Penny came to peer over her shoulder. "You have all that on the computer? Have you got child slave labour chained up in the stacks, or something? Who entered all this? I spend one hour reading one seventeenth-century ledger and my eyeballs are threatening to explode."

Maddy grinned. "We pay students to enter some of it, and we do some ourselves. But really, the bulk of the documents aren't archived in content, just in Records—a mere list of titles. We got lucky on some of this. It seems to have caught someone's fancy enough to take the time and trouble, very likely a student intern with time on their hands and a paper to write on the period. You said on the phone that you needed information about the arrest of Sir Hervey Leight, 28 August, 1629. I have a nice little hit list of documents here, including the full text of the parliamentary arrest record. That's the official charge, of course, and details of the actual crime. Would that help?"

"I'm not sure, but I somehow don't think so." Penny came round to peer over Maddy's shoulder. "I think what we really want is something about how things stood with the King, what was going on politically. The subtext, I suppose. I mean, Charles picked Hervey's son as a replacement so fast, he damned near left skidmarks. And there's no sign he'd ever even met the bloke. So— why? You're the historian, you tell me."

"Well, it was 1629." Maddy peered at the screen, her face intent. "I did a bit of looking this morning, getting the list together for you. This is really somewhat later than my particular area of interest. Politically, Charles the devout Anglican would have been doing a tricky dance with the Puritan types in Parliament right about then; the politics were intricate, to say the least, particularly where the religious aspect was concerned. But really, I'm thinking he'd have wanted as short a break in the continuity of the Speaker's chair as possible, especially since the chair was firmly anchored by his handpicked puppet. I'd forgotten, until I looked it up: the Leight family was straight Anglican, but the Arnolds—"

"Catholic. Yes, I know. We assumed the religious issue had something to do with it, with why whatever happened was distorted, or hushed up. But we're not certain how it fits."

"How about this?" Maddy clicked the mouse, and the screen flickered. She had a look of concentration, engagement, on her face. "Here's a supposition: Hervey Leight is Charles's special little Head Boy, his mouthy muscle in the Commons or wherever. He's also linked to one of the few really powerful monied Catholic families in England at that point. That covers two of Charles's bases. Then said Head Boy fetches up in the Tower, not for politics but for beating his wife to death. Immediate impact is, Charles is going to take a serious hit to his credibility."

"So you think the big issue would have been quick coverage of any chinks in the King's armour?" Penny asked doubtfully. "Basically, he would have wanted to allow virtually no time for the uppity blokes with the bad haircuts and the boring grey clothes to start rabble-rousing?"

"That's my thinking—keep the Puritans quiet. Look, here's the official note on the arrest, entered into the Records for 1629. God, it's lively! How can people think history is dry? Listen to this:

> " 'Noted, on the twenty-eighth day of August, that the demeanour of our Chamber was much disturbed by the incursion of armed Representatives of his Most Sovereign Charles I, who did carry warrants in the name of our most puissant King, that called for the arrest and removal of the Speaker, Sir Hervey Leight. When confronted, the Speaker was observed to have foam upon his lips, after the manner of a dog, and he did scream and rage most long and unseemly, threatening all who would dare to lay hands upon him with violence most extreme. We were sore bewildered and gravely taken aback to learn that Sir Hervey had done to death his wife, the Lady Margaret, in a foul and most grisly usage. He was removed forthwith from the floor, being driven to seeming greater fury by the reading of the charge, with not even—' oh my." Maddy broke off suddenly, and then resumed reading aloud. " '—the King's own assurance, writ down for all to hear, that the Speaker's own son would be brought with speed from Hampshire to take his father's place, serving to calm him.' "

"Well, that answers that. So it's 28 August." Penny was thinking hard. "Out with Hervey the Lunatic Wife Killer, and in with Andrew, who was rather worse, although I doubt the King knew that. I expect Charles wasn't thrilled by the whole thing, but keeping it quiet wasn't on the menu, not when Hervey'd beaten the lady to death. Hervey doesn't go quietly, he raises a huge stink, and everyone's left buzzing like mad horseflies over it. Lord, Commons must have been like the court of the Medicis by close of business, you know? All that whispering! So the King counters it—how? He sends his pet clergyman off to Hampshire with orders to get there as fast as he can, and to bring Andrew back with him, no ifs, ands, or buts."

"Right. Leight *père,* Leight *fils*—the King was trying to quiet things down." Maddy opened another browser window. "What next? I have a choice of document listings here. Give me a direction, a road to follow, and we'll try that."

"How about the timing? Hervey was arrested on the twenty-eighth, and apparently Bishop Wolvesley headed south at light speed, because he got to Callowen by 1 September. And the murder, whatever actually happened, happened on the second." Penny shook her head. "I don't remember anything in that journal entry Jane found that clarified whether or not Wolvesley went to Callowen first and then on to rest at St. Giles with the Reverend Lockereigh, or whether he stopped at the rectory first. And it's important, isn't it? Or could be?"

"Why? What are you thinking?"

"Motive. Did the Bishop tell Andrew about his father killing his mother, or did something else happen?"

"Are you thinking that hearing what his papa had done, along with being ordered to pack up and prepare to come up to London and leave Callowen behind forever, sent Andrew off his head? That it was actually Andrew who committed murder, and not the outraged husband?"

"It would make sense, wouldn't it? But damn, this is so frustrating. We don't actually know what happened that day. We don't even know who got killed and who did the killing. And we don't know why it was so urgent for the truth to be hidden behind a pretty piece of music that's as false as a political ad during an election."

As Maddy opened her mouth to reply, Penny's phone suddenly vibrated. She murmured an apology, flipped it open, and listened for a moment. When she hung up, her face was chalky.

"That was Ringan. They've found a child's coffin, and they think it's got Matty Groves buried in it. He was buried in the Folly, close to Susanna, under a stone." She swallowed hard. "Maddy, Charlotte was right. Matty Groves wasn't Susanna's lover. He was just a little boy. And they buried him in with her."

"Then what actually happened at Callowen?" Maddy stared at her friend. "Whatever it was, we know Susanna died. We presume Matty Groves died. Why was he not given a proper burial, and why was he put in near Susanna? What happened to Andrew Leight, and why is he still there? And for heaven's sake, who killed who, and why?"

Twelve

*"Oh I can't get up, I won't get up
I can't get up for my life
For you have two long beaten swords
And I but a pocket knife."*

In St. Giles's sunny churchyard, Jane Castle was searching for graves.

She'd left Walter Hibbert ensconced in his rectory, looking with painstaking thoroughness through the church records. He was scanning every line for any clue as to what might have happened to the Gedlington line. They'd agreed that the division of labour—Walter indoors with a genealogy search, Jane amongst the neatly tended headstones in search of relevant names—made sense in every way.

Jane, feeling the warmth of the day on her bare arms, was conscious of mild guilt at being happily out of doors while poor Walter ground through decades of that tiny handwriting and archaic language. She pushed it away; this was efficient, after all. It cut the working time in half and anyway, Walter had suggested it himself . . .

She peered at a small, unpretentious marker, with streaks of churchyard moss at its base: *Susan Anne Hilton, born July 1806, died September 1806. Rest eternal in the loving arms of God.* Poor thing, Jane thought idly, lasting just long enough to be baptised and head off to those eternally loving arms.

She moved on. She'd begun by searching for Andrew Leight or Matty Groves; a few minutes into her hunt, she'd mentally added anything with the surname of Gedlington on it to her list. Of the first two, there had been no sign, and after Ringan's call to tell them about the find in the Folly, she'd crossed Matty Groves's name off the list. It didn't matter that the coffin bore no name; there was simply no one else it could be.

Jane reached the end of a row, and knuckled the small of her spine as best as she could reach. It was lovely to be outdoors, but her back was getting tired of the kneeling and straightening. Perhaps it was time to take a break from the sleepers in the ground and investigate some of the mausoleums.

The first was an unimposing building, decorated with two small but ornately carved cherubim. They flanked the heavy door, which seemed to made of the same dark sturdy oak as everything else in and around St. Giles. She stepped back for a better look, and read the name "*Gedlington,*" carved deep into the stone.

Luck, she thought. Luck at last. She grinned ruefully. Had she thought to ask Walter Hibbert or even Charlotte about the existence and location of a Gedlington family mausoleum, she could have saved herself some work.

The door was latched and locked. But the heavy iron flanges were nearly free of their moorings; years of neglect showed as the original screws holding the hasps in place had been pulled mostly loose by the weight of the heavy antique lock.

"Damn." Jane spoke aloud, and with feeling. She needed to get in; the door was locked. A swift pull would probably give her entry, but did she have any right to do that? The question was unavoidable. Generations of respect for the houses of the dead told her, no, she didn't. Yet she'd been given a mandate to find the Gedlingtons. And, well, here they were . . .

"Jane?"

She jumped. "Walter! I didn't hear you. Look, I've found some Gedlingtons. Have you found something? And I don't suppose you have a key to this thing, do you?"

"Nothing yet—I'm just having a break. I'm afraid I've got a bit mired in reading the bloke who replaced Lockereigh after the murder. He wasn't nearly so interesting as Lockereigh was. Not to worry. The key will either be round the side in a small covered pot, or else possibly in the pile in the rectory mudroom. Let's have a look."

He ducked around the side of the structure, and returned a moment later, holding a large iron key. "Ha! Here we are."

The inside of the Gedlington mausoleum was a shadowed affair of stone benches and simple coffins. The stone coffins, four of them, were spaced a few feet apart; on the shelves were six wooden boxes. The place was cool, and smelled dry and clean.

"It's peaceful in here, isn't it? Tranquil." On the face of it, Jane's words were absurd, but Walter nodded. The absence of human presence in this vault for so many years could be felt in the quiet, the lack of footprints, the sense of everything at rest.

Walter squinted at a plaque on one of the stone coffins. "Oh, look, here's someone from a bit further on down the road from poor Susanna: 'Peter Gedlington, born 1620, departed this life 1682.' It shows that the family was still about after Susanna died."

"The bit the Callowen archivist found, Roger Searle?" Jane said. "Penny mentioned it had to do with Susanna's mum weeping like a willow when the Callowen steward handed over her daughter's tats and bobs, about a month after the schemozzle. If Susanna was in her twenties, her mother might easily have been barely forty."

"If she remarried . . ." Hibbert broke off. "Right, let's see about saving ourselves some bending and peering. She was still Dame Gedlington when she took possession of Susanna's things. That was the autumn of 1629. I wonder if anyone's thought to put the records for the county—nothing mysterious, just marriages, births, vital statistics—into a nice database yet?"

Jane's eyes widened. "You mean, one phone call, hours and hours of messing about with ancient ledgers averted?" She fumbled for her phone and held it towards him. "Yes, please. Here, ring someone up, quickly. Who would know? Who do we ask?"

He laughed. "I'd imagine the county archivist for civil historical documents would be the person, and I'm betting Roger Searle will know who that is. In the meanwhile, let's finish up. We might find what we need right here."

Five minutes later, reading the name on the fourth and most recent stone coffin, Jane Castle exclaimed out loud.

"What is it?" Walter kept his voice pitched low, and made his way to her side. "What have you found?"

"A marriage, I think. At the very least, it's a connection, I know it is. Look: Elizabeth Mary Anderley Gedlington, died August 1703." She stared at the plaque, shaking her head. "Anderley—why does that sound so familiar? I've heard the name recently, and I can't place it."

"Anderley? Really?" Walter pursed his lips. "Now, that's a surprise. I didn't know they were connected with the Gedlingtons. We've had Anderleys until recently, good solid yeomanry—the last Anderley died just about a month ago. An elderly woman; I presided over her funeral. In fact, haven't you spent a night at Annie Whitlaw's? Jenny Anderley was Annie's grandmother. Jane, good heavens, what is it?"

Jane was swaying on her feet. A memory, sharp and clear, of voices in a charming bathroom with chintz curtains, male voices. She couldn't remember the words, only their urgency. And counterpointing that, Annie Whitlaw's voice as she welcomed her guest. What had she said? How she'd be hard-pressed to offer rooms to more than Jane because she only had three rooms and one of them was filled with her late Gram's effects . . .

"Walter," Jane said abruptly. "Listen. You know I heard those voices at Annie Whitlaw's, Lord Edward's voice and Matty Groves?" He nodded, and she took a deep breath. "Well, she's got a bunch of boxes of her grandmother's things, in the bedroom next to mine."

"Does she?" He sounded puzzled.

"You think there's a connection between those two facts?"

"It's possible surely?" Andrew kept calling her lowborn, and peasant scum. Suppose the Gedlingtons and Anderleys were connected by marriage?"

"You think Susanna's mother may have been born an Anderley?" He'd caught up with her, and was startled to find his own heart thumping. "You think that's what Andrew meant by lowborn?"

"Yes, I do. And if I was catching those echoes that strongly, just from there being some personal mementos in the next room—can we find out, about Susanna's family? I want to know, one way or the other, before I go back to Annie Whitlaw's and commit the un-speakable cheek of asking her to tear through her dead grand-mother's effects for something, anything, that might explain why I heard those voices when I was nowhere near Callowen."

"We can, yes." Walter was already at the door. "That much should just be a phone call or two. But I think we're going to find that you're right. Would you mind very much if I come along for this? For one thing, I think any request to deal with her grand-mother's papers would be best coming from me, or from Lord Cal-lowen. And for another thing"—he grinned at her suddenly, a genuine smile that held a touch of rue—"well, I'm curious. I want to be there and see what's what."

Walter's first phone call, to Roger Searle, was a productive one. He was able to tell them there was no database with births and deaths that far back. Having dashed their hopes for an easy resolu-tion, he then produced a name, Peter Dilley, and a phone number. Dilley, it seemed, was a friend of his at the County Archives in Winchester. He would, Searle assured them, be able to find the in-formation they needed without trouble.

He was quite right. Walter phoned, listened, waited, nodded, asked, waited again. Jane sat across the table, her hands clenched tightly in her lap. If she'd been wrong, if in fact there was no con-nection between Susanna and the Anderley family . . .

". . . yes." Walter set his pen down, and took a deep breath. "Thank you very much. This is exactly what we needed to know. Thanks so much. Cheers."

He hung up the phone, and stared at Jane.

"Jane Anderley, of Purbury," he told her. "Born 1583. A mar-riage was recorded in the summer of 1600, to Robert Gedlington, also of Purbury. He looked a bit further for me; there were two births and baptisms recorded for that union. A son, William, born in 1602, and a daughter, Susanna, born in 1604."

"Well." Jane got to her feet. Something was moving in her, a sense that things were nearing completion, finality, resolution. "Then I suppose we ought to go and impose on Annie Whitlaw's good nature."

"My grandmother's things? You want to see them?"

Annie Whitlaw's bewilderment showed plainly, in face and voice alike. She was also clearly off balance, which was probably due as much to the peculiar nature of the request as it was to finding her sitting room inhabited not only by the local clergy but by two members of the aristocracy, as well.

"If you please, Mrs. Whitlaw." Miles Leight-Arnold seemed somehow enormous, edging on overpowering, in the small room, with its over-stuffed chairs and its endless trinkets. "I wouldn't ask, but I doubt I could explain what we're looking for. Easier if we look ourselves. Take us up, will you?"

Annie Whitlaw opened her mouth, then shut it firmly on what she had, presumably, been about to say. Albert Wychsale hurried into speech.

"Of course, it's amazing cheek on our part, Mrs. Whitlaw. But it really is very important—honestly, Lord Callowen wouldn't dream of asking something so outrageous if it weren't of the first importance." He sent Miles a look. "Would you, Miles?"

"Of course not. But this—well. For one thing, if those papers are there, they're Leight-Arnold history, and would need to be put back where they belong." He finally noticed the conflicting emotions on Annie's face. "Ah. You've no clue what I'm on about, have you, Mrs. Whitlaw? We think you have a family connection with us."

"But—but—" Annie Whitlaw swallowed. Her voice was faint. "I really don't see—"

Jane touched her hand. "Your grandmother was an Anderley,

wasn't she? Well, the Lady Susanna—the poor young ghost up at
the house—it seems she was an Anderley as well. Susanna's mother
was born an Anderley, and she married into the Gedlington family.
And her daughter Susanna became Lady Leight-Arnold."

"But what does that have to do with my grandmother's things?
The Lady Susanna, she was hundreds of years ago, surely." Annie
was gaining some courage. "Lord Callowen, you said it was papers
you'd be looking to find?"

"Papers, yes. Cut very carefully from one of the Arnold family
journals, from the year 1629." Miles explained about Roger Searle,
and his discovery of the nineteenth-century mention of papers in
the Anderley family's possession. "So you see," he finished, "there's
a good chance those papers are up there."

"And it's urgent, Mrs. Whitlaw." There was no point, Jane
thought, in beating round the bush; as small as Purbury was, and as
central to the village's life as the manor house was, the story of the
cataclysm in the ballroom must surely have made the rounds by
now. "Things have been happening at Callowen," she said simply.
"A very nasty ghost, not the Lady Susanna. He—it—is damaging
people. We want to stop it, get rid of it. I wish I could tell you
more, I truly do, but I can't. We're trying to find out the truth,
that's all. The papers are likely to have the true story, if they're up
there. And really, there's a good reason to think they are, more than
one reason. So please, Mrs. Whitlaw, may we look?"

"Well, yes. Surely." Something in Jane's speech seemed to have
reassured her. "There's a good dozen cartons or so, and I've not yet
gone through any of them. They aren't marked, except by number,
to match the inventory from the solicitor, so I couldn't guess what's
where. But you're welcome to look for yourselves, of course." She
hesitated, then looked directly into Miles's face. "You'll take care,
My Lord, won't you? My Gram and me, we weren't close these last
years, but I'm all the kin she had, and she trusted me with what's
left."

"We'll be very careful." Miles, understanding, spoke with un-
wonted gentleness. "I promise. Don't worry."

The boxes, fourteen of them, were stacked in neat piles, varying in no particular order. There was also a trunk, roped shut, sitting beneath a small window framed by curtains that were the twin of those in the room Jane had slept in.

"I'll be downstairs if I'm wanted." Annie Whitlaw turned back at the door to survey the room, which between the boxes and the people, seemed overfull. "Gram was a careful woman," she remarked unexpectedly. "Very tidy-minded. I hope you find what you need."

She left the door open behind her. They listened to her footfall die away down the stairs.

"Sensible," Miles grunted. "Wish more people were. I'm thinking we save the trunk for last; if there's nothing in the boxes, we can take that on. We'll need to empty the things out, and we want to make damned sure what comes out goes back in its proper box. Let's get started."

They began with a box each, carefully lifting out the contents and setting them to their right-hand side. Jane, whose first box contained no paper but rather an assortment of vintage costume jewellery, as well as an exquisite and probably valuable painted chamois fan, found herself hoping that the search would bear early fruit. There was something almost unnerving about this sifting through the accumulation of someone else's memories. She touched the baubles with a gentle fingertip, envisioning a woman with Annie Whitlaw's face, slipping off to the nearest large town for an illicit evening at the local dance hall . . .

"I hope we find something soon." Albert Wychsale shifted his weight, and looked at the careful stack of postcards and letters, all obviously twentieth-century, beside him. "I feel like a ghoul. I'm done, and ready for another box."

"Take a breather. We'll keep it organised; all start together, all repack together. Works better that way." Miles watched Walter Hibbert effortlessly repack his carton. "Right, and Jane's done as well. Ready for the next lot?"

Jane slit the tape on her second carton, and prised open the covers. This box was only half full, and padded at the top, with towels worn soft with time and use. Probably china or crystal, she thought, although it seemed light for that. She pushed the layer of linen and toweling to one side, and reached inside.

Susanna oh sweet merciful Christ no, I'll kill you kill you

"Jane, what is it?" Albert was staring at her. "Something?"

You leave my lady be, take your hands away from her, no no no

"I—" She tried to speak, swallowed, tried again. Her hands rested lightly inside the box, touching a packet of some kind. "Voices. I can—Edward—I think I can hear—"

She began to tremble.

"Out you go, lady." Miles had moved before anyone else had time to even think. He stooped, got his good hand around her waist, and with no apology pushed her back and away from the box. "Out into the hallway."

"No. Wait a bit. I'm not in any danger, none at all." She breathed heavily. "Listen to me. I heard Edward, I know it was Edward. He said—he called her name, *Susanna.* And then something like, *oh Christ,* and then he said, *no, I'll kill you kill you.*"

She closed her eyes, bringing the second voice back to her mind. "And I think—someone else, trying to protect her. But not from Edward—how could it be from Edward?" She heard the anguished words in her head, fainter and less shocking than they had been that first afternoon in her bathroom across the hallway. The words looped and spiralled: *Susanna no I'll kill you kill you.* "I don't think Edward was talking to Susanna."

"One way to find out." Miles reached into the carton, and carefully pulled out a small bundle tied in silk. The fabric, which had once probably been a rich purple, was streaky and iridescent with age. "Let's see if we can convince Annie Whitlaw to trust us with this on more neutral ground than a cottage that's belonged to the Anderley family damned near forever."

Albert Wychsale, thankfully replacing his own unopened carton in its original place, looked surprised. "Is this cottage so old? It looks very late Victorian to me. I mean, I'm not an expert like Ringan, but still . . ."

"It is Victorian. But there's been Anderleys living on this bit of land for nearly as long as Purbury's been part of the Callowen holdings, and that goes back to Edward the Second, early fourteenth century or so. This is one in a series, this cottage. There's always been a house on this patch."

"Blood calling to blood." Jane spoke softly. "This is where the steward would have come, then—to deliver Susanna's things to her mother, after she was killed. Or no, wait, that's all wrong, isn't it? She'd married into the Gedlington family. She wouldn't have been living here. Where do the Gedlingtons live?"

"That entry, the one Roger Searle found." Miles brows jutted with furious concentration. "If I remember right, the steward said he brought them to her house in Purbury. The Gedlingtons didn't live anywhere near the town proper—they were landowners a few miles south of it."

"She came home." Jane felt the truth of what she was saying, a quiet certainty, beyond questioning. "Susanna's mother. When her daughter died so horribly, and everyone was talking—and perhaps the lie already going round the place like a virus, the lie that Susanna was a harlot—her mother came home to her own house, where she felt safe. She couldn't sit there, secluded out in the countryside, hearing bits and whispers, knowing that once the story spread that Susanna had been caught with another man, she couldn't stop the talk. So she went home. It was the only thing she could do, and stay sane."

She looked at the three silent men. Her eyes were luminous. No wonder, she thought. No wonder the sense of Susanna here is so strong; this is where her mother came, to deal with her own heart breaking. Maybe her only place of safety . . .

"Let's take that package to the rectory," Albert Wychsale said quietly. "If Mrs. Whitlaw will allow it, of course. I think Miles is right. It needs to be looked into on neutral ground."

The pile of papers, fragile and yellowed at the edges, lay in sunlight on the rectory's long table. Carefully folded to one side was a length of silk, its colour intact in some places, as streaky as a sun-bleached abalone in others. From one edge of the silk dangled the remnants of what once must have been a carefully knotted fringe.

The room was crowded with people. Yet it was quiet, the sounds of individual breathing clear in the warm air. There was something about that bit of silk shawl that brought the events of 1629 into the realm and the reality of now.

"Well." Ringan, the dust of his efforts against the Folly's stone floor showered away, stared at the array of history. There was a hot, troublesome place in his chest, where pity and sympathy and regret for something long past might be clustered. He was suddenly aware of how fiercely he was missing Penny, and spared a quick thought for her, working at the Library with Maddy Holt. "Who wants to do the honours? I'd be afraid to touch any of this, myself."

"Roger, I think. He's trained to understand the language, as it's written." Miles caught the archivist's eye. "Unless you'd rather not? I'll have a shot at it, if you want to pass. Understand this isn't easy on the eyes, and you've done most of this, so far. Want me to take it?"

"No, My Lord, I'll be glad to read—I'll confess, I'm quite curious about all this. This first pile looks awfully familiar, doesn't it?" Searle placed his chair, arranging himself for the best use of light, both artificial and natural. He then took the pile of papers in hand. His touch was light, steady, reverent. He looked at the uppermost sheet, and his eyes widened.

"Well, here's a surprise." He gently lifted the upper edges, scanning each page for the dates of the entries. "This first lot wasn't written by Lady Susanna. These are by the steward, Lord Edward's man. I recognise the handwriting. The first entry here is dated 1 September—it's from the day before the murder. Quite long, too, at least two pages."

"Our missing pages?" Miles was staring. "What in hell are they doing in a trunk in Annie Whitlaw's second best bedroom?"

"Oh, for heaven's sake, Da, don't be dim." Charlotte, seated with Julian at her shoulder, sounded cranky. "He hid them, of course. Gave them back to Susanna's mum—a perfect place to stow the stuff, really. I wonder if Edward told him to? After all, things were awfully tricky, weren't they? And remember, Roger read us that bit, about the Widow Anderley trying to sell this back to us about a hundred years ago, and our berk of an ancestor not wanting to part with the lolly. We'd have had all this sussed out days ago if Great-Great-Lord Whatsis hadn't been so mean about a few paltry quid." She shook her head. "Damn. I've got quite disillusioned with our ancestors these past few days."

"Read them, Roger, will you?" Miles thrummed his fingertips on the table, a sharp impatient tattoo. "Let's get this out in the open. Everyone sit down."

Albert and Julian, still on their feet, found chairs. Roger Searle slipped his palm under the first sheet, lifted it carefully aside from the rest, and began to read aloud.

1 September. I am today in some perturbation of mind, word having come from Purbury that the Reverend Lockereigh is playing unexpected host to a most august visitor, no less a personage than Bishop Wolvesley himself. While the nature of this visit is as yet unknown, I fear that this can portend no good for the house of Callowen, for it is clear that my lord had no notion of the Bishop's coming. Indeed, Lord Edward is, himself, most unpleasantly surprised. Having let fall the news in a most innocent manner, I was at first taken aback at the sudden blanching of Lord Edward's cheek, the fashion of his receiving it serving to show most clearly that he feared such secrecy, and what this might portend. Indeed, as I write, I find myself uneasy in spirit, for I have yet to learn of a visit of this kind that was made in such haste, and in disregard of all usual custom. I suspect grave matters of state weighing on this circumstance.

"Well, there's that question answered, anyway." Ringan sounded satisfied. "There was no advance warning sent to Callowen. Edward didn't have a clue, and whatever it was likely to be, he knew straight off he wasn't going to enjoy it. Grave matters of state? He wasn't wrong."

"No, he wasn't," Miles said grimly. "He was right to be worried; that sort of secrecy meant something big was up. Go on, Roger. What's the next bit?"

"Here's the second entry for that day." Searle's voice was steady and uninflected.

1 September. I am grown deep in my belief that some dark misfortune is set to fall upon Callowen. The morning's business taking me into Purbury, I chanced upon Peter Strough, whose business it is to procure provisions for St. Giles. No sooner did he lay eyes upon me than his entire visage assumed an aspect of secrecy, most unlike to that openness of countenance which, over the course of long dealing, I have come to expect of him. I raised a hand in greeting, and did offer him a smile. He said nothing to me that was distinguishable, and instead hunched his shoulders, his unwillingness to raise his eyes to mine writ clear, and hurried off. I am left with no other choice than to believe that Reverend Lockereigh, and the occupants of the rectory of St. Giles, have knowledge of whatever business has brought the Bishop to Purbury. Surely only a fear that I might press him for information would send so genial a man away in such unmannerly haste.

Searle stopped. "That's all for that entry, but he's got rather a lot more to say later that day, as a separate bit. It looks as though something may have happened farther on in the evening." He glanced down the page, and his eyebrows went up. "Oh, my. Yes, indeed. We're coming to the grist of it, I think."

Char bounced a bit in her chair. "Well, read it, then."

"Certainly." Searle cleared his throat.

My deepest forebodings, of disaster for this house which I serve, weigh heavily. His Grace, Bishop Wolvesley, has come, most unexpectedly and unattended, to meet with Lord Edward. My lord did summon me, that I might attend him at this conversation, in my capacity as his secretary; he was most firm in his instruction to me, that everything might be transcribed, with the most exquisite care and attention to completeness. It pains and disgusts me to write down the news the Bishop did share, that Andrew Leight's father rests in the Tower of London, put in that grim place for bringing about the death by violence of his lady wife. The Bishop has come, in silence and haste, at the order of His Majesty King Charles himself, for Sir Hervey Leight has with his arrest left empty a most important Speaker's seat in Parliament. The Bishop's demeanour spoke clearly what his words did not, that this may come hard on good Anglican supporters of the King, and on Catholics most heavily indeed. Those Puritans who number so many among this governing body have much mistrust, and many a true hatred, for the King's preferred men. This being so, it comes clear that this seat must not stay empty, but must indeed be filled in haste, with as little attention as these circumstances permit.

Searle paused. "There's more here. Might I get a glass of water, Reverend?"

"So, Charlotte was absolutely right." As Hibbert got to his feet to pour water, Albert looked at his goddaughter with respect. "Hervey Leight's arrest upset the balance between the Anglican factions in Parliament. Charles wanted that balance restored. And he wanted it done fast, and without a lot of fuss."

"He couldn't afford fuss." Charlotte had a strand of hair twined around one finger and was tugging it hard, seeming not to notice. "Not by that point. If my memory of school is at all accurate, he'd called a few sessions of Parliament and then dissolved them almost at once, because they did nothing but fight with him. They didn't like him, they didn't like his demands for money, they didn't like his assumption of royal privilege, and they really didn't like his spendy French Catholic queen."

"Wow." Jane looked fascinated. "With all that dislike, I'm surprised they waited for a civil war to bung his head off."

Charlotte ignored this. "The point is, Charles simply couldn't afford the aggro. Facing another forced dissolution, he'd have been snookered. He had no room left for manoeuvring."

"I want to hear the rest of it." Ringan glanced around the table. "Well, I can't be the only one, can I? Can we get the full story before we start saying what if and maybe?"

"Good idea." Miles nodded at Searle. "If you've had enough water, read the rest, Roger, will you? Ringan's right. Let's have the whole thing."

"Of course." Searle set his empty glass aside. "Here we go.

It is the King's belief that Andrew Leight, in name and countenance his father's son, would be best fitted to take Hervey's place in Parliament, and the Bishop did produce the royal order, with this demand so signed. At this provision, Lord Edward did evince some signs of relief. He expressed his satisfaction that this solution to His Majesty's problem would at one stroke provide resolution to Andrew Leight's dispossession of his longstanding blood claim to Callowen. This sinecure being given to Andrew will bestow upon him at once high rank, position, and honour."

Searle glanced around the room. Seven pairs of eyes were fixed on him. He set the page aside, and picked up the next.

The Bishop accepting an offer of refreshment, Lord Edward dispatched a servant, to find Andrew and bring him to this discussion concerning his future. Though I write this as one who should not, I freely confess my own relief, that Andrew Leight would soon be gone from our midst. There is something to the man that bespeaks a carping envy and dissatisfaction with his lot in life; perhaps this tale of the father's violence is less shocking to those who have acquaintance with the son.

"Oh, good grief." The exclamation was surprised out of Miles. "The steward, the local vicar—did everyone who wasn't Edward understand what a menace Andrew was? Sorry, go on, Roger."

Andrew having been brought into the presence of his cousin and Bishop Wolvesley, it fell to Lord Edward to inform his cousin of his mother's death, and of his father's arrest. Andrew showed no emotion at this news, but his seeming calm was belied by his unquiet hands, which clutched at air, again and again. We were all of us most taken aback, therefore, when, upon Bishop Wolvesley giving him to understand that King Charles had commanded his immediate presence in London, he suddenly lost all command over himself and seemed to go mad, screaming and raving most unpleasantly. All manner of filth and absurdity streamed from his lips, making a most horrid and clear picture of his resentment.

Jane, halfway down the table, was nodding to herself. It came as no surprise to her, that breakdown of Andrew's.

He swore that all were in league against him, that the House of Callowen was meant to be his, that Edward had married the Lady Susanna—whom he shockingly insulted, calling her a village whore, and a scut of low birth—for no reason better than that he might cut Andrew out of his rightful inheritance. He berated my lord with words, the substance of whose ugliness I would not put down here, but the worst of his distempered tirade was aimed at the Lady Susanna. Lord Edward, at first utterly at a loss, would not bear this slur upon his wife, and did in the heat of his anger lay hands upon his cousin, striking him a hard blow across the face.

For Ringan, his eyes closed and his vision turned inward, the events in Lord Edward's study came acid-etched in their clarity. Andrew, his unmatched eyes first narrowing as he fought to conceal his feelings, then bulging as those feelings consumed him. And Edward, his eyes opened at last to the darkness and madness that had been infecting his house, knowing that the Leights, father and son, had by their actions brought trouble to the Leight-Arnold line that might well be past mending.

Roger Searle, even-voiced and clear, read on.

At this display of fury from his cousin, Andrew went so still as might a viper, poising to strike at its prey. He then turned on his heel and stumbled from the room, saying no other word, leaving behind him a deep silence. Lord Edward, seeming of a moment to suddenly grow much older, told the Bishop that he and the King were most welcome to Andrew, and that he had little understood what a poison he had harboured under his roof. It was settled between them, that Bishop Wolvesley will return to Callowen on the morrow, to take up Andrew in his entourage. The Bishop then took his leave, and Lord Edward bade me describe these events, while they remained fresh in my memory. As I came away, Lord Edward did summon young Matty Groves, my lady's page, to see how she did.

Searle stopped, and looked up. "That's all for that evening. Do you want me to read the next day's events?"

"For heaven's sake!" Char spoke before her father could open his mouth. "We've agreed we can't pitch Andrew out without knowing what actually happened, and why. So why are we messing about, holding back and asking silly questions? Read it. Then we'll know, and out he goes."

Searle, as if in the grip of some odd form of reluctance or reticence, looked mutely at Charlotte's father. The nod he received was a clear command to continue.

He took up the remaining pages, and began to read the steward's account of the events of 2 September 1629.

Penny, behind the wheel of Ringan's elderly Alfa Romeo, left London for Hampshire right after breakfast.

She was short on sleep, not enough to impair her driving, yet enough so that her mind, crammed full of information from a long night at the Library, wandered and bucked. Random facts from the archives that Madeleine Holt had found weaved in and out of her brain, maddeningly refusing to connect.

She owed Maddy, Penny thought. Everyone involved in this mess owed Maddy, in fact; she'd stayed with Maddy in her office until after three, reading the parliamentary records, the individual notes, piecing together and trying to understand the after-shocks of Sir Hervey Leight's crime. Maddy, that consummate researcher, had been slow, patient, meticulous. Every record had been checked, and every reference cross-checked. Penny, tired and impatient, felt a kind of awe at Maddy's unflappable thoroughness. No thread of evidence, it seemed, was small or insignificant enough to ignore. In Maddy's eyes, every written word, every opinion, every possible fact, merited a second look. And if that meant staying at it until sunrise, then stay they would.

And, in fact, they had—or close to it. They'd ordered curry for takeout, allowed themselves a short dinner break, and then gone back to it. The small stack of printouts on the Alfa's passenger seat, each page enhanced with notes in Maddy's elegant handwriting, was the fruit of a long, hard night of work.

"... the primary seat of speaker for the King's Party being empty, the Opposition speaker of commons, the Puritan John Howell, did stand and speak, most insinuatingly, of His Majesty's weakness of choice, hinting at his poor judgement. ..."

Penny took the A3, heading towards the south-west, driving well within the posted limits. Normally, three in the morning would have been no problem; late nights are an unavoidable part of life in the theatre. But the past week had been wracking—mentally, emotionally, physically—and she was suddenly aware of just how drained she was. Four hours' sleep was not enough today.

Maddy had been amazing. With only Penny's story to go by, she'd found the kind of things that Penny herself would never have thought to look for, the hidden gems and tantalising nuggets of information buried deep in the official records. They'd had some luck; the Official Registrar for the House of Commons in the year 1629 had been a chatty bloke, unable or unwilling to keep his own perspective away from the official archives he was supposed to be recording. His voice, his opinions, kept sliding through the drone of the bureaucracy he'd recorded.

"... this speech a great furore did provoke, those members of the commons loyal to the King's Party standing as one, shouting down John Howell, calling his words and demeanour an insult ..."

Water spattered the Alfa's windscreen, startling Penny. Away towards the south coast, the huge puffy clouds of summer had taken on the purple tint of storm and rain. There was water in the air; she could smell it, moving to the north-east from the Channel.

Penny rolled up her window. She was still a solid distance from Purbury, and bad weather would slow her down even further. There was also the fact that she had no idea where to make for. Calls to both Jane's and Charlotte's phones had resulted in voice-mail requests for a message; a call to Callowen House had produced an unforthcoming secretary, informing her that Lord Callowen was unavailable. So far, no one had called her back. She decided that her most sensible move would be to head for St. Giles and the rectory. If they weren't there, Walter's housekeeper would be able to tell her where to find them.

"... there is much whispering in chambers today, much dropping of voices and sudden pauses in conversation. A most ugly rumour has spread through the House, that Sir Hervey Leight has of a sudden fallen ill at the Tower of London. There is talk of sweating sickness, that mysterious flux of the bowel, that was in times past the merest euphemism for some deadly serum, served in food or drink to those for whom an early and quiet death

would benefit the Crown. Should Sir Hervey Leight fall prey to this, there
are many amongst the Puritans who would not hesitate to brand our King
a murderer, so hot is their venom and so deep their dislike. . . ."

Thunder, a long rolling explosion of sound, took Penny's full attention. The clouds to her left were now recognisably thunderheads. In the distance and growing ever closer, she could see straight sheets of torrential rain needling sideways into the countryside.

"Right." She spoke aloud, wincing at the electricity in the air; her skin was tingling with it. "That's it, then. Time to find a nice dry pub."

She took the next exit, following a roundabout that split into several country lanes, peering through the rain at the road signs: Chithurst, Iping, Trotton. She was still in West Sussex, albeit close to the Hampshire border.

The first place she came to was called Barleydown, a tiny picture-book village, the centre of which was a short High Street and an exquisite old church, of the kind often found in small villages. Penny saw a wonderful pub sign—the John Barleycorn, the swinging board exquisitely painted with a sheaf of wheat spouting a man's head—and heaved a sigh of relief. There would be beer here, and with any luck at all, a reasonable untarted-up lunch. A country pub was the perfect place to gather her thoughts, wait out the torrential drenching that was surely on the way, and perhaps doze a bit. She gathered the papers, stuffed them into her purse, and sprinted for cover.

The pub did not let her down. Provided with a massive helping of steak and kidney pie, a half-pint of local beer, and some hot crusty bread, Penny settled into a comfortable corner booth. The rain was coming down in sheets now; through the running rivulets of water streaming down the exterior of the mullioned windows, Penny saw the High Street empty as the villagers sought shelter indoors. The air became static and talkative, the wooden pub sign swinging wildly and lit by flashes of lightning.

Penny took a long swallow of beer, sighed with contentment, and closed her eyes. Maddy's findings, while containing nothing startling, nevertheless had provided a satisfying confirmation of what they'd already suspected: the political aspect, the danger King Charles had seen as the consequence of his favourite's appalling crime, the sending of Wolvesley into Hampshire within hours of the news breaking. What was new to Penny was the level, and urgency, of mutual loathing between Puritan and Anglican. If this nameless gossipy chronicler was to be believed, the Puritans had jumped on Hervey Leight's arrest as a perfect weapon against the King they despised. Hindsight, Penny thought, was a very useful thing; the social and religious blister that was the English Civil War had broken in 1642, a scant thirteen years after King Charles had sent his pet bishop off on a damage control mission.

Penny brought her plate back up to the bar. It had occurred to her that the pub, following licensing hours, might be closing shortly. The publican waved her back to her booth; apparently, she had a good hour in which she could snooze peacefully, before having to worry about closing until evening. Penny thanked him gratefully and went back. The pub was nearly empty, and she was alone in her corner by the bay windows. Thankfully, she leaned her head against the back of the upholstered booth, closed her eyes, and drifted off to sleep.

The imperative shrilling of her phone woke her out of a peaceful doze. She fumbled it open.

"Hello?"

"Penny?" Ringan's voice was taut, thrumming with an undertone of excitement. The Scots accent was very pronounced. "Thank goodness, lamb, there you are. Where are you? How far from Callowen? Is it storming where you are?"

"Halfway to dreamland, that's where. Give me half a moment to wake up, will you?" She rubbed her eyes and gulped the dregs of her beer. "Right. Sorry. Maddy and I were at the Library until nearly four this morning, and I'm tapped out. I'm in a pub in a tiny little village—Barleydown, it's called—probably an hour or so away from you. Maybe more, actually, considering this weather, because yes, it's soaking outside. I was going to let the weather lighten a bit and then head down. Are you at Callowen?"

"No, the rectory. Listen, lamb, things have been happening." He rapidly filled her in on what she'd missed while in London: discovery of Susanna's lineage, the tracking down of the missing register pages to Annie Whitlaw's bed and breakfast, the full story of the murder.

"What!" Penny was well and truly awake now. "You found an actual account?"

"We certainly did." Ringan sounded grim. "My God, Andrew Leight was a weed. I'm more interested in what he is now, and how we're going to get rid of him. Charlotte seems to have some notions in her head. So, if you'd hurry down—"

"But I want to know what happened!" Penny almost wailed. "Damn it, Ringan, don't be such a tease!"

"I'm not, Pen, I swear. But I can't read it to you over the phone, can I? For one thing, the account is two pages of that tiny spidery handwriting. Besides, Miles Leight-Arnold is not letting it out of his sight—I think he's mentally filing it under 'Family Treasures Reclaimed.' And by the way, there's still something missing, nearly a week's worth of entries. The last page of the eyewitness account—it's had a bit torn off at the bottom. But you need to read what there is."

"You're damned right I do." Penny was on her feet. "Right, look, I'm taking off now. For heaven's sake, promise me something. Promise you won't go near Callowen, or try to do anything about Andrew Leight, until I've got back and read that register entry."

"I promise. And Penny? Drive carefully, sweetheart."

Two hours later, having forced herself to drive sensibly in as torrential a downpour as she had seen in years, Penny had finished a cup of hot tea, rubbed her hair dry with one of the rectory's soft worn towels, and read the account of the events of 2 September 1629, as set down for posterity by Lord Edward's nameless steward.

Thirteen

So Matty struck the very first blow
And he hurt Lord Arnold sore
Lord Arnold struck the very next blow
And Matty struck no more

3 September—It is with the deepest of grief and pain that I must transcribe the events of yesterday. Though it is anathema to me, to write such words as must scald, as do my tears, the very pages beneath my hand, yet such is my duty to this broken House. There is no other to set down this account, for Lord Edward is blinded by his sorrow, and crushed beneath the vast weight of his despair, and no one else who took part in yesterday's horror lives to speak of it. Therefore must I set aside my own feelings, and so perform my duty to my lord.

The bare fact must come first, for in the eyes of God, this simple fact is all the story: the Lady Susanna is dead, and her young page Matthew Groves and Andrew Leight with her. All of this did I myself witness. I will take with me to eternity the events of yesterday; my own inability to lift one hand in aid or prevention will serve as scourge and sorrow, without surcease.

The weight of grief is added to a hundredfold by the very irony of happiness that underlay the situation. Two nights past, after the confrontation amongst Lord Edward, Andrew Leight, and the Bishop, I did show the Bishop away, setting him on the road to St. Giles, and bidding him Godspeed, that we might see him safe on the morrow.

As I made my way back to my own quarters, passing close by the opened windows, I chanced to overhear Lord Edward having speech with his lady, telling her all of what was said, praying that she might forgive him for thus leaving her in proximity to such a one as Andrew. He spoke, simply yet with deep feeling, of his fear, that Andrew might have done her harm. She, in her sweetness of character, did assure him that she had taken no hurt of Andrew, and bade her lord not worry himself. Remembering those times when I myself had seen marks upon the lady's wrists, I understood that she would wish Edward to know nothing of Andrew's ill-treatment of her. So strongly did outrage at Andrew's escape of earthly judgement for his behaviour well up in me, I was most hard-pressed not to speak the truth on her behalf. Yet I refrained, knowing that on the morrow, Andrew would be forever gone from our company, and we should never again be compelled to suffer his poisonous presence at Callowen.

Yesterday morning dawned fair and bright, with no sense of foreboding to overshadow what lay in wait for us. My lord and lady, having partaken of breakfast together, rode out, as was their wont, Lord Edward having given me to understand that he would return before the noon hour, when Bishop Wolvesley had said he would return, to take Andrew Leight up in his train.

The noon hour had not yet struck when, as I crossed the south Lawn, I did espy them returning. My lady was perched atop Lord Edward's horse, while my lord led the lady's grey mare, who, having stumbled, had come up limping. Lord Edward led the mare off to the stables, to superintend her care, whilst my lady, who professed herself unharmed in any way, took herself off to her favourite seat, in the hedged rose garden on the western lawn. As she went, she asked me, most sweetly, if I would summon her page to her presence, as she had errands she wished him to run. I assented, and went to the House, in search of Matty Groves.

I could not know that I was never to speak with her again. I would surely not have believed such a thing, not with the sun shining down, and Andrew Leight set to leave us forever. A sunset after the events of yesterday morning, I still can find no way to believe or accept the suddenness of disaster.

I found young Matty in the kitchen, waiting on his mistress's pleasure. As I sent him on his way, I enquired, most casually, whether Andrew Leight had requested help in his packing, to expedite his trip to London. No servant had knowledge of such a request, and I found myself unexpectedly uneasy at this, and in a worry, for surely Andrew understood that his departure for London was imminent, and not subject to discussion? I determined to first make certain that Andrew Leight was prepared, and, if he was not, to broach the matter to Lord Edward with all haste.

Having set my knuckles against Andrew's door, and having received no response, I ventured to open the door, calling him as I did so. Upon entrance, it became clear at once Andrew, unless he planned to leave all his possessions behind, had in no way accepted that he could not remain at Callowen. His chamber remained as it ever was; even those articles he used for his morning toilette lay undisturbed upon his dressing-table. My sense of fret growing, I at once decided that Lord Edward should know of this, for Bishop Wolvesley was expected within the hour.

As I came out of the west wing doors, I heard a confusion of sounds coming from behind the high hedges that form the boundaries of the Lady Susanna's favourite spot. These sounds did for the moment root me to the ground, despite their lack of clarity, for I heard a sickening susurration of breath, as if being forced through a space too small to allow it passage, laced with a piteous whimpering. I heard, too, a grunting, both pleasurable and animal; for a most horrid moment, my mind's eye did perceive a picture, of a ravening beast as it ripped the life from its helpless prey.

The events which followed seem, even at this close a remove, to have happened during some period in which time ceased its normal rotation. All was dreadfully slow, and yet unnaturally quick. I find that my hands are shaking, and yet I must not stop, if I am to set these things down while they remain fresh in my memory.

From where I stood motionless on the bottom stair, I saw the stable doors swing wide, from which emerged Lord Edward and Matty Groves. They ran, as fast as they might go, towards the rose garden, my lord shouting incoherently as he went. Young Matty, as was natural for a lad so young and healthy, speedily outstripped my lord. The paralysis of limb which had overtaken me having passed, I ran as well, a terrible sense of foreboding riding the wind at my back.

I reached the charming curve of hedge nearest to me, in time to see Matty throwing himself at Andrew Leight. The horror of what I saw, imprinting itself upon my heart and memory, will be a chilly companion to dreams, forever after.

My Lady Susanna, her tongue protruding from blue lips, dangled limp as an old cushion from Andrew Leight's merciless grip. His hands were closed hard round her throat, choking her, stifling her. I heard him speak, in a voice more like to that of a hungry wolf than to a man; his words were jumbled and unclear, the stuff of nightmare.

Young Matty, defending his mistress, pulled most desperately at Andrew's hands, shouting all the while for Lord Edward, and screaming that Andrew must not hurt his mistress. I saw Andrew's arm flash out, and saw the edge of his hand catch young Matty a brutal blow across the throat. It was the work of an instant, and Matty sagged, and he fell, and I saw the glaze of death settle across his face.

I started forward then, but was brushed aside as if I were no more than a fly. Lord Edward came past me, the light sword he always wears out and ready in his hand. As he came up on Andrew and the Lady Susanna, Andrew released the lady from his other hand, and let her fall, insensible, to the ground.

I heard them speak to each other, if such ugliness can be called speech between men. Andrew Leight, his face livid and unrecognisable, his lips drawn back, foam at the corners of his mouth, giving him the look of Satan's own Hound of Hell. My Lord Edward, his own visage curiously blank, as if he understood what was about to happen, the crumbling of his world.

I heard words, the most vile words, pour from Andrew Leight's lips. Though I stood apart, they are branded into me.

"You filthy Catholic scum," he spoke, into Lord Edward's face, close to his own. *"You with your fine silks and your hawks and your hounds, you with all your privilege, you should have burned, all of you, this is mine, it should have been for me, 'twas meant for me."*

I saw the Lady Susanna, immobile at Andrew's feet. I saw one eyelid flutter, and I knew in that moment that some spark of life was left in her. I believe I called out; I am certain I made a move towards her, thinking, hoping, that I might yet revive her.

Lord Edward, too, saw that movement. As he made to thrust Andrew from his path, Andrew spoke again, vile words, dark in their import.

"All this time, having to mind myself, saying aye, surely Edward, and nay Edward, all this time and you knew nothing you sorry fool of a heretic, you can't do any harm to me, you'll not touch me for it, mine, your lady, your sons, your land . . ."

And here it was that something most extraordinary did happen, for the Lady Susanna, her half-opened eyes fixed on Andrew Leight and with the marks of his brutality livid at her throat, gave vent to laughter. It was the briefest of sounds, and yet it was unmistakeable. Something passed over her face, a mere flutter of muscle. Contempt, scorn, I know not what else it might have been. But it stopped Andrew in full spate.

Lord Edward lifted his sword. The passage of time was most unnaturally slow, so slow that a man might not measure it by earthly time. He brought his weapon down, slicing deep and sure in that vital spot where neck meets shoulder, killing Andrew where he stood. I wish I had not seen, and wish I might banish from my dreams, the memory of Andrew's face as he fell, for even in death, his mouth retained a vestige of a most hellish triumph, mixed with rage and hate.

But this thought haunts me, and will never leave me in this life, no, nor in any other, that as Edward killed his cousin, I saw the last of Lady Susanna's life flicker out, and her soul depart from her.

There is more to tell, and I will tell it; this is my duty to my lord, and to his sons, and highest of all, to the memory of their sweet mother. But tonight I find my hands are wont to shake, as would an old man with a fever, and my eyes blur. All else must wait until tomorrow.

"What are we going to do?"

"What? Sorry, love." Ringan, his capacity for paying attention shredded by bone-deep exhaustion, jerked his head towards Penny, who'd set the register page aside and was looking worried. The big windows at St. Giles's Rectory were streaked with storm-blown pollen; there was something fascinating about it, Ringan thought, all those tiny smears and sticky-looking bits in odd, earthy colours . . .

"Good question." Jane drummed her fingertips in a light, easy rhythm on the tabletop. "If anyone's got a clue what we ought to do next, I'd love to hear it. Because, personally, I'm stumped. Miles wants Andrew out of his house. We all want Andrew elsewhere, in fact, but it seems to me that our song is useless. Not a word of it is true. So how in sweet hell are we supposed to get rid of him? What weapons have we got?"

"And let's not forget that Char's terrifying Papa has threatened us with immediate retribution if we dump Lady Susanna's ghost in the process. I'd say that muddies the waters." Julian rubbed his eyes; his beautiful voice was roughened, a bit ragged around the edges.

They were all tired, Ringan thought. Exhaustion was no friend to clear thinking. "Look," he said slowly. "Let's put a bit of concentration into this, yes? On the one hand, we won't have any trouble getting Andrew to, um, show up. All we seem to need for that is either Jane or Penny walking into a room at Callowen. On the other hand, the song about him is going to be no help at all. The way we got rid of ghosts, the other times we've had to do it, it simply won't fly. Jane and I can arrange the damned thing into nine sections for the London Symphony and three groups of madrigal singers, and Andrew won't do anything more than laugh in our faces. So what do we do?"

"Hang on a minute." Penny's voice suddenly sharpened. "What you just said, about him laughing in our faces—there was the bit the steward wrote, about how she laughed at Andrew just before she died, and how it paralysed him, enough so that Edward could kill him. And there's something else." Her eyes were blazing. "Ringan, listen. When he went through you, and you—he—was about a millisecond away from killing me, I laughed at him. Remember? And he went. He faded out. And I told you, I thought he couldn't deal with being laughed at." She looked at Ringan, and spoke urgently. "I know you don't want to take a trip down that particular bit of memory lane, but it's important. I know it is. Do you remember that?"

Ringan was quiet. He had spent the previous week doing his level best to forget the events of that horrible evening. His reluctance to revisit it, even at this safe remove, was tangible. Yet Jane was right; the song itself was useless as a tool for exorcism. And if Penny was correct, if the bare notion of being laughed at was enough to drive off Andrew Leight or even weaken him enough to tackle him, then every bit of information they could lay hands on was vital.

He focussed his memory, forcing himself to go back. The charming, luxurious bedroom at Callowen. Penny, in her chic black silk. Something, just as they came to the door of the room, something, something—how had it happened?

It was there suddenly, the full memory he'd been thrusting away from him, vivid and potent in its horror. The need, the rage, the hate, the ravening hunger that had been Andrew Leight had slid into him like a fine mist. He remembered it now, a strange surreal moment, his sense of identity pushed roughly into some small corner of his own existence as something hideous looked through his eyes, looking at Penny, seeing—

"Ringan?"

What had he seen? What had that Other in him, that intruder with its black evil reek and ravening, insatiable hunger, wanted? He had seen Penny, but blurred, smaller, not the woman he knew. He had hit her—he had always wanted to hit her, trash from the village, completely unworthy. Aye, he'd hit her for trying to resist him. Stupid worthless little fool, resisting him; he'd teach her to mind him, show her who was master, and it wasn't Edward, for sure and certain not. He, Andrew, would show the lady of the house who she had to obey.

Edward wouldn't know, of course, it was shame and sorrow that Edward would never know, but that was fine, it was a fine thing, because power that was secret was still power, wasn't it? And every bruise he left on the scut from Purbury was a bruise on Edward, every time he forced his body to hers was a victory and another blow against Edward, but she was laughing at him, *at him,* the miserable worthless little girl, he could feel his pride and his manhood alike shrinking away to nothing, scorn, she was scorning him, weakening him—

"Ringan!"

He jerked his head, feeling the memory roll out of him and away. For a moment he was still, his stomach in an uproar, the lingering sense of guilt and self-blame that he'd been pushing down into himself since the night it happened as devouring as Andrew's hunger and hate had been.

Then it was gone, gone for good, and he was himself again, and free of it. The memory had been looked at, faced squarely; no matter what might happen, Andrew Leight could never touch him or use him again. He turned to face Penny, his eyes wet, and knew she understood what he'd just gone through.

"You wanted to know if your laughter was what stopped him. The answer is yes—he shrivelled like paper in fire." Suddenly energised, Ringan got to his feet and began pacing. "Right. I call that a weapon. So, your basic idea is that we all scoot on up to Callowen, get Miles to kick out the non-essential personnel in case of fireworks, hang around until Andrew starts growling and snarling, and then begin laughing like drains? Or—what?"

"I don't know," Penny said slowly.

Julian turned to stare at her. "You know, I don't want to sound too blighting, and I certainly don't want to sound judgemental, but honestly, this isn't very encouraging. You don't know? I thought you two were the experts?"

"We're not experts, damn it!" Ringan snapped. "We're a few people who've got unlucky. I don't know why this keeps happening to us. And honestly, I think I can safely speak for both myself and Penny when I say we're sick and tired of it."

"The problem is, Julian, this is new. This situation, I mean." Penny was working it out in her mind as she spoke. "The first time, at Ringan's cottage, we had a pair of lovers who were caught. They weren't threatening, they didn't mean anyone any harm, they were just sort of caught, stuck in place and stuck in time. They—I don't know if they wanted to go, but they certainly didn't put up any sort of fuss about it. And after Christmas, in my theatre, yes, she was a bit of a nutter and dangerous, but all she wanted was absolution, really, and we got her a priest, he did his thing, and off she went. Both times, we could use music to get rid of them, or at least to get them into the picture. But this? It's uncharted territory. This one's as bad as they come. And the song is going to be meaningless to him, and that means it's probably going to be useless to us. So we'll have to bodge something up instead."

"Laughter," Charlotte said. Her voice was dreamy. "Not a 'ha-ha, how awfully funny' laughter, though. More of a 'ha-ha, you worthless bastard, you're a big joke and no one's got time for you' laughter. You know? The kind you get with hate."

They all turned to stare at her. Albert Wychsale, in his chair beside her, seemed to know where she was going. He was nodding gently.

"A sort of concentrated malice, really deep, really nasty," Charlotte went on. " 'La la la, Andrew, you're worthless and useless.' What Ringan said, about laughing like drains? That's right, it's really right, only it has to be a huge, mean, public school sort of laughing. We all come at him together, one big group of concerned parties, and we simply point and snicker and say rude things. And it has to be genuine. We all have to feel it. No faking."

"At which point," Ringan said drily, "Andrew Leight probably goes berserk. Any idea what we do then?"

"Then we keep laughing." Penny's face was alight with understanding. "We laugh him straight out of Callowen House. We follow him out if we have to, and we keep laughing. We—we *decimate* him with laughter. We shred him with it. We make sure that the last thing he ever hears is the last sound he heard in life. We stand there and we despise him right into nothingness, because nothingness is where he damned well belongs."

"Penny's right." Jane broke in eagerly. "Scorn. Derision. We beat him back to the gates of Hell, and we do it with contempt. He can't stand that; what happened with Penny and Ringan shows that he can't stand it dead. He couldn't stand it alive either, apparently—it led to his death. If Susanna hadn't laughed at him, would he have weakened and been taken off guard enough for Edward to kill him?"

"One question, though." Ringan looked at Charlotte. "Your scary parent has basically threatened us with ruin and damnation and seven flavours of professional hellfire if we accidentally exorcise Susanna in the process. So—"

"Susanna isn't going anywhere." The certainty in Charlotte's voice was absolute. "Don't worry. Let's just concentrate on getting rid of Andrew Leight."

Every available light in the ballroom at Callowen House had been turned on.

The glaziers had done their job; the hundreds of broken panes, shattered the night of Julian's recital, had been replaced. The new glass was getting quite a workout; the sun had near sunk below the yardarm, the last of its rays glancing off the French doors in a dance of spectacular red, as the overheads, both chandelier and spots, pooled their collective energy against the interior of the doors.

"I think we'll want these propped open."

Miles Leight-Arnold, with Roger Searle at his side, was sweating. He was worried, visibly so, and that fact alone was more than enough to worry the rest of those gathered in the ballroom with him. The fearsome Lord Callowen was not a man one could easily associate with jangled nerves.

"Yes, could we?" At least Charlotte sounded much as she usually did, Ringan thought. "Far too warm, really, with them shut."

"I was thinking more about broken glass," Miles said curtly. He saw the quick, worried look his old friend Albert threw at him, and flushed. "Look, no point in trying to pretty it up. This is likely to be one hell of a mess. Dangerous, too. I'd rather not get carved up like a Christmas roast. In fact, the more I think about it, the more I think you ought to go, Roger. No reason to put yourself in harm's way."

"Thank you, My Lord, but I'd rather stay." The archivist was his usual placid self. "After all, my job is the Leight-Arnold family history. This looks to provide me with the sort of opportunity that most historians wouldn't even believe."

"Might get you killed," Miles said bluntly. "But you're a grown man. If you want to stay, I'll count us lucky to have you."

"Lord Callowen, do we need doorstops?" Julian had headed towards the far wall. "I'd rather the doors were secured, one way or another. But I doubt they'll stay open on their own."

"Don't need doorstops. There's a row of eye-bolts along the outside, one per door, fairly high up; they hook open."

They got all two dozen doors fastened, letting the night air into the room in a clean, easy rush. Behind them, the outline of Callowen House, stately and lovely, had somehow transformed itself into a dark, threatening hulk, looming over them.

"Do you know, I've never seen the house dark." Albert shivered suddenly. "It's easy to underestimate its size, isn't it, Miles? It looks enormous."

"I sent all the servants off for the night." Miles looked around the ballroom, noting its emptiness; the tables and chairs had, at his order, been carried out and stored elsewhere in the house, earlier in the day. His reasoning was simple, and a cold reminder of what might happen: there was no point in giving Andrew Leight any ammunition at all.

"We're ready, I think." Ringan's voice was very quiet. "I just want to say, I hate this. I don't want Penny within ten miles of this house; I don't much want Jane in here, either. But if we're going to do it, then let's get on with it."

Albert, catching Callowen's nod, hurried out of doors, disappearing into the deepening shadows, and off towards the stables. He came back with Jane and Penny trailing behind him.

They all felt the difference the moment the two women walked through the doors: a thickening, a cold impossible density, moving like an invisible ground mist, climbing higher, making it hard to breathe, hard to swallow . . .

"Damn." Julian gulped down on the word, and moved up next to Charlotte. "*Damn.*"

The lights seemed dimmer suddenly, insufficient; somehow, the bright rows of bulbs were losing their ability to keep the long shadows at bay. Ringan, his jaw hard and grim, went straight to Penny, and put his arm around her waist.

"All right?" he asked, and she nodded. Her storm-grey eyes were enormous.

"He's nearby." Jane, her hands clawed against shaking, came up beside them. Her voice was a rasp of dread. "I can feel him."

The lights flickered, oddly, in a sequence, the stage spots fading west to east, then coming up again. Something moved, shadow, or perhaps it was only the sudden drop in temperature. The summer had gone out of the room, out of the night, out of the world, and it was cold, it was freezing . . .

Tricks, Ringan thought, he's using tricks, to weaken us. And the bugger's succeeding, too.

"Andrew!"

It was Charlotte. Her voice rang out, amused, scornful, commanding. "Andrew! Come here, *boy*!"

The hush that followed was dreadful. There was no doubt that Andrew Leight, whatever he had become, was present. There was a pulse, audible to everyone: a deep, slow breathing.

"Come here, you! I have errands for you to run."

Ringan's head moved, slowly and painfully, until he could see Charlotte. There was something peculiar about her voice; he tried to pinpoint where the difference lay, but it was no use.

Around them, the pulsing grew louder, more shallow, a rapid predatory panting, the voice of some unspeakable beast slavering after its prey.

"Stop that noise at once, you impertinent scum!" Char's voice was a bolt of contempt, of power, the dominance of privilege. "What, are you deaf, then? I've orders to give you. Don't keep me waiting, unless you fancy being turned out."

"Female," Penny said incomprehensibly, and Ringan stared at her. He saw Jane, her teeth chattering, begin to grin, and remembered, suddenly, what their only weapons were. Surprise: well, they had that, all right. Whatever Charlotte was doing, it had surprised Andrew Leight, and the rest of them as well. And laughter. Contempt, disdain.

He threw his head back suddenly, finding his own voice, shouting: "Oi! Andrew! Andrew Leight! How d'ye enjoy knowing you'll never have Callowen? Hey? How do you like that? No inheritance for you!"

He laughed. He was remembering what Andrew had done to Penny, using him, what he had done to Jane. Rapist, murderer . . .

"You filthy penniless scum!" Ringan shouted, and heard Jane laughing behind him.

The bulbs began to go, popping like firecrackers, one after another. The main chandelier was swinging wildly, its dozens of hand-blown crystals shattering, spraying the ballroom floor with rainbow dust.

"Like father, like son!" Miles bellowed. "Useless, greedy, stupid little heretics. You're no kin of ours—you never were. You had nothing here, lad, do you understand that? Not a damned thing. Your name isn't even remembered; you're just a servant."

He began to rumble with laughter. Forced at first, it eased into something more real, as if Miles had somehow manifested the contempt he felt into the paralysing sound they needed. "Servant," he yelled, and laughed again. "Servant."

You lie. You filthy Catholic scum. You lie!

It came from the ceiling, from the alcoves, from the star speckled lawn outside: Andrew's voice, raging, yet weak. They could feel his confusion; they could sense the enormous will it took for him to exist at all in the face of their contempt.

And suddenly, high and clear, Jane sang. " '*A grave, a grave,' Lord Arnold cried,' To put these lovers in But bury my Lady at the top For she was of noble kin.*" She drew in ragged breath. "You have no grave here. You have no marker. She was nobler than you ever were. You have no part here, not any more. You're lost—you're not even an interesting memory."

Penny was laughing, a strong easy laugh. Behind them, Albert was snorting with it. Out of nowhere, they heard Roger Searle.

"My Lord," he called out. "There's something there—on the ceiling!"

It was the stuff of nightmares, of fever dreams. Black, leathery, made of the shadows and the night. It was human, not human, not meant to be seen by waking minds: Andrew Leight was a bad dream. The human eye could not properly parse his outlines.

It dropped, heart of darkness, hovering, massive. Were those wings? Ringan wondered dizzily, no, they couldn't be, and then remembered, horribly, how Charlotte had described the shadow that had moved towards Penny in this very room. Hands shaking, he tried to steer Penny away, out of doors—exorcism be damned, he thought, it didn't matter, nothing mattered but getting her safely away . . .

Charlotte stepped forward. She walked between Penny and Jane, her mismatched eyes impossibly brilliant, her hair loose in a red-gold cascade to her waist. She was no longer laughing.

"Do you think we're frightened of you?" She spoke as the lady of the great house, the *grande dame,* talking to someone so socially inferior that she couldn't be bothered with *politesse.* Her smile, twisted and amused, was devastating in its arrogance. "We're not. We're tired of you. You're a very silly, very annoying little man. And it's high time you moved on."

Behind them, Julian cried out. It was a single word only, Charlotte's name. She ignored him, and walked straight into the black devouring centre of Andrew Leight.

Nobody really saw what happened. It was odd, comparing notes after it was all over, that every person there had seen something different, or else they'd seen nothing at all.

From Ringan's perspective, what he had seen that night was something that would wake him, sweating and disoriented, for several weeks after the event: a blending of two forms into one, a swirl of red-gold hair, and two pairs of odd-coloured eyes, inches apart and then melding, one pair dominating, absorbing the other pair, shrinking them to nothing.

Penny saw nothing but darkness. The room dissolved around her, the walls melted, and she felt sky above her as she lay on her back. There was warmth, the smell of roses and then the reek of blood. She felt it splatter across her face, she heard Edward's voice calling her, *Susanna, no, my sweet Sue, come back to me,* and she wondered why she was blind, seeing nothing, until she understood that she was Susanna, and Susanna was dying.

Julian saw horror, a piece of the night coming to life to take Charlotte, but horror was only a moment, and then it was triumph, Charlotte on high, Charlotte victorious.

No one ever asked Roger Searle what he had seen, and neither Albert Wychsale nor Miles Leight-Arnold ever volunteered that information. So Jane never knew if she was the only one who had seen the small pale girl, blank-faced, startlingly similar in general appearance to Jane herself, move out of that zone of darkness, beyond the influence of pain and need and memory, off into the night, towards the marble angels that waited in the Folly, reaching for Heaven.

Two days had passed since the events in the Callowen ballroom. It was early evening, and the soft touch of a summer night was beginning to settle on the lawns and rooftops. Safe at home in Somerset, relaxing on one of the terraces at Wychsale House, Ringan and Penny drank beer, while Jane chugged at an enormous glass of cider.

Albert Wychsale, who'd been called indoors to take a phone call, rejoined his guests.

"That was Miles," he told them. "It seems they had a nice sensible idea, and went back through the rest of the boxes in Annie Whitlaw's guest room."

"They found the rest of the missing entries?" Jane stifled a burp. "Susanna's? That poor unnamed steward, bless his careful, informative heart?"

"Both, believe it or not." Albert sat down, stretched his legs out, and gave a long sigh. "The rest of the steward's notes were folded up small, inside what turned out to be Susanna's housekeeping book. No," he added, seeing Penny's eager look. "No, don't get excited. Miles said it was just that: day-to-day events. They've read all of it, and it's mostly about the children, the servants' health, an outbreak of smallpox in Purbury. Apparently, writing didn't come all that easily to her, poor thing; it wasn't a staple part of the training of girls from her societal class, in those days. Anyway, it stops—I think Miles said 1628, so there's nothing there, really. And nothing about Andrew."

"Disappointing." Ringan grunted. "But not surprising, you know? Considering the times and the social structure, I doubt Edward would have discussed politics and whatnot with Susanna."

"What did the steward say about the aftermath?" Penny, her glass empty, had one elbow propped on the table and her chin cupped in one palm. "Was there anything in there about Bishop Wolvesley, or the King? Did you ask?"

"I certainly did." The twilight had become gloaming, the last of the light beginning to leach free of the evening air. Somewhere off towards Glastonbury, a dog fox barked once, sharply. "Miles said there was something about the Bishop showing up as arranged, and being closeted with Edward, and then leaving in a hurry. There was a note that Miles repeated, about Edward being too grief-stricken to cope. But it seems the steward wasn't privy to the conversation—the Bishop dragged Edward off at once, and the house was likely in an uproar, so there wasn't much. Oh, I nearly forgot—he says to tell you, he's going to let Madeleine Holt have the papers for her collection."

"Excellent! She'll love that." Penny sat back, and closed her eyes. It was odd, she thought, but ever since their confrontation with Andrew Leight, she'd been wary of closing her eyes. The memory of feeling the last of Susanna's life slip away from her was still too close for comfort.

"So we're probably never going to know what passed between Edward and Wolvesley? Pity." Ringan, mellow with beer and the relief of having got clean away from Callowen, let his gaze rest on Penny for a moment. Ear and mouth were both healed completely. There were no scars, at least on the surface. What remained of the experience was likely to remain private to Penny.

As she often did, Penny seemed to catch at his thoughts, and turned to give him a brilliant smile. "I suppose we could continue to try and track down records," she mused. "You know, of some of the major players in politics at the time. Maddy did read me off some notes about the King dissolving Parliament, and then going without any Parliament at all for something like a dozen years after that. I'm betting his not being able to fill that Speaker's chair didn't help the situation. We could research it, but frankly, I'm not sure I care that much. I do have one question, though. Ringan, Jane, do either of you know when the song first appeared?"

"In its present shape?" Jane shook her head. "Not a clue. I'd always thought it was far older than seventeenth century, but now, with what we know, I suppose not. Yet one more thing I've taken as gospel all these years turns out to be wrong."

"The story's an archetype," Ringan said lazily. "There are versions of that theme—naughty wife, hot young stud, avenging older husband—in other songs. This just happens to be the most famous one, and of course, it's all rubbish. Tracking down when it first appeared sounds like far more work than it's worth. I do wonder if someone sat down and crafted it deliberately, with an ulterior motive, or whether the fake story simply somehow got stuck onto an existing melody." He yawned. "Not enough to hunt it up, though. Much too much effort. Is there more beer?"

"Lazy," Penny told him. "So am I, actually. At least we know the truth, and Edward knew it, too. Susanna never betrayed him; she was a victim, not a seducer."

"Damned right." Jane nodded. "Albert, are they sure Andrew's really gone? I mean, is it possible we just pushed him back to relative weakness, rather than shoving him out altogether? I'd hate to think there might be another Sinead McCreary someday."

"He's gone." Penny's voice held an odd note. "I felt him go, when I felt Susanna die. She was laughing, did you know? Laughing in her mind, in her heart. Her throat was crushed. I don't know how she managed to make even that small noise that she did, the noise that froze him and allowed Edward to kill him. But she was laughing at him, beating him, winning over him in the end. And he knew it. I felt the entire thing."

The others were quiet a moment, chilled despite the warmth of the June night. It was nearly full dark now, and in the treetops to the south of them, birds rustled and bats began their nightly hunt for insects. On the wide lawn, the Wychsale estate's magnificent Persian cat, Butterball, stalked with his tail high.

"There's something . . ." Ringan's voice trailed away. He cleared his throat, and tried again. "Something I've been wondering about. I hate to bring it up—"

"Charlotte?" Penny said quietly. "Yes, well, I wondered too. Why Charlotte? Why was she able to stop him so easily? There seems to have been some sort of connection there."

"You're wondering about paternity, aren't you?" Albert spoke with unusual directness. "Not Char's paternity—the paternity of whichever of Susanna's two boys the Leight-Arnold line came down through. You're wondering if one of them, maybe both of them, were Andrew's rather than Edward's. Is that it?"

"Yes." Ringan drained his glass. He'd grown very fond of Charlotte, in the way a man might grow fond of a comrade in adversity, and the thought of her having any blood connection with the monster they had lately driven into darkness was a disturbing one. "Sorry, Albert. But yes, I am."

"So am I." Albert's lips were pinched. "I've been wondering since the first. I mean, the odd-eyed thing, that could simply be one of those recessive gene deals, they happen all the time, you know? Everything from cleft chins on up. But when I add that to the fear Andrew so obviously felt of her, the triumph I got from her when she booted him out, her complete lack of fear . . ." He stopped, and shook his head. "Right," he announced firmly. "She's my god-daughter. Why should I give a damn about who her great-grandfather ninety times removed may have been? I'm never going to know, and I refuse to worry about it."

"Good call. Besides, there's an even more annoying bit of the puzzle no one seems to have been able to discover." Jane's glass was empty. "Unless I've missed something, that is. Has anyone been able to track down where they buried Andrew? Because Walter couldn't find anything anywhere. There's no grave in the family crypt at St. Giles. And we know he wasn't buried in the Folly."

"That's right, isn't it? We still don't know where they put him." Albert pursed his lips. "Damn. That's going to wake me up at night, wondering."

Epilogue

"A grave, a grave," Lord Arnold cried
"To put these lovers in
But bury my Lady at the top
For she was of noble kin"

One year to the day after the death of his wife Susanna, Lord Edward Leight-Arnold stood at the far end of the small bridge that led across a dancing stream, to his wife's tomb.

In the past twelve months, Edward had aged nearly beyond recognition. The vigorous, virile husband had somehow been buried along with his wife; Edward moved slowly now. His hair had dulled to a thin, listless grey. The things that had once brought him pleasure—riding out to the hunt, his hawk on his arm—were painful memories. He had become an old man.

The Folly, Susanna's tomb, was complete. The marble sarcophagus had stood in solitary splendour, alone on its water-edged patch of Callowen land, since her death. The building had gone up around her. Nor was she alone, a fact which, had he been capable of any comfort, might have offered some. Matty Groves, asleep in his small wooden coffin in the crypt of St. Giles this past year, had been entombed in the Folly. He had guarded his mistress in life, as best he could; he had died trying to defend her. It was fitting, Edward thought, that young Matthew should rest so near her.

He stared down at the patch of ground on which his feet rested, and smiled. The smile was a thing of horror, a twisted travesty, as dark as the events of a year ago had been. It was fortunate, perhaps, that no one living was here to see it. The ground beneath his feet was thin of grass, showing where it had been disturbed, now growing cover once again.

Edward lifted his eyes to the Folly once more, his face smoothing clean of expression. He remembered, only vaguely, his conversation with Bishop Wolvesley. Matters of state, certainly. But did the man really believe Edward, at that moment of his own loss, would care a tinker's damn about the balance of power between King and Parliament, between Anglican and Puritan? Edward had cared for nothing, and the words had gone over him in a wash: *Tell no one. Turn off this steward and bid him hold his tongue lest he lose it by chattering. I myself will see to Lockereigh at St. Giles. Not a soul must know that Hervey Leight's son has done what his father did before him. These are dangerous times.* And then more, as Wolvesley saw and understood Edward's inattention and the cause of it, the words coming more disjointed, more quickly: *Puritans in Parliament, the King's bad judgement, bury them quiet, put some tale abroad that holds no kernel of the truth, Archbishop Laud at Canterbury would agree, this could go hard for you and for all Catholics, let no word of the truth leak out, no word of the truth, no word . . .*

Edward wrenched his mind back to the moment. He stared down once more at the telltale patch of earth under his boots.

"Rot there." He spoke aloud, his words carried away by the cool autumn wind, scattered to the vast distance. "Rot there in unconsecrated ground, you scum. She sleeps close enough that you can always know what you can't reach, and may it burn your soul, shrivel you, torment you until time stops."

The final words echoed off the front of the marble building on the other side of the charming little bridge *until time stops time stops time stops.*

Lord Edward spat on the unmarked grave beneath his feet, and walked away from his lady, from her protector, from her killer, back to the world he no longer cared for.